COUPLES
WANTED

Also by Briana Cole:

The Wives We Play

The Vows We Break

The Hearts We Burn

The Marriage Pass

And
"Pseudo" from *Justified*

COUPLES
WANTED

BRIANA COLE

www.kensingtonbooks.com

DAFINA BOOKS are published by

Kensington Publishing Corp.
119 West 40th Street
New York, NY 10018

All Kensington titles, imprints, and distributed lines are available at special quantity discounts for bulk purchases for sales promotion, premiums, fund-raising, and educational or institutional use.

Special book excerpts or customized printings can also be created to fit specific needs. For details, write or phone the office of the Kensington Sales Manager: Kensington Publishing Corp., 119 West 40th Street, New York, NY 10018. Attn. Sales Department. Phone: 1-800-221-2647.

The Dafina logo is a trademark of Kensington Publishing Corp.

ISBN: 978-1-4967-2957-6
First Trade Paperback Printing: December 2021

ISBN: 978-1-4967-2958-3 (e-book)
First Electronic Edition: December 2021

10 9 8 7 6 5 4 3 2 1

Printed in the United States of America

I dedicate this book, like I am dedicating the rest of my life, to my beautiful sister in Heaven, Paige Christina.

You have inspired me to be the best version of myself and I hope I make you as proud as you have always made me. This is for the both of us. Love you always, my forever angel.

Chapter One
Bridget

If Bridget hadn't been so caught up in the moment, she probably would have turned just a little to the right and noticed the couple with their eyes fixed on her. She probably would have questioned their quiet exchange, sizing her up and nodding in shared approval. No, she was too busy with her own hidden agenda, her attention completely enthralled with one particular gentleman as he stepped into the restaurant.

Bridget noticed him first, and that element alone was enough to excite her. The thrill, the secrecy. Hell, the sexual tension between them was hypnotic, despite them being several feet apart. So much so, she had to stop herself from glancing around to see if anyone else was turned on by the apparent chemistry.

She shifted on the barstool and took another sip of the vodka and Sprite, continuing to eye the man over the rim of her glass. Expecting the interaction, she had dressed with care, the navy blue bandage dress clinging to the dips and curves of her five-foot, eight-inch frame. The sleeves hung off her shoulders to reveal a tapestry of butterfly tattoos shading the mocha flesh of her neck and collarbone an ombre of orange hues.

She lifted her hand to signal the bartender, the encrusted diamonds of her wedding band catching the pendant lighting from overhead. The bartender moseyed over, dragging a cloth along the marble bar top along the way. A gold tag with the name Alisha was perched on the breast pocket of her button-up uniform shirt.

"Another drink?" Alisha greeted with a knowing smile.

"Not for me." Bridget nodded in the direction of the man who was now being seated alone in a nearby booth. "Send a Hennessy and Coke to him for me, please. Tell him it's from me."

Alisha nodded and headed off to fulfill the request.

Bridget continued nursing her own drink as she waited. She felt eyes on her, and she tried her best to hide a gloating smirk. It was foolish to feel nervous. Yet still, she felt her heart racing with excitement, or maybe it was anxiety. Either way, she had done her part. It was now up to Mr. Handsome to take the bait.

"Excuse me."

The voice had a grin cracking Bridget's face, and she cocked her head, only slightly, to eye the visitor. He, too, was smiling.

"Yes?"

"I just wanted to thank you for the drink."

Bridget nodded, exaggerating a lick of her plump lips. "My pleasure," she flirted.

The man eased onto the stool next to her, and Bridget appreciated how he didn't bother hiding his visual assessment of her body. "How did you know I like Hennessy and Coke?"

She shrugged. "Lucky guess, I suppose."

"Either I'm that easy to read, or you're just that good."

Now Bridget did turn to face him, crossing her legs to allow a sliver of thigh to peek through from underneath the bar. "I'm just that good," she said with a wink.

He laughed and held out his hand. "I'm Chris."

Bridget already had her own lie ready. "Veronica," she said, accepting his hand.

"Well, Veronica. Are you always this forward? Buying drinks for guys in bars?"

"Actually, yeah. I like to go for what I want."

She caught the glint in his eye. "Is that so? And what exactly do you want, Ms. Veronica?"

"It's Mrs.," she corrected politely and held up her hand, fingers spread apart to give him full view of her wedding ring.

The gesture didn't seem to faze him one bit. "I apologize. *Mrs.* So what does your husband feel about you being alone in here? Flirting with me?"

Bridget giggled. "Flirting? Is that what we're doing? I just thought we were here having a drink, enjoying each other's company. No harm in that, right?"

Now it was his turn to shrug. "You tell me."

The liquor had Bridget feeling bold, and she leaned forward, a mere breath away from his lips. She could almost taste him as his Versace cologne assaulted her nostrils and awakened every inch of her body, that delicious musk of lust and desire like an intoxicating drug. To hell with it.

"I won't tell if you won't," she whispered and leaned forward, pressing her lips against his to drink his very essence. She swallowed his moan as he deepened the kiss, using his tongue to wrestle with hers. He broke contact first, resting his forehead against hers as they both tried to catch their breath.

"You don't play fair," he murmured with a low chuckle.

Bridget kissed him once more and pulled back to take a healthy swig of her drink. "Hey, I tried," she said. "But you came here looking so damn good I couldn't resist. What was the name you used this time? Chris?" She wrinkled her nose in distaste as she side-eyed her man. "That doesn't really suit you, babe."

"Well, *Veronica* was definitely throwing it at me. A few more minutes and you were about to hop on this dick right here at the bar."

Bridget laughed out loud. "I'm sure you wouldn't have minded. Lucky for you, that's been my dick since I married you."

Alisha approached again, a wistful smile already planted on her face. She set a bread basket between the couple. "Are you two done with your role-playing?"

Bridget jerked a thumb in the man's direction. "Yeah, girl. Roman here couldn't keep a straight face."

Roman smirked as he nuzzled his wife's neck, startling a squeal from her lips. "I'll tell you what I can keep straight."

"You are so damn freaky."

"That's why you love me."

Alisha poked out her lip, feigning a jealous pout. "You two are so damn cute, it's sick. You come in here every Saturday night with this little pretend thing you do. Are y'all newlyweds or something?"

"Or something," Roman said with a grin.

"We've been married for two years," Bridget chimed in, dropping her hand to her husband's thigh. "Just a little something to keep the sparks alive. It's like our little date night."

"Well, you two look so happy," Alisha gushed. "Whatever y'all are doing, it's working. Teach me your ways."

Bridget chuckled as Alisha strolled off to assist another patron at the bar. Roman took her hands in his, and it felt like bolts of electricity shot from her wrist to her shoulder and back again. Amazing. Even she was in awe her husband still had that effect on her. A simple look, touch, or whisper from him was enough to have her sprung ass melting like hot wax. In every way possible.

"I love you," Roman murmured, keeping his eyes level with hers. Bridget sighed as her heart fluttered.

"I love you, too," she whispered.

"I think *Veronica* still owes me some action."

Bridget rose to her feet on a laugh. "Let *Veronica* go to the little girl's room, and then you can take her home and get every piece of her."

He groaned inwardly and exaggerated an appreciative roll of his eye as she stood. Bridget took her time, sashaying her slender hips as she weaved through the maze of people on her way to the restroom. Oh yeah, she was certainly going to lay it down on Mr. Pierce as soon as they got home. Hell, the way she was feeling, she would be surprised if they even made it out of the parking lot. Bridget was all but chuckling to herself as her mind wrapped around a series of sexual contortionist positions that they could pull off in Roman's two-seater Mercedes.

Bridget stood in front of the mirror, readjusting the razor-edge bangs on the bob wig that framed her face. It was itching like hell, but she would be damned if she let the seventy-five dollars go to waste. Besides, the short look did give her a little more sass, more sex appeal than the waves of her naturally long tresses. She fished in her purse to find the nude lipstick she had applied earlier that evening. Apparently, what was left of it had made its way from her lips to Roman's.

The restroom door swung open on its hinges, and Bridget met a woman's polite smile in the mirror. She nodded a silent greeting of her own before turning back to the task at hand.

Bridget couldn't help but notice the woman's body was like a siren's. A voluptuous frame filled every inch of the maxi dress she wore, the material taut with curves and arcs thick in proportion. They were about the same maple syrup complexion, but the woman towered a good few inches over Bridget, even with the six-inch stilettos she wore. Stunning was a complete understatement.

The woman approached the sink and bowed her head, staring into the porcelain as if it held the answer to her prayers. Her curls shielded her face from view. It wasn't until Bridget heard the muffled sniffles that she even knew the woman was crying.

"Um, are you okay?" She didn't know why she felt compelled to ask. Call it the Pisces in her. The woman's head bobbed in response, but still she kept her face lowered, nor did she utter a single word.

"You sure?" Bridget questioned again, her voice etched in concern. "I'm sorry, I don't mean to keep bugging you. I just wanted to . . ." She trailed off. *She just wanted to what?* Roman always managed to remind her of how she could come across as nosy. Not that it was her intention. But here she was again, all up and through this poor woman's business. Some woman she didn't even know, at that. "Sorry," Bridget murmured and, pursing her lips together, turned back to her sink.

"Don't be sorry." The woman's voice was quiet, and she braved lifting her eyes to meet Bridget's in the streaked glass of the mirror. Tears trailed her ashen cheeks with mascara and glittered on her lashes like black diamonds. "I appreciate you even asking."

Bridget snatched a few paper towels from the dispenser and held them out to her. "Do you need me to call someone, or . . ."

"No." The woman bit off the one-word answer with a shake of her head. "It's nothing like that. My husband and I just had a little fight."

Bridget nodded. No, she couldn't relate, but relationship issues weren't a foreign topic to her. Especially with her checkered past entanglements with men. It was just that now with Roman, he was, thankfully, the exception.

"Are you married?" the woman asked.

"Yes. Two years."

"Six." Her sigh was heavy, as if weighted under every second of the past 2,190 days of matrimony.

"It'll get better," Bridget offered with a comforting smile. "Men, you know how they can be sometimes."

"Don't I know it."

"And marriage is tough. Just talk it out if you can. My husband and I are getting better with our communication and transparency. Even if the other may not like what needs to be said. And if you can't talk it out, just show it out."

The woman frowned. "*Show* it out?"

"Yeah, girl." Bridget gestured toward the woman's body. "Looking as good as you do, just pull out the tricks. It'll temporarily make him lose his mind, he won't even remember why he's mad."

The woman chuckled, a slight blush coloring her cheeks. "I wish it were that simple." She paused. "What's your name?"

"Bridget."

"Corrine. Are you a motivational speaker, Bridget? Or a therapist? You certainly have a way with words, girl."

Bridget chuckled. "Event planner. So my little gift for gab comes in handy."

Corrine's eyebrows lifted. "Really? I'm a caterer. We run in the same circles."

"Oh, wow. Small world."

Corrine was already fishing in her clutch, producing a crisp business card embossed in hot pink and teal. "Here, take my card. Never know when you'll need me for your preferred vendor list."

Bridget accepted the card with a nod. "Oh, damn, I don't have any of mine on me. But I tell you what, look me up. My website is Brinique Lux Affair dot com."

Corrine smiled. Bridget noticed the appreciative gesture didn't reach her eyes.

"For what it's worth," Corrine said, "I really appreciate this little talk, Bridget. It made me feel better about my situation."

Bridget's smile widened at the compliment. "Sometimes, it helps just to get it off your chest," she said. "Good luck with everything, Corrine."

Corrine nodded her gratitude once again, her eyes following Bridget's movements as she swept past and back out of the door into the steady hum of restaurant activity.

Roman was still perched at the bar when Bridget returned. He slid another drink her way. "You took a minute. Everything okay?"

Bridget lifted the glass to her lips on a nod. "I'm just horny," she teased with a wink. "Let's finish this up at home."

"My kinda woman." Roman lifted his hand, and Alisha eased her way back to their side of the bar. "We're ready to cash out."

Alisha pulled her billfold from the pocket of her apron and quickly scanned the ticket. "Oh, it's already taken care of," she informed them.

Roman frowned and glanced at Bridget, who shrugged. "You sure?"

"Yeah." Alisha placed the receipt in front of him where she had scribbled *settled* in a sloppy circle. "The couple at the other end took care of this for you."

Bridget turned in the direction she gestured, craning her neck to pick out the people who were gracious enough to pay for their tab. She didn't bother getting a look at the man, but the woman, the gorgeous Corrine, was taking her place at the table, already smiling in her direction. Bridget smiled back, shaking off the slightly uneasy feeling.

"Well, that was weird," she murmured.

"How so?" Roman was peering over her shoulder, trying to get a look for himself. "Who is that? You know them?"

"No, not really. The woman I met in the restroom. She was crying, and I just gave her a little sisterly advice. She's a caterer."

"Wait. You met a caterer in the bathroom, and she pays for your drinks?"

"Guess she just wanted to thank me," she said absently.

Roman glanced in Corrine's direction and merely shook his head on a laugh. "Only my wife."

Bridget shrugged. She had to admit, it sounded even stranger out loud. But still, she kept her face neutral. She wondered why she was having to convince herself the innocent gesture really wasn't that big of a deal.

Chapter Two
Corrine

"You should've just asked for her number when y'all were talking!" Patrick was gripping the steering wheel so tight his knuckles bulged through his skin. Of course, he was pissed. That was Corrine's new normal with her husband: the attitude, the yelling, the occasional slap to reinforce whatever nonsensical point he was rattling on about. Sure, the fear was familiar, but she was no longer surprised.

Corrine swallowed the plea for him to slow down for the hundredth time. So instead she held on to the seat belt strap pinning her body to the crisp leather seat. Patrick swerved the Escalade over the double line to narrowly pass a slow-moving car, and Corrine released the breath she hadn't realized she was holding. He always got reckless when he was drunk. Not that he was that much more careful when he was sober.

"You had one damn job, Corrine," Patrick rambled on, lifting his index finger in the air to emphasize his point. "One damn job. And you can't even do that. You're fucking pathetic."

Reasoning wouldn't do any good, but she tried anyway. "Pat, I told you I got her website, but no, I didn't ask for her phone number. How awkward would that have been? Women don't go making friends in the bathroom like that."

"Well, I guess you're the expert on *women* now, huh?"

Corrine closed her eyes against the sting of his words. Even six years couldn't dull the pain of her husband's snide remarks. Hell, a lifetime couldn't dull the pain. No, she wasn't defensive about her transitional journey, nor was she naïve to the ignorance that was usually attributed to her being a transgender woman, but Patrick's intentional insensitivity felt like hot coals on open wounds. And because there had been so many repeated instances, Corrine's soul was past numb; it was rubbed raw.

A few fleeting images seemed to play like a movie on the windshield, memories of a better time in her relationship, without the bullshit, without the extra. There was a time when Patrick had been happy with just her, and her alone. Days were spent sneaking snatches of times on breaks and lunches, nights were spent in every sexual position a public place allowed. Patrick was romantic, a little bit controlling, but laced with enough charm it made Corrine ignore the obvious red flags. It was what had drawn her to him in the first place when she'd catered an appreciation luncheon for the grand opening of his mechanic's garage.

After twenty years in the army, Patrick had found his second career in his love of cars, so the opening of Pat's Auto Body and Repair had been his excuse to go all out with his party. But one thing about Patrick, still very much true, was his notorious procrastination. He'd found Corrine's catering business, A Taste of Corrine, via a simple Google search, only calling because he thought the name of her business was "sexy as hell." Well, that and she was probably the only caterer in Atlanta willing to throw together a large-scale meal with less than nine hours' notice.

Either way, from the moment she showed up with her barbecue spread, enough to feed the whole damn neighborhood, Corrine was smitten with the short smooth-talker with the peanut-brown complexion, deep-set dimples, and mile-long eyelashes. She was flaunting every curve she had, and the fact that she always had been able to cook her ass off certainly didn't hurt.

Patrick had been putty in her hands, and Corrine couldn't get enough. She hadn't meant to keep her past a secret from him. But it was crystal clear, even two years after the big revelation, that her husband never forgave her. Nor did he ever stop resenting her.

The tenderness in the hand placed on Corrine's arm was so foreign it startled a gasp from her lips. Corrine turned to peer at Patrick, his side profile like a mask in the shadows of the spring night.

"Look," he said. "It's cool. I'm not mad."

Corrine ignored the irony and remained quiet.

"I just really want this, Corrine. Shit, we've been talking and planning it for the longest. I don't know . . . I guess the other times didn't really do it for me. I want this to be right. So we can get back to us. Back to loving us, like we used to do."

Even in the dark, she caught the wink of his dimple in the crease of his cheek. A charming smile. He knew how to lay it on thick.

The whole thing had been his idea, one she had merely gone along with for peace. And maybe a little love. God, it was a shame she really only felt love from her husband when she was compliant. No matter the absurdity of the requests. Which was why, two years and three months after they began their alternative swinging lifestyle, it was still an issue for her. But if it meant peace, and love, well, there was her little sliver of happiness.

So, because he now expected her response, Corrine turned her hand to link her fingers with his, giving him a little reassuring squeeze. "I want this for us," she lied. "And if you want her, I'm willing to make that happen for you. Okay?"

Patrick lifted her hand to kiss the back of it. That was enough to satisfy him for now. But for her, it was another admission to the nightmare. One that was just getting started.

⸙

Bubble baths were a signature Corrine ritual. Something about soaking in the Jacuzzi tub surrounded by candles and soft music, submerged in scalding hot water and bubbles that had the smell of peaches and lavender hanging in air. It was time to herself, and she appreciated Patrick letting her have these uninterrupted moments.

Corrine poured herself a glass of Roscato and let the wine and the soulful ballads of Jahiem give her the buzz she needed. It was time to do a little digging on the bathroom beauty Patrick had picked out in the crowded restaurant. Corrine wasn't sure if Little Miss Bridget was into the swingers' lifestyle, but now it was her job to find out. Their system was simple: Patrick would cast the lure, and she would reel them in. Her only reprieve, however minimal or untrue, was that *this* time would be the last time.

With sweat peppering her brow and candlelight licking the walls, Corrine positioned her body against the jets of the tub and began her due diligence.

First, she went to Bridget's event planning website and toggled to the *About Us* page. Sure enough, there was a professional photo of the woman from the restroom, sans the wig and heavy makeup. She stood back-to-back with another black woman, a little shorter, with a sexy pixie cut. Corrine used her thumb to scroll the page, her eyes skimming the biography.

Brinique Lux Affair was owned by Bridget and her best friend Dominique. The business name was a combination of theirs. Cute. They had been in business for nearly two years and had become pretty successful in that short time period, appearing in a number of wedding magazines, event blogs, and even receiving prominent accolades, such as hitting the upper ranks of *Atlanta's*

Up and Coming and *Who's Who of the Entrepreneurs of Atlanta.*
Corrine was impressed, but not surprised. A woman like Bridget
carried herself like she was all about business. It was no wonder
she was a success. And more so, thanks to her husband, Roman,
who she made sure to highlight in her biography. Even better.

Corrine expanded her investigation to social media, cross-
checking Instagram, Twitter, Snapchat, and Facebook handles
until she was able to run across Bridget's personal social media
pages. The entrepreneur was quite active online, with plenty of
selfies, motivational quotes, and captured memories of her and
Roman or her and Dominique.

Corrine clicked on pictures and comments, mentally keeping
tabs on everything she could find that would be of use.

Apparently, Bridget and Dominique had an event coming up;
some kind of women's conference. Corrine hadn't planned on
being there, but that was the perfect place to make an appearance. She was already working out the details long after the water
had begun to chill her skin.

Corrine emerged from the bath a few hours later, her body so
relaxed it felt like silk. Patrick was sitting up in bed, the light from
the TV playing on his downcast features as he did whatever he
did on his cell phone. He spared her an absent glance as she
crossed from the adjoining bathroom to the dresser, selecting a lotion from the many tubes and bottles littering the counter.

"Find anything?" he asked.

"I did."

"And?"

Corrine wanted to roll her eyes, but she kept her back to him
as she continued lathering her body in the cream. "And I'll probably see her again this weekend."

"Good." A smile was in his voice. "You always know just what
to do to make me happy."

Corrine turned, completely naked and headed for the bed.

Something between the bath, the wine, the music, and Patrick's now uplifted mood had her body awake and vibrating with anticipation. She crawled up the foot of the bed, swaying her hips side-to-side like an agile cat.

"And you know what you can do for me?" she whispered, licking her lips seductively.

Patrick smirked but waited as Corrine made her way up the bed until she was face-to-face with him, resting her hands on his bare chest.

"Oh, and what's that?" he teased.

Her hands slid up farther and linked behind his neck. She pressed her lips to his, at first ignoring the slight dejection when he didn't return the intimacy. She might as well have been kissing a statue. Corrine used her tongue to try to pry his lips apart. Patrick just sat there, unmoved by her sexual gestures.

Corrine sighed, pulling away with a frown creasing her face. "Come on, Pat." She tried her best to keep the whine out of her voice. But, dammit, she was horny and needed her man.

Pat lifted his hands to grab her wrists and pull them from around his neck. "Babe, you know I got an early morning, okay?"

Corrine nodded, swallowing another swell of disappointment. Her mental calendar checked off the fourteenth day in a row he had given some bullshit excuse. She should have expected this. She rolled off him onto her side of the bed.

"But you can give me some head, though," Patrick added, breaking the building silence. "You know how I need that to put me to sleep."

Of course he did. Corrine pulled up to her knees on a sigh, even as her mind was trying to fast-forward to the weekend, when she would see Bridget. The quicker they got this over with, the quicker she could get back to her happily ever after. At least, that was enough to fuel her motivation. For the time being.

Chapter Three
Bridget

Good day—I am Marco Richards. A friend referred your services to me for an event I am planning. I am interested in meeting with someone for assistance with an elite and exclusive anniversary affair for my club. Please give me a call at your earliest convenience. Warm regards.

Bridget skimmed the contents of the email again with a grin before screenshotting the message and texting it to Dominique, or Nikki, as she had been dubbed since their college days. Her girl's reply was quick and customary: *Yes, bitch! We doing the damn thang!* The comment was followed by some dancing emojis, then another message: *Check emails later and go get ready. We got a big day! Be there in an hour.* Obediently, Bridget set her phone down. Nikki was right. They *did* have a big day.

She busied herself at the kitchen counter, pushing buttons on the Keurig until brewed coffee trickled from the spout and caused a caramelized aroma of smoky and nutty flavors to waft in the air. She had woken up in a Jay-Z mood, so strains of *The Blueprint* filtered from the in-home speakers, taking her back to an era of Baby Phat, velour track suits, and Harlem shaking. Humming along to the music, Bridget welcomed the distraction of the mellow ambiance as she ambled around the gourmet kitchen.

It wasn't like she hadn't attended a conference before. Despite the initial apprehension of her mother and, hell, even Roman, she and her best friend had managed to carve out a little success with their event planning enterprise. And now, it was flourishing under her business leadership and Nikki's creative genius. Not to mention the referrals she had been getting. The proof was in the pudding. They were making a name for themselves and taking the industry by storm. Being able to relay her passion during her speech in a few hours shouldn't have put her on edge. So where the hell was this nervousness coming from?

"Hmm. What I tell you about wearing that?"

She hadn't heard him enter the kitchen. Roman's playful reprimand had Bridget grinning, not bothering to turn around as her husband's arms circled her waist from behind. The satin robe she wore clung to the spots of skin still damp from her morning shower and barely brushed the middle of her thighs. She felt his lips graze the back of her neck, and she giggled with the sensation that tingled down to simmer between her thighs. Roman had mastered the art of making her body react to his touch, or his look. It was as if she had now been programmed as some kind of customized Roman-edition. It was a nuisance, always being so turned on whenever he was around. An erotic nuisance, but a nuisance nonetheless.

She turned, letting Roman brace her against the marble kitchen counter, and lifted her legs to circle around his waist. "We don't have time," she murmured against his lips. "I have to go."

"I'll be quick."

"Your friend is downstairs."

"Man, fuck him. He's asleep anyway."

Bridget was tempted to give in. An early morning quickie

could relieve her anxiety and was probably just what the doctor ordered. And it didn't hurt that Roman actually was a doctor. The man certainly knew how to heal. As if on cue, her mind flipped from her long list of action items for the day and refocused on the budding orgasm. She was already moaning as he deepened the kiss, his fingers fumbling with the belt that held her robe together.

Footsteps approaching had a panicked Bridget snatching herself away and hopping off the counter in one fluid motion. So much for that idea.

The door from the basement opened, and Roman's friend Dorian shuffled into the kitchen, looking like death run over twice. His eyes bounced around the room before landing on Bridget.

"You made breakfast?" he asked.

Bridget rolled her eyes, not bothering to hide her annoyance. "No," she snapped. "But the Comfort Inn and Suites has breakfast included." Roman's playful swat on her butt had her swallowing the rest of the insults playing on her tongue and turning back to the Keurig to finish their coffees.

It was harsh, she knew. But she didn't like the man, and she sure as hell wasn't one to hide her disdain. Plus, the fact that he was camping out in their finished basement for going on five months was enough to heighten her disgust for his presence.

"Hey, man, you good?" Roman asked as Dorian made his way to the refrigerator.

"Yeah," he huffed.

Out of the corner of her eye, Bridget watched him rummage through the fridge, sift through the groceries she had just purchased, and grab the unopened gallon of milk, plus the to-go box with the leftover fish tacos from yesterday's lunch. *Her* tacos. Because she knew Roman was watching her, she kept her lips pursed together, though she really wanted to snap on his ass.

It wasn't until Dorian had disappeared back downstairs that

she let her thoughts loose. "I'm tired of his ass." She lowered her voice only slightly as she gestured wildly toward the closed basement door. "We work while he sits up here all day like some overgrown-ass kid. He eats up all the damn food and we never have any privacy. I'm sick of it!"

Roman nodded, rubbing his hands up and down her arms to calm her down. "Sssshhh, I know, babe. I know. But you know what he's going through."

Of course she knew. She'd had front row seats to the madness and had been hearing about it every day while he overstayed his welcome.

Dorian had some kind of marriage hall pass with his wife that gave him permission to go out and cheat for one night. The greedy bastard had decided to take advantage of their little arrangement and use his pass with his wife's sister, and the shit didn't end so well. Served him right, honestly.

Bridget had never cared for Dorian even before she and Roman got married, and she most certainly wasn't giving out sympathy after she found out everything that went down. So while he was bouncing between friends, sleeping on couches, and trying to get his "life together" as everyone tried to justify, she was just trying her best to keep the peace. Still, she couldn't wait for him to take his broken ass on to the next enabler.

Bridget handed Roman his mug of coffee and gingerly took a sip of her own. "I'm serious, Roman," she said. "You've been more than a good friend for letting him stay. He needs to go."

"Okay, okay. I'll talk to him. I promise."

Roman lifted Bridget's hand to kiss it, all the while giving her those puppy-dog eyes and pouted lip that made her melt every time. She smirked. Sometimes, she couldn't stay mad at the man if she tried.

"I recall a time you mentioned a marriage hall pass yourself," she teased with a wink.

"Yeah, but after I saw what the shit did to him, I'll pass. No pun intended. Besides," he added giving her another kiss, "your sexy ass is more than enough."

Bridget chuckled as Roman took the mug from her hands.

"Don't you need to get ready? You have your conference in a few hours. You nervous?"

Bridget drew in a breath and released a sigh, meant to emit some sense of encouragement. "I got this," she said.

"Exactly. It's you doing what you do best. You love what you do, it shows, and you're damn good at it! What could go wrong?" Roman's cell phone rang, and he angled it up to check the screen. "Oh, got to go, babe. Duty calls." He gave her a swift peck on the forehead and headed out. "Go make some luxe events," he called.

"Go save lives, babe." Another thing she could appreciate about her doctor husband, he certainly knew how to make her feel better.

Bridget picked up her cell and sent a quick email reply to Mr. Marco Richards, coordinating an in-person meeting with him. She was looking forward to the new business and was grateful to whoever sent him her way. It was the extra motivation she needed to show up and show out at this conference.

Being in the space was like a breath of fresh air. Atlanta's Fourth Annual Divas in Charge Summit was held at the Georgia International Convention Center in College Park. The place was packed wall-to-wall with female entrepreneurs from all walks of life, from makeup artists to investment bankers, and every creative, analytical, and social influencer in between. Bridget had been psyched when she secured a vendor booth for the normally sold-out event and even more so when the coordinator called her to ask her to participate as a speaker at one of the workshops.

It went unbelievably well, and Bridget managed to acquire

more clients for a few upcoming events. Plus, she had made some networking relationships for future business.

"Girl, how did it go?" Nikki asked as soon as Bridget returned from giving her speech. She had stayed behind to cover their booth in the exhibition hall, which housed all of the vendors. A maze of banners and products was on display as attendees volleyed between tables with goodie bags and giveaways.

Bridget grinned as she took a seat behind their table. "Do you really have to ask?" she gloated with a confident wink.

"Yes, girl, what I tell you!" Nikki did a little dance in the middle of the floor, which prompted a few amused glances from onlookers. "If we keep it up, I'll be able to buy myself two new Teslas for Christmas."

"Two? One for you and one for Jordan?"

Nikki laughed at the mention of her daughter. "Hell no. One for mama on the weekday, and one for mama on the weekend. Preferably in hot pink."

Bridget shook her head with a chuckle and lifted her crossed fingers. "We're getting there."

"I'm telling you," Nikki took a seat next to Bridget and handed her a bottle of water. "You should write a book or something on this shit, girl. You have a gift." Nikki touched her bottle against Bridget's in a mock toast as her words resonated in the air.

"A book? About what? Event planning?"

"Yeah," Nikki said with a slight shrug. "Or just business in general. Black female entrepreneurs are the most overlooked when it comes to being business savvy. Maybe you can give them the knowledge and confidence they need to pursue what they are passionate about. Like you."

Bridget nodded, the idea beginning to develop a little more. "Like us," she corrected.

Nikki's wink was one of appreciation as she rose to greet an attendee.

Bridget watched her girl work and had to swallow her own surge of triumph. Sure, she had the business side down pat, but she and Nikki made such a great team because they were both passionate, and it was more than obvious when they spoke to people.

Bridget leaned down to grab more business cards and brochures to replenish the table display when a familiar face caught her eye. She stared for a moment or two longer, pleasantly surprised.

The woman looked vastly different from when she was in the restroom back at the restaurant. This woman was professional and confident, smiling as she engaged with a couple raving about a plate of pastry samples.

Bridget walked over to her table and waited patiently while the couple made idle chatter, taking the time to survey the woman's setup.

Corrine, yes, that was her name. She did say she was a caterer, which was more than obvious by the large retractable banner she had set up at her booth. The vinyl had enlarged HD photos of gourmet dishes with the name A Taste of Corrine as well as her website and social media handles on display. She had set out various platters and bowls of samples to whet anyone's palate, and Bridget had to give her props for the indulgence. Two things she knew from her own experience that drew the folks in: freebies and food.

She plucked a sample cup with a sliver of salmon in it and used the accompanying utensil to fork the piece into her mouth. Absolutely delicious. Bridget let out a moan without even realizing it, savoring the Cajun flavors and spices that danced on her tongue.

"That good, huh?"

Bridget couldn't help the tiny flood of embarrassment at Corrine's knowing smile. "Actually, it is," she confessed.

"Thanks, girl. It's a little special recipe but definitely a favorite."

"I'm sure it is." And because Bridget didn't want to come across as sneaky, stalkerish, or crazy, she added, "Did we meet before? In the bathroom last week at Pappadeaux? You and your husband paid for our drinks?"

Corrine frowned, as if struggling to remember.

"I think you had had some kind of argument," Bridget reminded her. "We exchanged contact information."

Corrine snapped and her eyes brightened with recognition. "Oh yes, the . . . event planner, right?"

"Yep."

"Now I remember. You had some encouraging words for me that I really appreciated. What was your name again?"

"Bridget." Bridget reached across the table for a handshake.

Corrine accepted it with a vague gesture to her signage. "I'm Corrine, but of course you knew that."

"This salmon is so good, girl," Bridget complimented again. "I'm going to have to call you up to cook for me and my husband."

"Oh, yes, I do private events, too. Here, try my roast." Corrine was already pushing another sample cup in Bridget's hand before she had time to object. The aroma was rich with flavor and, by the looks of the slow cooker hooked up on a nearby table, Bridget knew this meat was about to be fresh, hot, and tender. She was most certainly not disappointed.

Bridget spent the next few minutes sampling everything from entrees to desserts, to Corrine's award-winning Better Than Yo Mama's Mac 'n Cheese. And dammit, she would never admit it to her mama, but the side dish definitely gave hers a run for the money. Plus, Corrine was so down-to-earth, with a warm and beautiful personality that was infectious.

"Hey, Bri," Nikki greeted, joining them both at Corrine's booth. "What y'all got over here that's smelling so damn good?"

"Girl, everything," Bridget said with a chuckle. "Nikki, this is Corrine. We met before, but I'm just now trying the food. We have to get her on the preferred caterers' list."

"Uh huh. I'll be the judge of that." Nikki helped herself to a sample of the peach cobbler, keeping her face neutral as she chewed.

"It's a little Hennessy in the cobbler," Corrine mentioned with a smirk.

Nikki swallowed, stifling a smile of her own. "Okay, I'm going to need to try one of everything at this table," she teased. "Just to confirm."

Corrine laughed. "I got a better idea." She glanced to Bridget. "There's this restaurant on the Southside where the owner is a good friend of mine. He has a few of my dishes on the menu. You ladies maybe up for a late lunch after this?"

Chapter Four
Corrine

At first, Coldwater Avenue didn't seem like the kind of place that would cater to a special caliber of people. The name alone was too vague to suggest it was an upscale gourmet dining establishment with signature seafood selections and premium imported wines. Patrons appeared average, albeit over dressed for an afternoon. Yet still, the fact that these folks were a part of the alternative lifestyle community wouldn't even register. That was how the owner, Marco Richards, preferred it. Some secrets were meant to stay hidden. But that was exactly where Corrine needed Bridget to be for the next part of the plan to fall into place.

The lodge-like restaurant gave the ambiance of a rusty cabin, adorned with exposed beam ceilings, plank flooring, and antler chandeliers with low-level mood lighting to add to the mystery. Shades were drawn to filter out the sunlight from the floor-to-ceiling windows. The showpiece was a huge stone waterfall feature in the center of the restaurant that poured into a surrounding fountain, the soothing noise of the water the only music needed.

"This place is gorgeous," Nikki commented as they were seated in an intimate booth in the back.

"I didn't even know this was over here," Bridget added. "You sure as hell can't tell it's a restaurant. How long has this been open?"

Corrine thought back to when she and Pat had met Marco. He was only talking about the restaurant then, making it an extension of his club. The time had really flown by. "About five years now, I suppose," she answered. "It's one of those places that's not highly publicized, but the food speaks for itself."

"Because your stuff is on it, huh?"

Corrine shrugged, feigning nonchalance. "Touché."

The server came over, greeting Corrine by name, and introducing herself to Bridget and Nikki.

"It's on me, ladies," Corrine offered after the server rattled off drink specials. "So get whatever you want. I want to make a good impression."

"No, you don't have to do that." Bridget waved away Corrine's gesture with a flick of her wrist. "You've probably hipped us to our new favorite place, so we'll be back."

Corrine was counting on it.

She felt her phone vibrate and automatically knew it was Patrick. She didn't bother acknowledging the call. In his usual controlling fashion, Pat would just be checking up on her, wanting a play-by-play to ensure she wasn't fucking everything up. Pat wanted what he wanted, and he was particular with liking things a certain way. Corrine had the aged bruises coloring her cocoa-brown skin to prove it. Unconsciously, she lifted her hand to readjust the collar of her chiffon emerald blouse, making sure it was hiding as much of her skin as possible. She turned back to her tablemates.

Nikki's eyes homed in on the menu, skimming each of the options. "Which one of these dishes are yours?"

"The braised chicken and the lamb. Also, the crab cakes if you want an appetizer."

Bridget and Nikki relayed their orders to the server before she flounced away.

"So, Corrine, tell us about yourself." Nikki spoke up first after their drinks were served. "After all, if we're going to be working together, we need to get to know you."

Corrine took a sip of her wine to stall a little. Out of the corner of her eye, she monitored Bridget, trying to gauge her interest in Nikki's inquiry.

"Of course, what do you want to know?" she asked finally.

"For starters, how long have you been a chef?" Bridget said. "And who you taught you how to cook?"

Do you mean before or after I was berated as a child for even wanting to cook? Corrine mused. After all, she was supposed to be outside, playing basketball or asking neighbors if she could mow their lawn for five bucks. At least that's what her dad made sure to drill into Corrine. And with her weak-minded mother too afraid to speak out against Mr. Jeremy Crenshaw, his word was as good as gospel.

"Let's see." Corrine chose her words carefully. "I've always known I had a passion for cooking. My sister used to teach me some things, but a lot I learned from reading recipes and watching shows on TV and YouTube. Then I started experimenting with different things until I found what worked."

"How long have you been in business?" Bridget asked.

"Almost eight years, but I recently started doing this full-time. Before that, it was just something for a little extra money."

"Yeah, we know how that goes," Bridget agreed. "But hey, girl, kudos to you for pursuing your passion. And your husband for supporting you."

Ha, Corrine couldn't agree so much on that last part, but she nodded anyway. "How do you two know each other? Other than business partners?" The question was more of an attempt to redirect the attention. She had done more than enough research on both women to know their friendship was rooted as far back as middle school. Yet still, she listened attentively and nodded politely as the two launched into their history, even tossed in some engaging chuckles as they reminisced. Corrine listened for what she needed, catching snatches of dialogue to piece together enough backstory to share with Patrick later.

A phone rang, and instinct had Corrine's eyes dropping to her purse. But it was Bridget who pulled out her cell phone, a goofy grin crossing her face as she checked the caller ID. She held up a finger to pause the conversation before putting the phone to her ear. "Hey, babe," she gushed. "It went really good, just came to lunch with some girlfriends." With that, she rose, signaling she was going to step away to finish her call.

Corrine hadn't meant her sigh to sound envious, but there was a time Patrick could make her feel those butterflies. That, too, had transitioned.

"Those two, I swear." Nikki shook her head with a smirk once they were alone. "When I get me a man that loves me like Roman does her, I swear y'all hoes ain't going to be able to tell me shit." She chuckled at her own joke. "Are you married?"

"Yep." *If you could call it that.*

"Good for you." Nikki lifted her glass in the air in a mock toast. "Hopefully you two haven't tied down the last two good ones left. I'm still holding out for my Prince Charming."

If Corrine could co-sign on that one, she would. She merely forked a piece of her crab cake in her mouth and chewed.

Bridget returned to the table mere moments later. "Sorry about that," she said. "Roman just had a little break and wanted to chat."

"Oh? What does he do?" Corrine asked, keeping her interest as mild as possible.

"He's an ER doctor at Southern Regional," Bridget said with a proud smile.

Noted. Corrine knew she would have to make a point to pay Mr. Roman a little visit. She remembered him vaguely from the restaurant, but it wouldn't hurt to get a more up close and personal consultation of her own to see what she would be working with.

Out of the corner of her eye, Corrine recognized her friend Marco speaking to one of the bartenders. She pushed back from the table. "I'll be right back," she said and rose to make her way over to him.

Corrine followed Marco into the kitchen, being met with the familiar organized chaos of cooking activity, noises, and fragrances. She lifted her hand in greeting to a few of the folks she knew before catching up to Marco at the stove and tapping him on the arm.

Marco turned with a huge smile displaying a row of pearly whites. His Hispanic roots colored his words with an accent that heightened his flamboyance. But it really came down to the tight pants and the white boyfriend he often toted on his arm to really solidify his gay sexuality.

"Corrine," he greeted with two air kisses on either side of her cheeks. "You should've told me you were coming up here today."

Corrine braced against the stainless steel prep counter, the small of her back pressed against the edge. "I wanted you to see the young lady I was telling you about," she said. "Plus, she wanted to try some of my dishes."

Habit had Marco rubbing his baby-smooth chin. The gesture would have made more sense had he not cut his beard. "Ah yes, the event planner," he said with a recollective nod. "I sent her an email and she responded. We're meeting next week. But I can tell you now, she's as good as gold coming from your referral."

Corrine smiled. She should have known Marco wouldn't let her down. They had been friends for way too long.

Marco's eyes suddenly narrowed as he studied Corrine's face.

"How's Patrick?" He didn't even bother to hide the animosity. The question was less of a "how is he" and more so "how had she been with him."

Corrine's hands fisted at her sides to keep from making some obvious gesture to draw more attention. The last time she had so casually, or what she thought was casually, readjusted her shirt, the material had lifted just enough to expose the aging bruises on her stomach. That had been one of the only times they had argued. So, to keep from going down that road again, both just tiptoed around the elephant in the room.

"Everything is good," she lied. "Just working, as usual. Staying busy."

Marco looked as if he knew the ambiguous response was just a cover, but he didn't dig any further. "Well, you be sure and let me know if you need anything," he said instead.

Corrine grabbed his hand and gave it a reassuring squeeze. "I just need to get Bridget planning this party for you," she said. "So she and her husband can get in on all the fun at the club. That's all."

Marco looked as if he wanted to say something, his eyebrows creased in a troubling slant that defined his boyish features.

"Hey, I got it." Corrine went ahead and answered the question so evident on her friend's face. Whether she felt it or not, she didn't need Marco worrying about her and Patrick's issues. She couldn't handle disappointing him, too.

Chapter Five
Bridget

Bridget had to check and recheck the address just to make sure she was in the right place. She peered through the windshield at the wrought-iron gate and looked once more at the GPS on her phone. And, just to reassure herself, she quickly opened her email to the last correspondence she received from Marco Richards, setting up their little consultation. Trammel Road. She was in the right place. She had never been this deep in Cumming, Georgia, but when the email mentioned she would be coordinating for an exclusive membership club, she didn't expect the majestic mansion nestled some ways back from the road amid fall foliage and overhanging trees.

The email provided Mr. Marco Richards's phone number and said to call should she have any issues finding the place. Bridget punched in the digits and put the phone to her ear. If this was some sort of scam or human trafficking setup . . .

"Hi, Mr. Richards," Bridget greeted when the gentleman answered. "This is Bridget Pierce, with—"

"Yes, of course, I see you've made it."

Bridget froze, once again eyeing the gate through the windshield.

"On the camera." Marco's chuckle was light with amusement. "Come on in."

He didn't bother waiting for her reply before hanging up. As if on cue, the gate opened, exposing the winding stone driveway that led up to the house. Bridget debated for a moment or two longer. It wasn't like she had never met someone at their residence before to conduct business. Plus, both Nikki and Roman knew exactly where she was, should something happen. Could never be too careful.

There was no reason for the apprehension, she knew. Bridget had to admit she expected . . . well, hell, she really didn't know what she expected. And, because she knew she probably looked completely foolish on this man's camera just sitting at the edge of his driveway, Bridget eased away from the curb and turned into the residence.

The house, or club, or whatever the building was supposed to be was absolutely gorgeous, though, she had to admit. A large fountain dominated the manicured front lawn with professionally trimmed shrubbery flanking the European exterior. The yard stretched on for miles and miles in each direction, and the driveway looked like it had room to accommodate at least twenty cars. Right now, other than Bridget's Infiniti, a royal blue Benz glistened in the afternoon sun, parked under a porte cochere that led into the courtyard.

Bridget gave herself a final once-over in the rearview mirror, making sure her makeup was still just as flawless as when she applied it earlier that morning. She'd pinned her hair up into a neat ponytail at the top of her head and now it flowed to brush the shoulders of her navy pinstriped skirt suit. The yellow blouse was just the right pop of color. Her message was clear. She was fun, easygoing, but damn sure about her business. She smiled to herself and, grabbing her briefcase from the passenger seat, opened her door.

"Good afternoon."

Bridget nearly screamed at the sudden voice as she emerged from her car. She hadn't noticed the man standing mere steps away, dressed casually in black slacks and a black shirt unbuttoned enough to expose just a hint of his toned chest. He was barefoot, his hands shoved casually in his pockets, and his sleek black hair was wet as if he'd just gotten out of the shower.

"Sorry." He smiled as Bridget tried to catch her breath. "Didn't mean to scare you. Thought you saw me here waiting for you."

"No, I didn't." She felt the embarrassment color her cheeks. "Is Mr. Marco Richards in?" Dumb question, she knew, but at that moment, she was slightly flustered from the abrupt intrusion.

The man's smile was warm, immediately giving off a boyish charm. "You're looking at him," he said, holding out his hand. "Pleasure to meet you, Mrs. Bridget Pierce."

Bridget was slow to accept his hand, still scrutinizing. She had done some research before their meeting. Marco Richards was quite a wealthy investor with a number of successful businesses in his enterprise. This young man looked like he should've been frolicking on a beach somewhere offering mojitos or Jet Skis. He certainly didn't even look like he owned a suit, or a tie, that's for sure. For a moment, she wondered if he was just a silver spoon baby, having inherited all of his daddy's riches and companies. She quickly dispelled the thought. Money was money and business was business. And Mr. Marco here looked like he was ready to give her a lot of both.

"Nice to meet you, too, Mr. Richards," she said with a polite smile. "Forgive me, but I didn't expect we would be meeting at your home."

"Ah, I understand. This is my home and my business." His

chuckle was light. "What can I say? I'm a workaholic. And it beats having to drive to the office. Can I get that for you?" In classic gentlemanly fashion, he was already taking her briefcase from her hands and closing her car door for her. "Come inside so we can talk. I'm anxious to get to know you and tell you about what I have in mind."

Bridget nodded and followed as he led the way to the front door. Why did she get the feeling he was sizing her up? *Interesting.*

The interior of the home was just as impressive as the exterior. Immediately upon walking through the front door, they entered a two-story foyer with marble floors and the letters *SL* encrusted in the unique design. Overhead, a Swarovski crystal–trimmed chandelier glittered like a million gold diamonds illuminating a grand marble staircase curving up both sides of the entry and closed off with velvet ropes. Right in the center, which seemed unusual, was a tempered glass–topped reception desk, again with the initials *SL* etched in silver on the front panel.

"Would you like something to eat or drink?" Marco offered, passing Bridget's briefcase back to her.

"Um, no thanks."

Marco gestured toward a closed door off to the right-hand side. "We'll take this in my manager's office. She won't be in until later. Why don't you wait in there, and I'll be right with you?"

Obediently, Bridget crossed into the room. It was large, but simplistic in design with a standard desk and two chevron chairs in front. Filing cabinets and bookcases covered an entire back wall, and a bay window was open displaying a prominent view of the front yard.

Bridget opened her briefcase and pulled out some folders of paperwork she had prepared in anticipation for their meeting. Optimism had her already drawing up the contract, but she decided to leave that in the briefcase until he was ready to move forward. Didn't want to jump the gun. She shot a quick text to Nikki to let her know she had arrived and would call afterward with the details, and then turned her phone on silent.

Marco entered with two glasses of red wine, setting one in front of Bridget as he took a seat behind the desk. "I know you said you didn't want anything," he said. "But I didn't want to be rude."

Bridget nodded her thanks, but still, she didn't touch the glass. "So, tell me about your event, Mr. Richards," she started, uncapping her pen and positioning a spiral notebook on her lap. "What kind of event is it, what is your budget, theme . . . What do you have in mind?"

Marco relaxed in the wingback chair, taking a leisurely sip of his drink. "It's an appreciation-type of celebration," he said. "Sort of an annual thing I throw every year on the anniversary of when I opened the club. I like to go all out, so decorations, food, drinks, entertainment, the whole nine."

Bridget jotted notes as she nodded along. "And do you have a theme in mind?"

"Nope. Haven't thought that far."

"No worries." Bridget scribbled the word *theme* with a question mark and circled it so she would remember to revisit that topic later. "What did you do last year?"

Marco crossed his legs, resting the base of his wineglass on his thigh. "Last year, it was a masquerade theme. Before that, Vegas. Both were fun, so I wanted to stay in that same type of arena. Sexy, sensual, and completely uninhibited."

Bridget nodded, her brain already working in overdrive. "Well, I can come up with a few ideas in a proposal," she said. "But right off the bat, I'm thinking something like Cirque du Soleil. A sexy circus, if you will. Acrobats—"

"That's perfect," Marco jumped in. "Let's do that. I like it."

Bridget chuckled to herself as she made herself some notes. He was an easy one to work with. That would make her and Nikki's job even better.

"Usually, me and my team do all of this ourselves," Marco went on. "But damn, I'm so glad I'm hiring you. This is a huge thing, with over a hundred people, and I just don't have the time to worry about all of that."

"Fair enough. When are you wanting the party?"

"Week and a half."

Bridget's pen paused over the paper, and she looked up in shock. "Sir, you want me to put together a large-scale event for a hundred people in less than two weeks?"

"Yep." Marco leaned forward and set his glass on the desk. He began rummaging through drawers until he found a checkbook and a pen. "You already have the venue. Right here. And I have a phenomenal caterer already in mind. Just give her a call and tell her what you want. That should make it a little easier for you. So how much do you need to make it all happen?" he asked, opening the book to a blank check.

Bridget watched his movements, all the while trying to run some quick estimates in her head. Damn, maybe she should have insisted Nikki come with her. She had just figured they would be going over details so she could draw up proposals and estimations of costs after doing some research to make sure what he wanted was even feasible. But, Mr. Millionaire Marco was sitting here with his pen on the dotted line, waiting for whatever figure she tossed his way.

"Um, Mr. Richards, I don't want to misquote you," Bridget said. "I would have to get with my business partner so we can see how to pull off your vision. I do have a contract you can sign to lock you in and then we would get some packages together—"

"That's not necessary." Marco was already shaking his head as he signed his name on the check and ripped it from the perforated edge. He slid the check across the desk. "You came highly recommended from a very good friend of mine, and let's just say I trust this friend's word. So do whatever you need to do to make this happen. No budget. And I'll double the commission for you and your partner. How about that?"

Bridget looked at the blank check and back to Marco. He was completely serious.

"Who recommended me?" she asked. Not that it mattered. She would be a damn idiot not to take him up on the offer. Nikki would have called her every name in the book if she let her rational side interfere with this opportunity.

"Doesn't matter," Marco said, rising. He gestured to the glass Bridget had left untouched, right beside the check. "Shall we make a toast to a wonderful party?"

She hesitated, only briefly, before grabbing the glass and standing up across from him. Marco smiled and clinked his against hers, and she took a sip, letting the smooth taste of Merlot slide down her throat.

A light knock on the door had Marco looking up. "Come in," he called.

The man, dressed in matching black slacks and a button-up shirt padded into the room with a folder in his hands. Typical blond hair, blue-eyed type with his sleeves rolled up to the elbow to reveal chiseled arms. "Excuse me," he said, nodding first in Bridget's direction before crossing to Marco. "Here's that guest list you wanted, Marco."

"Thanks." Marco accepted the folder, flipping it open to skim the documents inside. "Oh, I'm sorry," he said with a chuckle, as if suddenly remembering. "Where are my manners? Jonathan, this is Mrs. Bridget Pierce, our new event coordinator."

Bridget exchanged a friendly handshake with the man.

"She's handling the anniversary party for the club," Marco added. "And if we play our cards right, we might be able to convince Mrs. Pierce here to handle all of Shadow Lounge's events."

"Oh, that would certainly be fabulous." Jonathan grinned. "Glad to have you on board. The club is known for its phenomenal parties. Well, that and other things." He chuckled and nudged an elbow at Marco, as if sharing some secret joke.

Bridget wasn't really sure how to respond, so she simply said, "I'm excited to work with you both."

"Oh, I like her, Marco," Jonathan said, nudging Marco again with a coy smile. "And she's cute. You'll fit right in." He turned back to Marco. "Anything else, sweetie?"

"No, this is perfect. Thank you."

Bridget watched as they shared a quick peck on the lips before Jonathan left them alone once more.

"Sorry about that." Marco gestured to the closed door. "My husband can be as much of a workaholic as I am."

So he was gay. She'd had her suspicions when she first met him outside, but hadn't wanted to harp on it for fear of making him uncomfortable. Not that she cared, but her mind couldn't help but wonder back to Jonathan's words. *Among other things.* So did that mean . . .

"So Shadow Lounge is the name of the club," Bridget said casually as she began to put her things back in the briefcase.

"Yep. This is my baby. It's for a very *niche* type of crowd."

"You mean like for you and your husband?"

Marco smirked. "Something like that. But I hope the fact that we're gay doesn't make you feel any different about—"

"Oh, no, no, not at all." Bridget quickly waved away his assumption. "I apologize. I didn't mean it like that. I just have never heard of the club, and if you were thinking I could plan some more of the events, it would help to know the clientele. That's all."

Marco paused, his face creased in consideration.

"Or, if you would prefer I didn't, that's completely fine," Bridget rushed on.

"No, no, you're right. I should've thought of that earlier. That makes perfect sense." He gestured toward the chair behind Bridget. "Please, sit back down for a moment."

Bridget lowered herself back to the chair and started to pull out her notebook once again. She laid it on the desk, and Marco placed his hand on top of it to stop her from writing, his fingers spread to block the page.

"This is not really something for the notes," he said with a gentle smile. "More of an off-the-record thing, if you will. Just listen for me and I'll be happy to tell you all about the Shadow Lounge."

Bridget nodded and sat back. Well now, he had certainly piqued her interest.

Bridget was in the bed working when she heard the garage door open. The computer was open on her lap, and her planning notes lay scattered across the sheets. Since Nikki was putting the final touches on a wedding they had coordinated, Bridget had offered to take the lead on Marco's event, especially because they only had a couple weeks to make it happen. She hadn't been able to get out of the door quickly enough before she was already putting in calls to her connections, working out the details for the Cirque du Soleil theme she had suggested. Truth be told, it was very ambitious and, looking back, Bridget would have opted for something simpler had she known of her very limited time constraints. But then again, the more lavish the better, and Marco had specifically instructed her to "go all out" with no budget. And now, knowing what kind of club Shadow Lounge was, they were looking to use all the bells and whistles. Because she was counting on that fat-ass commission check, Bridget planned on pulling off nothing short of a miracle. The challenge was thrilling. And in Jonathan's words, "That among other things." She couldn't wait to share the news with Roman. As soon as he hurried his ass and came upstairs.

She heard him in the kitchen, messing around in cabinets and rattling dishes, obviously looking for something to eat. She doubted the soul food plate she picked up from Anna Laura's Kitchen on the way home was even still down there considering Dorian had done his own rummaging for food only a few hours before. She wasn't trying to be smug, but a few more days and nights of cereal and maybe Roman would finally talk to his friend and kick him the hell out.

"Hey, babe," Roman greeted, entering their bedroom. He looked completely worn out as he started peeling off his clothes. "You're up late."

Bridget glanced at the clock on the nightstand. Yeah, she was definitely engrossed in work. When did it turn three in the morning? As if on cue, she yawned and stretched her tightened limbs. "Just wanted to get some things done," she said, powering off her computer. "But I'm calling it a night. You look exhausted. Long day?"

Roman nodded as he trudged into the adjoining bathroom. He didn't bother elaborating, and Bridget didn't push any further. It took a while for her to get used to her husband's nonverbal communication regarding his job, and she was resigned that it was his way of dealing with the trauma of working in a hospital. Of course, he had his share of minor emergencies like fevers and pains. But she knew to exercise caution after witnessing how shaken up he could get when the issues were more serious, such as car accidents and heart attacks. She would never forget hearing him cry in the shower after he lost an eight-year-old on the operating table trying to treat him for a gunshot wound. A tragic case of being in the wrong place at the wrong time. It had rocked Roman to his core because the little boy had been the same age as his daughter, her stepdaughter Maya.

Roman emerged from the bathroom a few minutes later, completely naked, his delicious body still sprinkled with water from the spots he had missed with the towel. Bridget waited until he climbed in the bed and automatically she turned to snuggle into his arms. His sigh was one of relief.

"How was your meeting?" he murmured.

"Good. It was at Shadow Lounge."

"Never heard of it."

"Yeah, I hadn't either." Bridget paused, before adding what she had been itching to reveal. "It's a swingers' club."

"Oh, wow." Roman chuckled in amusement. "What are you planning for a swingers' club?"

"Some kind of anniversary, client appreciation party." Bridget tried her best to take the enthusiasm out of her voice.

Ever since Marco had revealed the information, the idea had been bouncing around in her head. Not necessarily being a swinger—she was perfectly satisfied with her husband so that had never crossed her mind. But the swinging lifestyle and the people involved. Marco had mentioned the non-disclosure agreement, membership, and exclusivity aspects because he assured her there were notable people that frequented the club. Lawyers, politicians, executives, and a number of the who's who in the elite circles. People she wouldn't have suspected and who were determined to keep this part of their lives away from the limelight. Maybe that was it. All the secrecy and mystery surrounding the arrangements made it all the more fascinating.

"You and your husband should come one night," Marco had suggested, which Bridget had immediately declined. It wasn't like she and Roman were swingers, nor were they open to the idea, she didn't think. So she didn't even think the invitation was worth mentioning. But still, something clawed at her, like the embers of a campfire with crackles of tiny flames threatening to intensify. She just had to be sure not to blow on the fire.

Roman was beginning to doze; she could hear it in his breathing, as it got heavier. Bridget turned her attention to something else that had been festering ever since the conference. "Babe, what do you think of me writing a book?" she asked. "Nikki brought it up and, I don't know, it sounded interesting and I wanted to look into it."

"I wouldn't worry about all of that now, honestly," he said. "You're busy enough as it is." And that was that. Bridget hadn't known what to expect, but support was definitely on the list. Hearing his apathetic dismissal of her idea, well, the shit hurt. But then again, maybe he was just tired.

It took her back briefly to when she first mentioned to Roman that she and Nikki wanted to start their event-planning business. She was wanting to leave her boring job at an insurance company and pursue her passion. He hadn't been as supportive as she would have liked, even then. Job security, he had mentioned. Being an entrepreneur required a lot of time and work with so many variables that could contribute to its success or failure. Whereas her corporate job was steady, a nine-to-five routine with a salary check every two weeks. But Bridget had always been a risk-taker. It was the thrill for her. Hell, why else did Roman think she had accepted his marriage proposal after only four months of dating? Because it felt right. And Bridget moved accordingly, even if others disagreed.

Roman didn't have many faults that she could tally. But one thing for sure that came up sporadically was his lack of support for her ventures. He was more old-fashioned in that regard. He, being the husband, would provide and take care of the household. His job was demanding enough, so he wanted his wife's main focus to be the home and children. He needed that stability for his own peace of mind. Anything outside of that neat little box tended to make him uncomfortable. And Bridget, well, she was anything but traditional in that sense.

Of course, he finally came around to her wanting to quit her job and pursue entrepreneurship full-time, but it sure as hell had been a fight. It wasn't until Brinique Lux Affair had scored some pretty big clients and was raking in profits within the first six months of business that Roman gave her the credit she deserved.

The book idea was just that, an idea. Had she really expected her husband to go for yet another business venture of hers? The answer was yes, she had. But being perfectly honest with herself, she should've known her husband wouldn't immediately concur.

Even as the thought crossed her mind, Roman's light snore filled the darkened room. Bridget sighed, lying awake, pinned between him and the bed before she eased her body from underneath his arm. He didn't so much as stir.

Bridget picked up her laptop from the table and powered it back on. This party wasn't going to plan itself. But first, she wanted to see what else was out there about Shadow Lounge. Sure, she had been interested. But now, she felt vested.

Chapter Six
Corrine

Corrine's hand paused an inch away from the door. She didn't feel up to mingling. She was more in the mood for solitude. A long bath mixed with scented oils, maybe a glass of wine to mellow out and take her mind off of everything. Patrick was working late, so she was sure she could find something unexpired perhaps, somewhere among the instant dinner boxes in the overstuffed freezer. She let her hand fall back to her side and stared at the closed door. She didn't want to. Period. That didn't make her some kind of villain just because she didn't want to go to her mother's birthday dinner.

The door swung open, the unmistakable scent of a fresh pot roast beckoned her like a seductive finger, and Vanessa stood with her gap-toothed smile warm, inviting, and expectant. All prior thoughts settled in the recesses of her mind as Corrine smiled back down at her niece.

"We've been waiting for you, Auntie," Vanessa squealed, grabbing Corrine's hand and pulling her inside. "Mommy said you were going to change your mind."

"Well, your mommy needs to have a little more faith." She spoke loud enough for Gina to hear her over the music filling the tiny apartment. As expected, her sister's round face poked from the kitchen, and she narrowed her eyes, looking all too much like an expression Corrine had seen on herself many times.

"Oh, I have plenty of faith," Gina responded with a smile. "I just know my sister."

They could almost pass for twins. Same peanut butter complexion, same jet black eyes that seemed to pierce when focused, same pouty lips with the one dimple winking at the right cheek with every curl, snarl, and smirk. Nevertheless, even though Gina had tried to put the pieces of her life back together, Corrine could see past the visage. She could see the permanent worry lines creasing her sister's forehead, the bags under each eye that evidenced many a sleepless night, and all her other physical attributes that came not with age but with stress. It made her look much older than the three years that separated them.

Vanessa pulled Corrine into the dining room, the round table already set for four. She glanced around, noting the intimate, comfortable atmosphere over here compared to her own home. Where Corrine had tried to pamper her neglect with expensive furniture and trinkets, Gina's place was elaborately decorated with vibrant colors and foolish thrift store and yard sale accessories that didn't match. Style had never been her sister's strong suit.

Corrine glanced around and let out a relieved sigh when she realized her mother hadn't arrived yet. Gina bumped her playfully as she walked by with a dish of mashed potatoes in hand.

"I heard that." She grinned, setting the dish on the table. "And look, if it's any consolation, I appreciate you coming tonight."

"I know." Corrine sat down in her usual spot, stretching her legs underneath the table. "And that's the only reason why I came."

"Mama appreciates it, too. She just doesn't know how to express it."

Corrine rolled her eyes at the excuse. "Well, she sure has no problem expressing anything else that's on her mind."

Gina glanced at Vanessa, who was all but hanging on every exchange of their words. "Go wash your hands," she instructed.

Vanessa pouted but, obediently, she climbed from the chair and scurried toward the back of the apartment.

Gina waited, listening to the fading scramble of feet. When she was sure the little girl was out of earshot, she leaned toward her sister, lowering her voice. "Look, I'm not saying you have to sit here and have fun," she said. "But please just try to be cordial. It's her birthday. And you know how she hasn't been the same since Daddy died. This is hard for her."

Corrine was tempted to remind her how hard they had it growing up, first with Corrine coming out as transgender and then poor Gina, as a cisgender woman, having to be subjected to equal ridicule because their parents feared she was "confused" too. The only difference was that Gina had forgiven them. Corrine hadn't.

She had never been one to celebrate death, but oh, did she rejoice when that bastard father of hers passed away. Now, with their mother still wrestling with stretches of grief and adjusting to her new normal as a widow, Corrine didn't have an ounce of sympathy. Served the bitch right.

Corrine glanced away from Gina's pleading gaze and shrugged a half-hearted shoulder. She felt Gina's gentle hand cover hers, firm enough to draw her eyes back.

"Promise you'll be good, Sis. Please?"

"As long as she stays in her place," Corrine stated, slightly relieved when the doorbell interrupted her sister's objection. Gina cast one more desperate look her way, silently begging for Corrine's cooperation, before disappearing from the dining room.

Corrine remained seated, idly fingering a napkin. The beginning of a dull ache was already throbbing at her temples.

She tolerated Paula, plain and simple. Sure, there may have been some fraction of love somewhere in her heart for the woman, but that was out of traditional obedience. Too many years of Paula's conditional love and judgments had strained their relationship; so much so that Corrine could've gone the rest of her life without seeing her and not cared one bit.

Corrine heard the front door open and close, then the click of her mother's shoes headed down the hall. She sighed, already knowing this evening was not going to be as peaceful as Gina had hoped.

"I'm surprised to see you." Paula's voice was curt and laced with a chill of arrogance, a complete contrast to the overjoyed warmth she had just displayed in the other room. Corrine was not surprised when she didn't bother addressing her by name. Neither she nor their father had given her that much respect.

Paula stepped around her daughter and sat down at the table, the creased tan slacks not so much as wrinkling with the brisk movement. Paula looked thinner than Corrine remembered, but it wasn't like she saw her mother often enough to know for sure. Paula made no move to speak further, and Corrine could only shake her head.

"Just surprised?" she asked. "Not, happy, not appreciative?"

Paula glanced up, a phony smile touching her lips. "Well, I didn't know you were coming. But it's good to see you anyway," she responded flatly.

The cold response should have hurt. Would have hurt in the past. However, Corrine had grown numb to the attitude.

They remained quiet, and for a while, all that could be heard were the R & B instrumentals Gina had playing on the Bluetooth speaker. Corrine watched her mother pick at some invisible lint on her shirt, averting her eyes and making it more than obvious she wanted to do everything but engage with her daughter. Funny how a casual dinner among family could be so awkward.

"So . . ." Corrine sighed when Paula continued to pay entirely too much attention to the buttons on her shirt. "How has everything been with you, Mama?"

"Fine."

"Gina told me you were planning on taking a cruise at the end of the year with some ladies from the church."

Paula didn't bother to voice a response, just merely nodded absently.

Corrine shut her eyes and took a labored breath. "Where do you think you'll go?"

Paula shrugged, her silver-streaked curls bouncing off her shoulder.

Corrine rolled her eyes. "You know, I'm trying to be nice here. The least you can do is pretend to have a decent conversation with me."

Her mother frowned, parting her lips to toss back what was sure to be a snide remark when Vanessa came running into the room. Corrine watched the familiar transformation. The warmth lit Paula's eyes, the genuine smile blossomed, and for a moment, she actually seemed angelic.

"There's my 'Nessa." Paula pulled her granddaughter to sit on her lap. "Tell Granny what you've been learning in school."

And just that quick, Corrine knew she had been shut off. She watched them laugh, joke, and bounce from subject to subject as if they were the only two in the room. At least the stifling tension had disappeared.

Corrine rested her head in her palm, gently massaging the headache with her fingertips. Just until dinner was served, she promised herself. She would stay long enough for Gina to serve the pot roast, then she could escape to her own safe haven and shut herself in with some aspirin. She eyed her mother out of the corner of her eye. If she could last that long.

The succulent scents of a gourmet meal perfumed the air as Gina carted in dish after dish and arranged them in the center of the table. Corrine spooned healthy servings on her plate, halfway listening to Gina and Paula engage in some small talk about their phone conversation earlier. She was starving and at that point didn't care if neither one of them addressed her. Just let her eat herself sick and doze into an overfed coma right there at the table.

"So, Corrine," Gina prompted, expertly steering the conversation, "tell us something interesting. How is work? How is Patrick?"

Corrine glanced up and could only smile at her sister's attempt. "The usual," she answered. "Work is pretty steady. And Pat is good. He's working late at the garage or he would've joined us."

Paula snorted as she poured herself another glass of lemonade. "Of course he's working late."

Corrine narrowed her eyes at the pointed statement. "And what's that supposed to mean?"

Paula glanced up from her plate, feigning innocence. "No need to be offended."

Corrine opened her mouth and shut it again when she felt the slight nudge of Gina's foot on her leg under the table. *Lord, please give me strength.* Obediently, she swallowed the response on the edge of her tongue and instead took a bite out of her roll. She glanced over in time to see Gina's expression of gratitude before she cleared her throat and spoke up again.

"Didn't you attend some kind of conference?" Gina inquired with a knowing nod of her head. "How did that go?" The question was almost desperate.

Obliging, Corrine sighed and took a sip of her sweet tea, choosing her words carefully. "It went good. Met a lot of other entrepreneurs. Did some networking. I probably have a few more events coming up soon." The Shadow Lounge party crossed her mind. She had spoken with Marco shortly after his consultation with Bridget, so she knew they were planning to pull it off in a couple weeks. She also knew Marco requested her catering services, so it was only a matter of time before Bridget called her so they could chat about the menu.

"I'm glad to hear business is doing well." Gina's lips curved in amusement. "I remember when you first told me you wanted to be a chef, I thought you were joking to get out of homework."

"Yeah, we thought *he* was joking about a lot of things," Paula mumbled under her breath, bringing her glass to her lips.

Corrine felt the anger beginning to boil, hot and familiar as it bubbled up to warm her neck, right under her collarbone.

Gina spoke up first, lifting her hand to silence Corrine before she could open her mouth. "Mama, we talked about you using the incorrect pronouns," she said, her voice firm. "Corrine and I both have corrected your error multiple times, so to keep doing it is blatantly disrespectful."

"No, don't worry about it." Corrine pushed her chair back and rose to her feet. "She does this shit every time and then wonders why I don't want to be bothered." She was so damn pissed she hadn't even tried to curtail her language, knowing Vanessa was in the room.

"Corrine, please sit down," Gina pleaded. "Let's try and do this for Mama's birthday."

"Oh, give me a break," Paula snapped, throwing up her hands. "Everyone wants to do something for my birthday or think they know what's best for me, but no one has bothered to ask me what I want."

"Okay, fine." Corrine sat down and pulled her chair up to the table. She held her hands out in Paula's direction. "What is it that *you* want, Paula?"

"You see that, Gina?" Paula's accusatory finger shot out in Corrine's direction. "You want to talk about respect, but look at how this child talks to me."

"This *child's* name is Corrine, but you can't even bring yourself to acknowledge that, can you?"

"Okay, you two, enough!" Gina was nearly in tears as she pulled Vanessa up from the table. "Sweetie, go to your room for a second and let Granny, Mommy, and Auntie talk, okay?"

Vanessa nodded, her eyes ballooned in wonder. She dragged her feet down the hall toward the bedrooms in the back.

"Look at that," Paula went on. "My grandchild is only seven and you have her confused. Telling her to call you *Auntie* when you're really her uncle."

Corrine's lips trembled open and, like so many times before, she felt the tears beginning to burn her eyes. "I am a woman," she said through clenched teeth. "Why can't you see that?"

"Because you're my son, *Christopher.*" Paula was on her feet, nearly shouting in exasperation. "I had a boy. Just because you put on a dress and heels doesn't make you a woman. I've put up with this shit for far too long."

Gina put her hand on Paula's arm to stop her rant, but she merely snatched it out of her grasp. "No, I need to say this," she said. "Now, your father and I gave you everything. You and your sister. But you want to be so ungrateful, so defiant as to keep up this *make-believe* for all of these years. You already gave your father a heart attack, and now you're trying to kill me, too?"

"Mama, you are completely delusional." Corrine watched the woman in front of her, the woman who birthed and raised her, yet a complete stranger. She managed to keep her voice calm, but the anger vibrated through each syllable. "I am who I am. That's something you're going to have to accept."

"I don't have to accept shit," Paula snapped. "I was pregnant for nine months and in labor twenty-six hours before giving birth to a *boy.* That's the reality we're living in. Now if you want to wear your sister's clothes, fine. If you want to be gay, fine. Just stop dragging this family's name through the mud and confusing my impressionable granddaughter."

Corrine was visibly shaking. Their mother's words were ripping her to shreds, and she could almost feel the bleeding.

"Mama, please," Gina spoke up now, her voice cracking. "You're sadly mistaken about the LGBTQ community. Transgender and gay are not the same. Corrine has tried to get you to go to therapy so you can get educated—"

"Therapy? I don't need no damn therapy. *He's* the one that needs help. And you too for engaging in all of this foolishness. How can you sit here and be okay with this negative influence on Vanessa? You want to show her how it's okay to lie, sneak, and manipulate people because it's what you want?"

Corrine lifted her head, struggling to put the crumbling confidence back in her voice. "That is completely untrue, Mama, and you know it."

"Oh, yeah? Isn't that how you got Patrick to marry you, by thinking you were a woman?"

Corrine let the last statement hang in the air like a putrid smell before she spoke, rising once more. "We're done here," she stated simply and walked from the dining room. She couldn't entertain Paula anymore. It was too exhausting, mentally and emotionally, and she would be damned if now, after finally coming into herself, she'd allowed the woman's willful ignorance and venomous remarks to put her back into that depressive state. It had taken her too long to find her way out of the dark.

Corrine stood in the hallway and shut her eyes on a sigh. Tears were futile, and she hadn't shed any about her parents in years. But, once in a while, the feeling was tempting.

"Corrine."

She hadn't heard Gina follow her. She took another breath, her lungs tight with the repressed tension. Satisfied that she was going to be able to hold it together, Corrine turned to face her sister.

"I'm okay," she assured her before Gina could do her famous consolation speech. "I promise. I'm just really tired and I have a bad headache."

Gina nodded her understanding. She knew her sister was strong and needed a little space. Smothering would do no good. "Call me tomorrow," she replied simply, with a comforting smile.

Corrine nodded and, turning, all but fled from the apartment. The door closed at her back and shut out all thoughts of the dinner and Paula, even as the first few tears glistened on her cheeks.

Chapter Seven
Bridget

"So, wait, back up." Nikki was completely tickled as she leaned across the counter. "It was what kind of club?"

The two were working at Bridget's house today and had decided to take a break to grab some lunch. They now sat in the kitchen while Bridget finished pulling out the makings for turkey sandwiches and chips.

Bridget turned, setting the mayonnaise and knife in front of Nikki on the island. "You heard me," she said. "Swingers. As in, you-and-your-partner-can-switch-with-me-and-my-partner."

"Wow. I know I'm way out the loop. I didn't even know they had clubs for that sort of thing. Did you see anything while you were there?"

Bridget chuckled. "See anything like what?"

"Girl, I don't know. A bunch of drunk, half-naked hoes fucking on the floor while the men watched."

"Uh, first of all, I said swingers, not an orgy." Bridget took a seat on the barstool next to Nikki and grabbed the bag of Lay's salt and vinegar chips. "And second, no. I was there on business, so the club was closed. But it's a reason why it's membership only. I doubt they would just get buck wild right in the lobby like that."

"Damn, I knew I should've gone with you."

"Why do you say that?"

"Because"—Nikki popped a chip into her mouth and washed it down with a swig of her Coke—"you got a man, so you're sexually satisfied. I am the one that's on a drought and have to find my way to release. Shoot, I needed to see a little dang-a-lang. That'll be the closest I can get to one." She poked her bottom lip out and had Bridget laughing aloud.

"Well, we only have a little over a week left for this party, so you can get as up close to the *dang-a-lang* as you want then."

Nikki exaggerated a roll of her eyes. "Fine. Be stingy."

The two joked a little longer before the conversation turned back to work. Bridget was too psyched with the way the planning was coming along. Marco had been right. Money talked. Even on short notice, folks were suddenly available for the right price. So far, they had secured the DJ, an emcee, aerialists and acrobats, and a host of other performance artists to create the perfect immersive experience. She had thrown a shit ton of money into décor, having planned to turn the interior and exterior into an over-the-top circus extravaganza. Nikki had solidified some sponsors for giveaways and Bridget had confirmed with Marco that the invitations had already gone out to the guest list, over half having RSVP'd their expected attendance within the first hour. All that was left was to confirm with Corrine to finalize the food.

Bridget had tried to call her twice, but she hadn't returned her call just yet. Definitely strange, but since Marco insisted Corrine had already verified her availability to handle the catering, Bridget would just keep trying to get her on the phone.

The door from the basement opened, prompting Bridget to smack her lips. She didn't even bother turning as she heard Dorian pulling open cabinets. Nor did he bother speaking. A few minutes later and he was headed back downstairs, a bag of cookies and a Dr Pepper in hand, closing the door behind him.

"Girl, he's still here?" Nikki turned up her lips.

"Yes. All he does is eat, sleep, and shit. I'll be glad when he's gone."

"I kind of feel bad," Nikki said with a look over her shoulder. "He's kind of cute in a homeless-y kinda way."

Bridget couldn't help but smirk. "Careful," she teased. "That drought is starting to look like desperation. Want me to hook you up?"

"I'll pass, thanks."

The distant chime of her cell phone had Bridget hopping off the stool and trekking to her office, where she had left it on her desk. She answered without bothering to check the caller ID.

"Hello?"

"Hey, Bridget? It's Corrine."

Bridget smiled. Thank God. One more thing she could scratch off her list of action items. "Hey. I've been trying to call you about the Shadow Lounge party."

"Yeah, I know. Sorry about that. It's just been a little crazy here." Corrine's voice sounded distant and heavy. Bridget couldn't tell, but she could've sworn it sounded as if the woman had been crying.

"Is everything okay?" she asked. "Is now a good time? We can chat later."

"I'm good," Corrine insisted. "Just wanted to touch base because I saw you had called and wanted to let you know I was putting a few items together. Can I get you a finalized menu tomorrow? Marco told me the theme was Cirque du Soleil."

"Sure, that's fine." And because she sounded like she needed it, Bridget went on. "Listen, me and Nikki were going to go out later and grab some drinks. Why don't you join us?"

There was a pause before Corrine spoke up. "Actually, I was going to go to Shadow Lounge tonight. You should come by. You know, check out the scenery. Feel the vibe. Meet a few people."

Bridget chuckled, the rejection already formulating on her tongue before she had time to actually consider the offer. "I can't," she said. "Roman is spending time with his daughter, so he won't be home until later."

"So?"

Corrine made it sound so easy. And, Bridget hated to admit it, so right. She had given a complete bullshit excuse and it was more than obvious.

When Bridget didn't reply, Corrine spoke up again, her voice sultry, almost flirtatious. "You know what? Just think about it. And hopefully, if you decide to come, I'll see you there."

"I'll talk to you later," Bridget said and disconnected the call. Damn, why was she suddenly so curious? And turned on?

"Everything okay?" Nikki asked as soon as Bridget re-entered the kitchen.

She nodded and leaned back on the counter, still mulling the idea over in her head. The more she harbored it, the more excited she felt. She had been right. Roman was spending some father-daughter time with Maya. And afterward, he did say he might go in to work. So she was as good as free for the rest of the night. And what would be the harm? For the briefest of moments, she debated extending the invitation to Nikki as well. Her girl did say she wanted to go to the club and get in on some action. But for some reason, Bridget dispelled that thought just as quickly.

"Yeah, everything is good," she said with a smile. She resumed eating her food, but her mind was already working over the show-stopper outfit she would pull out for the exclusive patrons at Shadow Lounge.

———>-o-<———

It was a vastly different scene from the first time Bridget had arrived at the club for her meeting with Marco. Now, there was a line of cars from the house, outside of the driveway, and halfway down the block. Someone was checking identification at the entrance gate before letting people in.

Bridget waited in line so long she debated turning around and saying to hell with the entire idea. There was no way this place was worth it. But curiosity, or maybe that nosiness of hers, refused to let her leave. Not without going inside to see what it was all about.

She eased up to the gate and, mimicking what she had seen others before her do, she rolled down her window and flashed her driver's license. The gentleman, a big burly guy with a body that looked too big for his head, looked at the clipboard in his hand. "Are you a member?" he asked.

"No."

"You're not on the guest list." He stepped back to begin directing her out of the way.

Bridget held up her hand. "Wait, I'm Bridget Pierce with Brinique Lux Affairs. I'm coordinating an event for Marco. Corrine suggested I come by."

The man paused, narrowing his eyes. He shifted to the side and spoke directly into a radio on his shoulder, angling his ear to the device to listen to the response. Bridget held her breath. Damn, she wished Corrine had told her it was like getting into Alcatraz. If she couldn't get through the maximum security, so be it. She would have to just take her disappointment and go home. She couldn't stop the grin when the guard nodded and waved her through.

Bridget followed the steady trail of cars around to the back of the house. Yet another guard in a yellow reflector vest was using safety sticks to direct cars to the numerous parking spaces that had been sectioned off with cones. Bridget eased into a tight spot alongside a Tesla and couldn't help but think of Nikki. Oh, what would she say if she knew where Bridget was now?

She flipped down her visor and took a quick peek at her makeup. Then, shooting a quick text to Roman, she stuffed her phone in the silver wristlet that hung from her arm, readjusted the top of her tube dress, and stepped out into the cool night air.

Bridget wasn't trying to be nosy, but she caught herself sneaking looks at the other clubbers as they all made their way to the front. There were a few solo guests, but the crowd consisted mainly of couples, huddled together against the bite of the cold air, dressed for an evening out on the town in blazers, party dresses, and heels. No one was really scantily clad, which she found surprising. An innocent bystander could assume everyone was on their way to the theater, or to have drinks at some siddity country club.

One woman in particular caught Bridget's attention, and she had to do a double-take. Judge Lancaster. She almost didn't recognize the woman off the bench. Another guy Bridget realized played for the Atlanta Falcons only because of the couple of games she had conceded to watch with Roman. She was tempted to tell her husband about the player's alternative lifestyle, then remembered her ass was sneaking around at the club herself and probably shouldn't have been privy to this classified information. Marco had been right when he'd relayed the club's popular motto: *What happens in the shadow stays in the shadow.*

Along with the others, Bridget was ushered into the same front lobby as before, but now, under the veils of night sky and dim lights, the ambiance was more mysterious. And forbidden. Adding to the allure, a thin curtain of fog from a machine greeted her and collected in the lobby, enveloping the guests in a gray film that shielded their bodies until they were nothing more than silhouettes. Strobe lights filtered fluorescent colors of red and gold that tinted the room, and the smell of vanilla, jasmine, and peaches assaulted her nostrils.

Bridget approached the desk where three young women who looked like triplet Black Barbie dolls expertly juggled the line, answering phones, and the computer check-in.

The woman who beckoned her had a dazzling smile and piercings in her deep-set dimples that creased each cheek. "ID, please," she greeted.

Bridget pulled out her driver's license again, but, remembering the slight confusion at the gate, didn't bother passing it across the desk. "It's my license," she explained. "I don't have a badge or membership card or anything. I'm Bridget Pierce." The woman squinted to eye the identification Bridget held up to her face and then typed on the computer.

"Yes, Marco heard you were here and indicated I should give you a visitor's pass. I need to scan your ID and collect a little information from you."

Privacy and security was clearly of the utmost importance. Never had she been to a club with such measures in place. Bridget grabbed one of the colored mints from the glass bowl at her elbow and popped it in her mouth while she waited.

After volunteering some general information and passing over her ID, the woman clipped a white beaded bracelet around her wrist and passed back her license clipped to a small stack of papers. "What's this?" Bridget asked, thumbing through the paperwork.

"A membership application. In case you want to join us, you'll have to bring this back. Visitors are only allowed one free entry without membership and dues."

Bridget started to pass the papers back. She started to insist she didn't need it and only planned to return for the party and that was the last time she would set foot in the Shadow Lounge. For some reason she didn't object, merely folding the papers until they were small enough to fit in her purse. Her eyes shifted to the couple next to her, arms extended for the red beaded bracelets being fastened on their wrists. A glance at the desk showed more bracelets in other colors: white, red, purple, gold, and black.

"Visitors only have access to the first floor," the woman said, bringing Bridget's attention back to her. She tapped the white bracelet to indicate her limited admittance. "The second floor is for members only. You must keep the bracelet on at all times. The bar is open until eleven tonight, and then it's a cash bar. Hor d'oeuvres are complimentary. Enjoy."

The woman winked, and Bridget could only smile in response. She supposed being here meant she was free game. Why did she feel like a fawn in a lion's den?

Music guided her steps toward the back of the house, which opened into an open, two-story great room. Floor-to-ceiling windows displayed a magnificent backdrop of stars glittering off a lake. In the daytime, Bridget was sure it was brilliantly inviting, giving off that natural light. A set of large, glass, accordion-style doors were open to expand the living space, connecting the outdoors with the indoors in a seamless feng shui of breezy cohesion. People were peppered around the room, chatting and laughing, while more had spilled outside onto the veranda and extensive acreage of backyard.

Classic R & B drifted from some hidden speakers and had a few couples grinding against each other on the dance floor. Or what Bridget assumed was the dance floor. Really, it was just the central space in front of some large white leather sectionals.

"Lobster toast, miss?"

Bridget turned to the server, the tray of hors d'oeuvres expertly balanced on the tips of his gloved fingers. Tiny, bite-size squares of avocado toast each had a spoonful of lobster meat stacked on top. She accepted one on a nod and placed it on her tongue, letting the rich flavors of the delicacy sweeten her buds.

She was tempted to track down the server for another one when she turned and spotted Corrine strolling into the great room, arm-in-arm with someone who Bridget assumed was her husband.

Bridget felt a swell of relief at the sight of a familiar face, and without hesitation, she strolled up to greet them. She didn't notice the man's eyes devouring her body like it was his next meal as Corrine pulled her in for a hug.

"You made it," she said.

"Yeah," Bridget said. "Figured I would come see what the place was all about."

Corrine stepped back and gestured to the man. "This is my husband, Patrick. Pat, this is Bridget, the one I was telling you about."

"Pleasure to meet you," Bridget said, accepting his outstretched hand.

In an exaggerated motion from some royal courtship, Patrick leaned over, bringing the back of Bridget's hand to meet his lips. He held it there for a few seconds before breaking the contact with a smile. The prolonged gesture was slightly awkward, but Corrine didn't seem to mind.

"Rinny has told me such good things," he said. Bridget saw his eyes flicker briefly behind her before meeting her gaze again. "Where's your husband?"

"Oh, he was busy, so I'm solo tonight."

If she didn't know any better, she could've sworn she saw Patrick's eyes light up like Christmas. Bridget had to remember her environment. And with Corrine and Patrick there, it was clear they, too, were in their element. It was she who would have to get used to the extra . . . what was this even considered? Flirtation? Attention? Sexual advances?

"Come on, girl," Corrine said, grabbing Bridget's hand. "Let's go get a drink."

Bridget let herself be led away, grateful for the temporary relief.

Corrine was already flagging the bartender as they took seats on the leather barstools. The man to Bridget's right grinned in her direction. He was short, she could tell, and a lot older. Perhaps in his fifties. She returned a polite smile, immediately regretting it when he took that as a sign to proceed with his approach.

"I've never seen you here before," he said, licking his lips in a way that was intended to be sexy but only made Bridget's skin crawl. He reeked of Old Spice and cigar smoke. "What's your name, pretty lady?"

Corrine's hand covered hers, almost possessively. "She's with me, Earl."

Bridget had to stifle a chuckle. Even if she were interested, how the hell could she sex a man named Earl? It even sounded old and perverted.

Earl's smile dipped a few degrees, but he leaned back, thankfully giving Bridget some space.

"Corrine," he acknowledged. "How's Pat?"

"Good. How's Lucille?"

"Good." Earl picked up his beer and rose. "Well, let me go find her. Y'all take care." And with that, he made his way over to another woman. A woman Bridget could only assume was *not* Lucille.

Suddenly finding the entire interaction extremely hilarious, Bridget burst into giggles. "Girl, are they always like this in here?" she asked, accepting the drink Corrine slid in front of her.

"Only when they see something new that they like."

In another setting, or maybe at another time, the wink Corrine gave her could've been flirtatious. Bridget couldn't be sure. She took a sip of the drink, wincing at the strength of the alcohol.

"It's good to see you. Here, in this environment," Corrine went on. "I'm glad you were able to make it. Where did you say your husband was?"

Bridget tried to think of a credible lie. "With his daughter," and then for good measure she added, "and plus he's on call throughout the night so, it's just me."

Corrine's knowing smile spread slowly, but she didn't comment on the excuse. She grabbed one of the colorful mints in a nearby glass bowl, popped it in her mouth, and chased it with whatever shot of liquor she had ordered. When she lifted her arm, Bridget noticed she wore a black beaded bracelet. Her eyes flicked to her own white bracelet, which she had deduced was for visitors. She was tempted to ask Corrine what her black color meant, but then again, she wasn't sure she was ready for the answer.

Behind them, the music was lowered, replaced with raised conversations heightened with excitement. Everyone seemed to be getting themselves situated for something, shifting furniture and finding seats.

"Musical Shadow," Corrine responded to Bridget's questioning stare. "One of the many games we play here."

"How do you play?"

"It's like musical chairs mixed with speed dating, couples style, if that makes sense. You shift down the row of seats until the music stops, and the couple you're sitting with your back against, that's the couple you switch with."

Bridget watched the game get underway. The liquor had her feeling slightly light-headed, but still, she couldn't help her fascination as she watched the couples begin to rotate through the seats as an upbeat New Edition hit filled the air.

"So, you and Patrick?"

"Yeah," Corrine said. "Me and Patrick, too. But we don't really do the speed dating type games anymore. If we see something we like, we just go for it."

Something flicked in Corrine's eyes, something wildly erotic, and Bridget couldn't help but blush. She blinked, struggling to clear her wavering vision. As turned on as she was, her head was starting to feel like it was full of helium. It must have been the combination of the drink, the club, the sexual chemistry she could all but taste in the air as it dripped from everyone's pores, or a combination of all three. Corrine was looking absolutely delicious, and Bridget had the sudden desire to touch her, in more ways than one. She reached for her hair, letting her fingers tangle in the curls.

"You are so sexy, Corrine." Bridget was all but singing the words like a lullaby.

Corrine's smile was one of confusion, her eyes narrowing as Bridget inched closer.

"Can I kiss you?" Bridget's voice was a seductive whisper as she leaned closer. Just a taste. Those lips looked so soft, so inviting. Her mind flipped to all the places on her body she yearned to feel them.

Corrine grabbed Bridget's shoulders, halting her presumptuous movements. "Bri," she said gently. "You're not ready for this."

"I want you." Bridget's tone was pleading as she lifted her hands to frame Corrine's face. She was acting on pure impulse, yielding to the flaming desires erupting from between her legs. Bridget could tell Corrine was still hesitant, but she thought she saw the lust in her eyes, even as her lips trembled open. Then, as if a light bulb had gone off, Corrine's eyes slid to the bowl of mints on the bar.

"Shit." She was on her feet in an instant, and Bridget had to brace against the abrupt movement. "Bri, did you take the X?"

Bridget stared in confusion. Here she was wanting to sex this goddess on the floor and she was talking about her ex?

"Bri, listen." Corrine slowed down her speech, enunciating

each word as if she were speaking to a child. "Did you take the Ecstasy pills?" Corrine pointed to the bowl of colorful mints, her expression fearful.

"No, I ate a mint." Bridget giggled at the absurdity. Why the hell would she take Ecstasy anyway? She didn't even know they had drugs here.

"What mint?"

"I love you, Corrine—" Bridget leaned in for a kiss, dammit, she just wanted one kiss. To her surprise, Corrine stood her up.

"Sweetie, I need you to focus. What mint did you eat? Where?"

"At the door."

"Shit." Corrine was putting Bridget's arm around her shoulders, bracing her body against hers for support. Bridget didn't even know what was happening, but she heard the restrained panic in Corrine's voice. "Melly, get Jonathan. Bridget accidentally took X."

Chapter Eight
Corrine

Shit, shit, shit.

Corrine tried her best to remain calm as she paced. She felt horrible. Jonathan had assured her everything would be fine and to bring Bridget someplace quiet to let her come down off the high. That had been an hour ago.

The bedroom suite was dim, only illuminated by a small desk lamp on a side table. In the center of the room, Bridget lay sideways across the king bed, finally having dozed off. Probably exhausted from coming on too strong, Corrine mused with a shake of her head. She had to admit, even in her wrong state of mind, the girl was persistent. In any other circumstance, it probably would've been funny. And Corrine probably would have taken full advantage of the opportunity to go ahead and get it out the way. But it wasn't right to do that to Bridget. Corrine's heart wouldn't let her. Unfortunately, she couldn't say the same for her husband.

Corrine remembered how anxious he had been as they lifted Bridget's arms across their shoulders and walked her to one of the first-floor bedrooms. He had been enraptured with Bridget's ine-briated state and was all too eager to get her back to somewhere private. His noticeable delight had made Corrine slightly nause-ated. And, if she had to admit it to herself, a little jealous.

Corrine glanced to the bed as Bridget stirred.

Patrick wasn't hiding his attraction to this woman, sexual or otherwise. There was something about her that was magnetic. Corrine felt it, too, though she wasn't attracted to her in the tradi-tional sense. But Bridget had a certain aura about her, different from most women. Corrine wondered if she spent most of her days fighting off unsolicited attention. Corrine had more of a brick house shape on her that could come across as intimidating. Plus, she was tall, always had been. She was just—what was the terminology someone had used to describe her before? A whole lotta woman? Yeah, that really didn't come with positive connota-tions.

Meanwhile Bridget, though somewhat tall herself, was slim like a Victoria's Secret model. All that was missing were those big-ass feather wings. Sure, the woman had thighs, ass, and titties, but her curves were more subtle, like a tease. Corrine had been around enough women now to know the differences. And to know a man's preference. Especially Patrick's.

Bridget was just his type. She'd had to all but push him out of the room to get him to leave. If he'd had his way, he would've had Bridget bent over the bed right then and there. It didn't surprise Corrine. It wasn't like Pat had never raped before.

He had finally left, pissed, but left just the same. She would probably catch all kind of hell tonight and would still need to fol-low through eventually. But at least for tonight, she wouldn't have to torture herself watching Pat sleep with another girl, pouring into her everything he had been denying his wife.

The first few drizzles of envy felt gritty and bitter, like saltwater on skin after emerging from the ocean. Now, suddenly, everything about Bridget was captivating, from the hair that had escaped from the ponytail to fan out across her face, to her tube dress that accented her curves, to the butterfly tattoos, beautiful and colorful, flecking the back of her neck.

Corrine's gesture was subconscious, lifting her hand to her own neck. Her own mane was curly and wild, a stark contrast to Bridget's. She lifted it up in a makeshift ponytail and positioned her back to the mirror, craning to see the little peek of neck exposed. Maybe she would look good with a tattoo herself. Maybe she could get some straight extensions, or a wig that would temper her own mane. Maybe . . .

Corrine caught Bridget shifting again in the mirror, and she quickly let her hair drop back into place, all thoughts dispelled as Bridget sat up and looked around.

"Hey." Corrine slid a hip on the side of the bed. "How are you feeling?"

Bridget yawned, giving answer enough. "I have a headache," she murmured, her eyes sweeping the room. "Where am I?"

"We're still at Shadow Lounge. Just one of the guest rooms."

"What happened?"

For the briefest of moments, Corrine considered not telling her. She relented on a sigh. "You took Ecstasy," she said. "Not sure when or how many, but you just had a little crash."

Bridget's eyes ballooned. "What? Oh my God, Corrine!"

"Calm down—"

"I don't do drugs!"

"I know. Just stay away from the mints in this place, okay?"

Bridget sprang to her feet. "I need to go to the hospital," she said. "My husband needs to—"

Corrine placed her hand on Bridget's arm to extinguish her rising panic. "You're fine, Bri. I promise. Marco's husband, Jonathan, deals with this kind of thing. He checked you out and said you're good. May feel a little yucky as you come down. But still, it's all over."

Bridget eased back to the bed with an apprehensive nod. "Roman is going to kick my ass," she mumbled with a chuckle.

"Don't tell him. What happens in the shadow stays in the shadow."

Bridget's lips curved in humor. "Okay. Well, what all happens in the shadow?" she asked.

"Maybe if I can convince you to stick around long enough, you'll find out."

Corrine caught Bridget's eyes lingering on her black bracelet. It was evident she was dying to know, but uncertainty had her mouth pursed shut. Corrine relaxed in relief. For a moment, she thought the little episode would scare Bridget off or, worse, that she would be vehemently upset and not want anything to do with Corrine again. In fact, that last thought had scared her a little too much for her liking. She didn't like acting on desperation, but at this point, she needed Bridget. Hopefully, she would be the key Corrine needed to breathe life back into her own languishing marriage.

Corrine fingered the beads of the bracelet, and for a moment, the baubles knocking against each other was the only sound in the room. "You and your husband ever . . . ?"

Bridget chuckled. "Swing? No, we've never."

Corrine nodded, not commenting.

"Don't get me wrong," Bridget rushed on. "No offense to anyone that does. Hey, that's your thing. But we just try to keep it exciting between us, you know?"

"I get it. It took me a moment to come around to the idea myself," Corrine said with a nonchalant shrug. "But now, I don't know it, it works. It enhances trust between us."

"How?"

Corrine had to mask her own feelings as she launched into the same speech Patrick had given her time and time again, enough so that she partially believed it herself. "Think about it, Bri," she

said. "If I loosen Patrick's leash and let him play on the edge a little and he doesn't cross his boundaries, I can trust him under any
circumstances." She watched Bridget nod, digesting the information. "Plus," she added, "it's adventurous. You can have your
cake and eat it, too, and both parties are in agreement. Patrick
and I never cared much for tradition anyway." At least that part
was half true.

"My husband's friend had a marriage pass in his relationship.
Let's just say it didn't work out too well for them."

"And it won't if *all* parties involved are not on the same page,"
Corrine said. "Not sure what happened with your husband's
friend, but you can rest assured that everyone who becomes a
member here knows and plays by the rules." Corrine paused, all
but watching the gears turn in Bridget's head. And just because it
was the perfect time to make her next move, she added, "You
know, Pat and I are looking for a new couple. Maybe it'll be easier for you and Roman if your first time is with people you can
trust."

⟶•◦•⟵

Patrick had left. Corrine figured as much. On a shake of her
head, she pulled her cell phone out and toggled to the Uber app
to request a ride home. It had gotten late, but Corrine had insisted on staying with Bridget until she was sure the Ecstasy had
completely worn off. It was worth it, though. They had ended up
staying in the VIP room talking and shooting the shit for hours.
After Corrine had planted the few seeds, she knew Bridget had
heard enough to pique her interest. So they had switched to other
topics: work, the party, kids, friendship, and relationships in general. And by the time Corrine had invited both Bridget and her
husband over for dinner one night, Bridget had agreed. It felt surprisingly comfortable.

Corrine hadn't had many friends. The public humiliation and

ridicule of her childhood had been exhausting, and without her parents to help, Corrine had just stayed to herself. Thank God for Gina, because she probably wouldn't have survived childhood without her sister.

Two unsuccessful suicide attempts later, Corrine had done some research and discovered the truth about herself. And she had been living in it ever since, despite the judgment. So friends were not something she came across too often.

Corrine remembered one time she had done some research online and found a few transgender communities and support groups. It felt good being welcomed and surrounded by the love of people who could relate. Who understood her. She had met a trans woman there, Tangie, and the two had clicked almost immediately. Tangie was young, about twenty, an only child with both parents deceased. She was struggling as a bartender, barely able to afford the rent for her tiny apartment, let alone the costly medical procedures to transition like she wanted. Tangie had reminded Corrine so much of herself that she was drawn to her. Outside of the group, she had no one else, a fact mirrored in Corrine's own circumstances at that age. Tangie saw Corrine as a big sister, and to be honest, Corrine thrived in the fulfillment of being looked up to. Being needed.

She hadn't bothered telling Patrick where she spent her Saturday mornings. This was a part of her that he probably would never understand. Nor did she think he really cared. But the more time she spent away, the more pissed Patrick became. Until she finally revealed the support group, the tribe she had found, and Tangie. He was pissed. But his blatant ignorance came from his far-fetched accusations that she was actually cheating with Tangie, using the "transgender thing," as he called it, as a cover-up.

She had never been more disgusted with her husband than she was at that point, and if there were ever a justification for leaving him—well, *one* justification for leaving him, rather—it was most surely that. But the ultimatum wasn't much of a choice at all, and she hadn't seen or spoken to Tangie, or the support group, since.

Corrine sighed as she hopped in the back seat of the Uber outside of the Shadow Lounge gate and nestled in the plush leather seats. Instinct had her opening her messages and shooting a quick text message to Patrick: **ON WAY HOME.** She watched the notification pop into view, showing he had *read* the message. Still, he didn't respond.

He hadn't bothered leaving any lights on, Corrine noticed as the Uber pulled into her driveway. She thanked the driver and pushed the garage door key on her keyring. Sure enough, Patrick's truck was parked right next to hers in the two-car garage, affirming his insensitivity. It had been his idea to ride together to the club, only to leave her stranded without so much as a text message or phone call. Typical.

Patrick didn't say anything when Corrine walked into their bedroom. He didn't even look over from the TV. Corrine rolled her eyes, tossing her keys on the dresser as she passed. "Thanks for staying," she said, sarcasm laced in her words. "I really appreciate you making sure I got home safely, too, since we, you know, rode together."

"Well, I would've looked out for you if you'd looked out for me."

He said it so apathetically, it was nearly sickening. Corrine shook her head as she plopped down on the bed, bending over to take off her heels. "If you wanted me to let you rape her, just say that," she mumbled.

"It wasn't rape. She wanted it."

Corrine cringed. Yeah, she had heard that before. It was times like this she felt completely foolish for still loving this man as much as she did. Foolish, and desperate.

Corrine peeled out of her clothes, tossing them on the floor.

"They're coming for dinner tomorrow night. That way, she can see about you and we can meet Roman."

She would never admit it out loud, but that was the real reason for the dinner invitation. Bridget had bragged all night on her husband. Roman this, Roman that. She talked him up so much Corrine was anxious to meet her future sexual partner. She wondered what kind of lover he would be. Probably a complete contrast to Pat. No, Roman sounded like the patient, tender type. He would know his way around a woman's body, know those strokes that could make her quiver. How long had it been since sex had actually turned her on?

Corrine climbed in the bed and turned over, her back to Patrick. He didn't waste any time getting into the spoon position, molding his body to hers to enter her from behind. He was rough, unusually so, and Corrine could only grimace against the pain piercing her backside. His fingers dug into the flesh at her sides, and his stabbing thrusts had the headboard bumping violently against the wall in a monotonous tempo.

Corrine closed her eyes and succumbed to her usual fulfillment when Pat took over. She checked out. In her mind, she went to someplace tranquil, someplace soothing with the warmth of the sun kissing her skin and drinks too weak to let the men take advantage of her sobriety but still strong enough for them to try. And when she felt her body begin to purr in response, it was Roman's name that dribbled from her tongue and had her erupting in a fluid of ecstasy.

Chapter Nine
Bridget

A dull headache snatched Bridget from sleep first. The sound of laughter and something sizzling in the kitchen prompted her to risk opening her eyes next. Sure enough, the distinct smell of burning bacon lingered in the air, followed by more muffled laughter. Which could only mean one thing.

Bridget swung her legs over the couch on a groan and took her time, rising to her feet. She was still in her club attire, and she could only assume she looked as rough as she felt. A shower would have been more appropriate, and an aspirin. Both of which would have to wait. So she put on her best morning smile and went into stepmommy mode.

"Miss Bri!"

Roman's daughter, Maya, was all but squealing as she hopped down from the barstool. Bridget opened her arms just in time to catch her as she came barreling in for a hug in a blur.

"Hey, Maya. How are you, darling?"

Maya angled her head up on a snaggle-tooth grin. "Good. Me and Daddy are making breakfast."

Bridget nodded. Their customary father-daughter bonding over cream of wheat, scrambled eggs, and bacon was a staple in the Pierce household on Roman's weekends. Speaking of her husband, she felt his inquisitive stare and kept her eyes downcast, averting her gaze. "You've gotten so big since the last time I saw you." Bridget held her hand on top of Maya's head, then lowered it to show the difference in height. "Weren't you about . . . five inches shorter last time?" she teased.

"I'm a big girl, Miss Bri. My birthday is coming up."

"I know. Won't you be fifteen or sixteen?"

"Eight." Maya chuckled.

"Maya, sweetie, do me a favor and go see if your uncle Dorian wants some breakfast."

Bridget recognized the request was only to get his daughter from the room, because Roman sure as hell knew they always fixed Dorian breakfast as well.

Maya was gone in an instant, and Bridget used the excuse to pour herself a glass of juice. She eyed the plate of bacon on the counter, or what was probably supposed to be bacon. The meat was scorched beyond recognition. "You know you got it stinking in here, right?" she said.

"Ha, ha. For your information, we like our bacon black."

"Uh huh." Bridget took a seat at the bar, welcoming the acidity of the orange juice pulp as it stung her throat. Thankfully, it was enough to overpower the putrid taste of day-old alcohol that was still lingering on her tongue. "If I had known she was coming over, I would've come back earlier."

That wasn't entirely true, but it sounded good. Truth was, no offense to Maya, because she was a sweetie pie, but Bridget just really didn't care for kids; a pill she had to swallow when Roman finally revealed to her he had a daughter. But by then she was already head-over-heels in love. It was a fact that was easy to tolerate because, as active as Roman was, he was still a weekend father.

Typical every other weekend, alternating holidays, a couple weeks in the summer kinda father. So it wasn't like the arrangement was overwhelming, because it really was doable. Any more than that and she probably would have felt compelled to speak up. Plus, Roman with his baby girl brought out another side of him that just made her heart smile.

Bridget was the youngest of seven, and she loved it that way. Pampered, yes, spoiled, absolutely. As the baby of the family, and much to her siblings' discontent, she had always gotten everything she needed, and then some. Even still, her parents had made sure to ingrain her with an independent work ethic to be able to afford her appetite for the lavish lifestyle and lofty career goals. Which was why kids didn't fit into that plan. They were a hindrance. She had never considered herself a selfish person, but she could admit, if only to herself, that she wasn't entirely selfless enough to give up her body, her time, and money to a child. Maybe one day Roman would see that.

They didn't disagree often, but the subject of children was one they both tiptoed around, because each sat on complete opposite ends of the spectrum. She knew he wanted another child, and maybe it was her fault for not making her intentions completely transparent before they were married. Especially knowing what she had done to permanently ensure kids would never happen for her. That little surgery she had neglected to tell her husband about, of course. But here they were. And no matter how much he liked to hint and throw little slick comments about the son that would take his name, Bridget knew it was only a matter of time before she would have to break his heart, or end up resenting him and their child later.

"April had to work today." Roman spoke of his ex-girlfriend and baby mother as he began pulling plates down from the cabinet. "I'm taking her home later this afternoon."

Bridget nodded, understanding the rationale for the impromptu visit. In another time and place, if she had had that motherly instinct, she was sure the perfect daddy gesture would send her ovaries into overdrive.

"You went out with Nikki?" Roman inquired. "I called you a few times to let you know we were coming over."

"Actually, I went by Shadow Lounge."

"The swingers' club?" His eyebrows lifted in surprise.

"Yeah, you know we have that party coming up. So I thought it would be cool to check out."

Roman chuckled. "How was it?"

Bridget opened her mouth to respond and stopped short when she heard the rapid footsteps bounding up from the basement. She winked at Roman as Maya reentered the kitchen in a huff.

"Let me shower and change clothes," she said. "I wanted to talk to you about it anyway." She left them to their little bonding thing and journeyed upstairs to her own place of solitude, if only for a ten-minute shower.

Bridget thought better of her options when she walked into the bathroom, instead relishing the thought of a soothing bath. She felt soiled, having slept in her clothes and still reeking of substances and Shadow shenanigans.

Bridget stripped naked, leaving last night's clothes in a pile on the gray hardwood floor of their contemporary en suite bathroom and flipped on the faucet in their garden tub. She adjusted the water until it was scorching, just like she liked it, and poured in some of her bath milk, turning the water a translucent white. She shuffled to some random R & B playlist on her cell and set it on the lip of the tub. Keyshia Cole began crooning about how she should've cheated, and Bridget murmured along as she made herself comfortable against the porcelain. As her body began to relax muscle by muscle, she finally let her thoughts trail to last night and Corrine's subtle, but not so subtle, offer.

Bridget had to admit to herself, somewhere between the hors d'oeuvres and the Ecstasy episode, her mind had already wandered to the possibilities of swinging. Not that she wasn't satisfied with Roman. The man was a sex king who sure as hell knew how to put it down in the bedroom. Well, any room—Bridget had to smile to herself as the thought had her kitty purring. But there was something potentially exhilarating about swinging with another couple. Something uninhibited and erotically thrilling.

She thought of Patrick from last night, kissing her hand like some Prince-Charming-in-training. He seemed nice enough. Handsome, sure. Was she attracted to him? No, not really. But then again, was she supposed to be attracted to him to have sex? And it was just sex, pure and simple. An adventure, nothing more. Like seeing an active volcano or ziplining in the tropics.

She and Roman had always been thrill-seekers. From the time he approached her at the club, their cylinders had been firing on all levels. By the end of the night he'd had her bent over the toilet in the men's restroom, her short Versace dress bunched around her waist. Four months later he had proposed. They had been inseparable ever since.

Their sexual compatibility was part of what magnetized them to each other. They could play out their fantasies. Tricks, toys, BDSM, kinks, it was like a high, and they both loved the adventures. But swinging, this was something even she had a little apprehension about. Fascination, yes, but apprehension nonetheless. Still, Bridget's curiosity was outweighing logic at this point. She would gauge his reaction first, see if he would be interested. Corrine had invited them to dinner, and Bridget figured that was as good a time as any to really feel the whole situation out.

What had Corrine said? The lifestyle bred trust. *If I loosen Patrick's leash and let him play on the edge a little and he doesn't cross his boundaries, I can trust him under any circumstances.* Interesting way to think of it, but she wasn't entirely wrong. Bridget liked to think she and Roman had a very trusting relationship. But if something like this could bring her and Roman even closer together, surely that made the ordeal worthwhile.

Bridget turned her attention back to the music, belting out the first few bars of some popular Rhianna joint, before it was interrupted with the familiar jingle of her ringtone. She leaned up to glance at the caller ID, smirking when the name flashed across the screen.

"Girl, where have you been?" Nikki didn't even bother with a greeting as soon as Bridget picked up. "I was calling you all night and this morning. Wanted to see if you and Roman wanted to double date with me and Dennis."

Bridget lifted an eyebrow. "Dennis?"

"You caught that, huh?"

"Yeah, I don't know too many black men named Dennis. Unless you're talking about Dennis Rodman. In which case you've got a lot more explaining to do before I go anywhere with you two."

Nikki's laughed bubbled through the phone. "Okay, okay," she relented. "We matched online about a month ago and we've been kinda hitting it off when we talk on the phone. I figured it was time to meet up and, girl, you know I don't want to meet him by myself. What if he's crazy? And yes, since I know you're thinking it, he is white."

Bridget's lips curved in amusement. She guessed it was the season for everyone to try a little something new. "No judgment," she piped, the water sloshing as she shifted her legs. "I just never thought you would be interested in a white guy. Or online dating, for that matter. How long have you been doing that?"

"Just a few months." Nikki sighed heavily with the admission. "It's hard out here for a single mother. You wouldn't know this wild-ass dating scene, since you're all married and shit," she added in jest. "But seriously, I've had so many terrible dates, I figured, what the hell. Open up a little. Plus, I've heard so many people have found their husbands through online dating. You would be surprised."

Bridget was quiet with understanding. For some reason, Nikki had the worst luck when it came to men, starting with her deadbeat baby daddy, Kenard. Not to mention the revolving door of unsuccessful relationships with the cheaters, don't-wanna-work bums, or misogynistic assholes threatened by a strong, successful, independent woman. The pickings were slim, and it was pathetic.

"I'll let Roman know," Bridget answered. "Yes, girl, we need to check him out together. He's not uncomfortable around a bunch of black people, is he?"

Now it was Nikki's turn to laugh. "I hope not. Because he sure as hell wouldn't be able to hang at one of my family reunions. Now you didn't answer my other question," she said, changing subjects. "What's up? Where were you last night? I figured you and Roman were somewhere practicing for my godson."

Bridget smirked, not bothering to correct her inaccuracy. She opened her mouth to disclose all the details about last night, but stopped short. She really couldn't put her finger on why she couldn't bring herself to tell Nikki. It wasn't like she would judge her. Maybe part of the allure was the mystery. Plus, Nikki was fiercely protective, and knowing her, she wouldn't waste time going down the gauntlet of cons and considerations that would have Bridget second-guessing the idea. So she would wait to tell her, at least until she and Roman had made a decision.

"Maya came over last night," she said, expertly skirting around the lie. "So, you know how that goes."

"Aw, how is my baby?" Nikki gushed, and that was all it took to steer the conversation to safer corners.

By the time they hung up, the water was lukewarm, peppering

chill bumps on Bridget's skin. She let the water out and switched over to the glass-panel walk-in shower, which was where Roman found her.

She smiled, watching the bends and angles of her husband's toned physique as he undressed. He stepped into the spacious shower stall with her, immediately pulling her body to his under the rain faucet.

She expected hunger, but his kiss was gently passionate, his touch soft, as if he were experimenting with a long-lost lover. Bridget felt her legs quiver, and she wrapped them around his waist, partly for support and partly to keep from melting into a puddle on the tiled floor. His hands circled around to grip her cheeks, and he braced her against the wall. Bridget felt her delicate folds parting for him like the Red Sea, and she moaned his name as he entered her, inch by delicious inch. He had her pinned, and each stroke was slow and deep. Oh, she loved how this man knew how to explore every spot that had new and unfamiliar sensations erupting with each thrust. She clung to him, her breathing roaring in her ears. Or maybe that was his, she couldn't be sure. He quickened his pace, her ass bouncing against the shower wall in increasing frequency.

She caught her orgasm first, clutching the euphoria full force with a startled cry and soaring on the wave until it began to ebb. He followed right behind, emptying himself until the cum spilled out and dribbled down her thighs. He sighed in content.

"Well, I missed you, too," Bridget said, stepping down on legs that felt like jelly.

"I figured you needed a little pick-me-up."

"The best part of waking up is Roman in my cup," she teased, her singsong voice pitched in the best Folger's commercial impersonation she could muster.

Roman stepped under the spray to rinse off, then got out first. He handed her a plush towel from the rack. "You missed breakfast," he said. "Maya wanted to wait, but I told her I didn't think you were hungry."

"Yeah, thanks," Bridget said, stooping to dry herself off. She didn't catch the flicker in Roman's eyes at the nonchalant statement. "Where is she?"

"She's in her room, watching TV. I was thinking we could do something together today. A movie or something."

"Aren't you on call this morning?"

"I was, but I went ahead and took off since she's here."

Bridget nodded, wrapping the towel snugly around her body and securing it under her arms. "I would, but I'm working today, sweetie. I didn't know you would be home."

Roman stuck his bottom lip out in an exaggerated pout. "Come on, babe. Just for a few hours."

Bridget couldn't help but grin. He was too adorable when he begged. She lifted onto her tiptoes, braced against his chest, and planted an apologetic kiss on his downturned lips.

"Go enjoy your day with your daughter," she said. "I don't want to intrude on your daddy day." It was an excuse, but a believable one, and much better than the truth. She really wasn't feeling the "kiddie" activities today. She hadn't planned on spending her afternoon watching princesses, or sitting bored at the playground. It was better for all three of them if she left that parenting part to Roman.

When she turned around, he grabbed her from behind, placing his hand on her flat stomach. "I don't know how you're going to manage work when little Romi comes along," he said with a smirk. "You're really a superwoman, babe."

Bridget's back was to him, and she couldn't help but roll her eyes, though she didn't directly respond to the baby comment. "You know I like what I do so it doesn't even really feel like work," she said instead. "And thankfully, Nikki holds it down for me, so we make a great team. Speaking of which,"—she chuckled at the conversation she was about to relay—"how about Nikki done went and got herself a white boy."

"What? I didn't know your girl was down with the swirl." They shared an easy laugh.

"I know, so we have to vet him for her. You know how some of these men can be. There's not too many you can trust."

"What's his name?"

"Dennis."

"Yeah, this should be interesting." Roman shook his head. "I don't know if Mr. Dennis can hold up against Nikki's mouth, though."

"I guess we'll see." Bridget paused before she changed subjects. "So, you got any plans later?"

"Not really, why?"

"You remember that caterer I was telling you about? Corrine? The one that's helping me with the party at Shadow Lounge."

"Yeah."

"She invited us to dinner tonight. I told her I would check with you, but I figured it would be fun to get to know her and her husband."

Roman turned to the sink, meeting Bridget's eyes in the mirror as he reached for his toothbrush. "You trying to set me up on one of those men playdates or something?"

"Boy, whatever. She's cooking some sample dishes she wants me to try so we can finalize the menu for the party."

"Okay, sounds cool," he agreed on a shrug. "She can cook, for real, though, right?"

Bridget groaned and smacked her lips. "Wait until you try it. She took me and Nikki to this restaurant that's owned by the Shadow Lounge guy. Food was amazing."

"Speaking of which, you didn't tell me. How was the club anyway?"

Bridget feigned nonchalance. "It was okay," she said simply.

She would wait until after dinner to bring up the swinging idea, after she saw how they vibed with this couple. For all she knew, they might not even get along, in which case the entire idea would be scrapped and there was no sense in mentioning it anyway.

"You see anything interesting?" Roman asked as he disappeared into the closet. "Sounds like one of those places where a bunch of crazy shit goes down."

"Nah, not really." It was probably best to withhold her little experimental drug consumption. Besides, what happened in the shadow stayed in the shadow.

"Where is my grandchild?"

The greeting had Bridget grimacing, even as her mother folded her into a hug.

"Mama, I wish you would stop saying that," she murmured.

"Girl, you know I don't give a damn what you say." Vernita nudged the door closed and led the way into the kitchen. "You married that man knowing he had a kid, so that girl is yours, too. Period."

All of a sudden, the impromptu visit didn't seem as appealing as it did earlier. But Bridget had wanted to see her sister Ava, and she needed to kill some time after being buried in work for the better half of the day. And with Roman out with Maya, she figured a quick pop-in would be a welcome distraction. She should've known that since Ava had moved back home with her parents, she would have to grin and bear her mother's temperament. As much as Bridget loved the woman, Vernita knew how to push buttons. Whether intentionally or unintentionally, Bridget couldn't be certain. But it was aggravating just the same.

One thing everyone who knew Vernita could agree, she always said what was on her mind, no matter how uncomfortable it could, or often did, make others. Bridget knew she had inherited her mother's same candor, and it wasn't so bad when it was to her advantage. When she was on the receiving end, however, not so much so.

Growing up as the baby of the family put Bridget in a strange position: volleying between her father's coddling generosity and her mother's conservative logic. But with six older siblings to emulate, Bridget had mastered what to do, and what not to do, to stay in her folks' good graces. So much so that by the time she graduated high school, Bridget's honed manipulative tactics had her dubbed the model child, much to her siblings' animosity. Though Bridget's behavior made her the favorite among the adults, it did put her at odds with her siblings, so she wasn't very close to any of them. The only exception was Ava, who was the closest to her in age and attitude.

Everyone knew Bridget was the daddy's girl, and she sometimes questioned whether her relationship with her father fostered a certain strain between her and her mother. Vernita was quick to argue against Bridget having certain luxuries because she would "never know hard work." Granted, as Bridget matured, she understood where her mother was coming from. It built a certain ethic and even more fulfillment when she could work her ass off and see the fruits of her labor. But she sure as hell hadn't wanted to hear all that bullshit when she was sixteen with the keys to a new Mercedes that Vernita had spent two weeks refuting.

It had taken years before Bridget came around to understanding her mother a little more and, therefore, being able to tolerate her shenanigans. It was just Vernita being Vernita. Love her or hate her, people had no choice but to admire her authenticity.

They had done some renovations. Bridget had noticed as soon as she'd driven up to the European-style home. Fresh paint adorned the exterior, and whoever their landscaper was had the immaculate lawn looking like something out of the glossy pages of a *Better Homes and Gardens* magazine. Through a backyard wrought-iron fence that hadn't been there last month when she came to visit, Bridget had seen the demolition in the early stages for construction of an in-ground pool.

Now, Bridget took a seat at the breakfast table as Vernita reentered her gourmet kitchen. Bridget's eyes swept over the new gray cabinetry and matching hardwood floors that looked slick from a recent mopping. "You've been busy," she noted.

Vernita picked up a spoon and began stirring whatever was boiling in the pot on the stove. "Yeah, I've got a little more work to do on the pool," she said.

Bridget craned her neck to peek again at the backyard through the bay window. "I see. Mama, you don't even like swimming. Or anything that means getting your hair wet."

Vernita lifted a hand, almost unconsciously, to rub the soft body waves of her shoulder-cropped 'do. "Who said I was planning on swimming?" she countered in amusement. "I just wanted a pool."

"Uh huh. And what did Daddy say?"

Vernita smacked her lips. "Fuck him."

Bridget didn't mean to chuckle, but the flippant remark was humorous. Her parents had been married for nearly forty years, and it seemed they'd had this love-hate relationship as long as she could remember. Apparently, she had come on a hate day.

Vernita and her dad, Kirk, sometimes acted like they couldn't stand each other. But the few times they did follow through with threats of separation, the two were miserable while feigning that the liberty outweighed their loneliness. It was never long before she would see Daddy shuffling his suitcases back up the stairs because they had decided to "work it out." Sure, it was exhausting to watch, but that was why Bridget opted to mind her business, because she knew, deep down, the two were sickeningly in love and had been since high school.

So instead of engaging her mother to expound on her little midafternoon attitude, Bridget changed subjects. "What are you cooking?" she asked, rising and crossing into the kitchen, sniffing the spices and peppers tinging the air.

"I had a taste for some chili."

"Mama, it's seventy-five degrees outside. Chili?"

Vernita didn't respond, merely stirring the bubbling stew in slow, meticulous circles. Her obvious disinterest in the task had Bridget frowning. Maybe it was deeper than she thought.

She placed her hand on her mom's arm to halt that annoying *tink* of metal against metal as the spoon touched the sides of the pot. "What's wrong?" she asked carefully. "Is it work-related?"

Vernita was a Realtor, so it was far-fetched to assume work was putting her in this type of funk. But still . . . "Mama," Bridget spoke again, her voice was more firm at the continued silence. "Seriously."

Vernita sighed and placed the spoon on the granite countertop. She turned slightly to face her daughter with eyes sharpened in sympathy. Something was there, something Bridget couldn't put her finger on, and it was making her nervous.

"Kirk and I are probably getting a divorce, sweetie," she said, her voice neutral.

The admission had Bridget's lip twitching. She couldn't possibly be serious. "Yeah, right, Mama. What's really wrong?"

"I just told you."

"Where is Daddy? Does he know about this alleged divorce?"

Vernita lifted her shoulder in a half-hearted shrug. "He moved out."

"Again?"

"For real this time."

And here they were again. Because she didn't want to make her mom feel bad by downplaying the validity of her comment, Bridget merely nodded. "I'm sure it'll work out fine, Mama. You two just need some space, but y'all know how you do. You love each other."

Vernita squeezed her eyes shut, as if blocking out the painful truth. "Lord knows I do," she whispered.

"See? Whatever it is, I'm sure it's just a little misunderstanding that you can talk out and move on from." She paused, then added, "I honestly would question your love if you two weren't fighting."

"I can't take the infidelity anymore, Bri."

The words hung suspended between them like a putrid pile of rubbish. Bridget opened her mouth, then closed it again. She watched Vernita's face for any sign of humor. But all she saw reflected in her eyes was hurt. Pure, raw hurt.

Bridget opened her mouth once more, her own questions stinging her throat like bile. She dreaded saying it out loud. That would confirm the validity. As absurd as it sounded. "Daddy cheated on you?"

"I would rather you heard it from him," Vernita said. "But he'll never admit it honestly."

"How do you know?"

"I know," she stated with enough conviction that she put all lingering doubts to rest. "A woman knows. I'm not stupid, and your father just figures since he has money he can do whatever the hell he wants. I'm tired of putting up with it." She turned back to the stove, as if the conversation was over.

Bridget stood, her eyebrows drawn together in confusion. She didn't know what to make of it. Her mother had plunged head-first into assumptions before, based off of her so-called intuition, and she wasn't necessarily correct each time.

Bridget remembered when she was eleven, her then best friend Sierra had come over to spend the night, and Bridget had divulged a huge crush she had on her lab partner, DJ. The next day, it was all over the school, and Vernita insisted Bridget cut off the friendship because Sierra had told everyone and couldn't be trusted. Bridget had refused to believe her best friend would violate their friendship, but her mother swore up and down it was the only justification that made sense. Plus, Vernita didn't really like Sierra because she thought the girl was jealous of her daughter. Bridget had never gotten that from their relationship, but in her young mind, her mother was absolutely correct. So Bridget had completely stopped speaking to Sierra. No matter how much the poor girl called, sent cards, and showed up at her locker to plead her innocence, Bridget had ignored all of her efforts.

A year later, long after rezoning jurisdictions had Sierra changing schools, it came out that Morgan, another girl they all shared class with, had actually seen the "Bri loves DJ" heart on her notebook and had spread the rumor because she actually liked him, too. Some classic Mean Girls shit that ended up costing Bridget her best friend.

The circumstance paled in comparison to this, but Bridget tended to not hold her mother's word as the gospel. Hopefully, she was completely wrong about this, too. Of course, everyone had faults and made mistakes, but Bridget didn't want to start doubting her dad. He had always been her rock, her foundation. When it came to trust, relationships, and the idyllic standard for men, Kirk was undoubtedly the reigning champion. He was a gentleman in every sense of the word, and though she had secretly overheard her parents' hushed arguments sometimes in the middle of the night, he never spoke any kind of disrespect toward her mother. He had always been big on communication and had even made her take a good, long look at Roman before she actually accepted his marriage proposal. She couldn't bear the thought of him, or anyone else, tainting that image.

Yet, the possibility was there. No matter how long people knew each other, they could still be complete strangers. And that was a pill Bridget wouldn't be able to easily digest.

A few moments longer with Vernita, and Bridget headed upstairs in search of Ava. Knowing her sister, she probably had her head buried in a book, studying for an exam for one of her many degrees.

Ava was the serial student of the family, having continued her education well past the expected four years. She had obtained numerous post-graduate degrees in various subjects that everyone knew she would never use. Their eldest sister, Felicia, had called it a "Peter Pan complex," a strategic way for Ava to keep from having to grow up. Bridget didn't understand it, because Lord knew she would go stir crazy having to always be under their mother's thumb and not having anything of her own. But it seemed to work fine for Ava. Plus, she usually kept a little job bartending or something to put money on a light or cable bill, just to say she was contributing.

Apparently, it was sufficient enough, Bridget mused as she poked her head into her sister's room. Because here she was at the ripe age of thirty, and it was clear she had no plans of deviating from her gravy train.

"Hey, Sis," Bridget greeted, plopping down on the foot of Ava's queen bed. Her sister sat Indian-style, a laptop balanced expertly on her toned legs as she keyed away at some document. A set of headphones dangled around her neck, the music blaring so loud Bridget heard every octave of the Mariah Carey song playing through the speakers.

"Hey, I thought I heard you downstairs."

"Yep. Mama was filling me in on the latest with her and Dad."

Ava snorted. "Yeah I'm you sure got a nice recap of *The Bold and the Boujie.*" She tossed her untamed locs behind her shoulder. "We'll deal with that saga later. I'm glad you came by. I wanted to talk to you."

Bridget kicked off her sneakers and made herself comfortable on the bed. "Of course, what's up?"

"Can you come with me to my group therapy next month?" Ava clasped her hands together in a pleading gesture. "And before you say 'no,' just please here me out."

"You don't have to sell anything to me, Sis. You know I'll come support you." She was proud of Ava for gaining enough courage to come out as bisexual to the family last year. Thankfully, no one cared, mostly because everyone had always had their suspicions about Ava well before her confession.

Ava grinned and threw her arms around Bridget's neck. "I appreciate you."

"You know I love and support you, Ava," Bridget told her sincerely. "I want you to be happy, whatever that looks like for you. Just let me know when it is, and I'll be there."

Bridget could appreciate how sexually liberated Ava was. She moved through life completely uninhibited with no worries and no care what anyone else thought. Her free-spirited nature was why Bridget even considered bringing up her own circumstances. If anyone would be the most understanding, it was certainly Ava. "Listen," she said, lowering her voice just in case Vernita was in earshot. "Do you know much about the swinging lifestyle?"

"Say what now?" The corners of Ava's lips turned up, just a little, as if she were trying to stifle a smirk. But the look she gave let Bridget know it was a stupid question. Of course, she knew about it.

Bridget didn't know why, but Ava's apparent amusement at the question had her blushing. "Look, don't judge me," she countered, standing up to pace the room. "It was just a question."

"No, I'm not judging you, Little Sis. You know I wouldn't do that. I'm just questioning why you would think *I* know about swinging." When Bridget cut her eyes in her direction, Ava finally let loose the laugh she had been restraining. "Okay, fine," she relented, holding up her hands in mock surrender. "What do you want to know?"

Good question. Everything there was to know, but that would

have been too much, Bridget was sure. Instead, she opted to start with the basics. "Roman and I are . . . considering it," she admitted, a little dance hitting her eye at the possibility. "I guess I just want to know more about what to expect."

"Oh, you know what to expect," Ava teased with a wink. "Have you vetted a couple?"

Bridget thought of Corrine and Patrick. She and Roman were going to dinner that night with them. And after that, well, it was looking fairly likely. "I went to a swingers' club," she divulged. "I met this couple and, yes, they're looking for some new partners. I haven't told Roman yet, though. Trying to decide if it's even worth pursuing."

Ava nodded. "My advice is to just make sure you know what you're getting into before you go down this road."

"Why do you say that? I thought it was more of a fun thing."

"For some." Ava sat back against her headboard, her shrug lighthearted. "You know I believe in soul ties. You have sex with someone, they leave a piece of themselves with you. I've never minded it so much with me, but you're leaving a piece of yourself with the other person, too. Everyone can't just walk away from that."

Bridget nodded along, but soul ties, or any kind of ties for that matter, were the least likely piece of the puzzle, as far as she was concerned. Corrine had already made that clear. Ava's spiritual jargon was commonplace, but going in one ear and out the other. Sometimes, the girl was too deep, and her theories were rarely substantiated. Bridget preferred to stay on the logical side of the spectrum. It made it that much easier to feel at ease with her decision.

<hr/>

What do you wear to meet a potential swinging partner anyway?
Bridget put her hands on her hips, turning in the full-length

mirror on a frown. At first, the burgundy off-the-shoulder blouse and slim hip-hugging jeans seemed like a good idea. Especially when she remembered the sleek matching pumps still in the original box at the bottom of her closet. Now, though, she wasn't so sure.

She turned from the mirror and headed to the jewelry box on the dresser, flipping it open to rummage through for the best accessories. Honestly, she was just nervous as hell. Why? She didn't know. She felt like she was going on a job interview or some kind of freaky audition. And though usually she didn't mind attention, Bridget got the feeling that tonight she was going to be subjected to even more scrutiny. Her adrenaline was kicking in high gear because, deep down, she knew part of her wanted this. And chances were if Corrine and Pat didn't like them, she didn't know if she were brave, or trusting enough, to swing with another couple. So it was either all or nothing.

"Look at my sexy lady." Roman wrapped his arms around Bridget's waist from behind, nuzzling her neck. The ticklish gesture startled a squeal from her lips before she slapped his arm.

"Boy, move," she chided playfully. "We have to get ready to go."

"Oh, I'm ready to go all right." He slapped her ass, licking his lips as he watched the juicy flesh jiggle in response.

She eyed him in the mirror, approving of his casual outfit of black slacks and a black button-up. The man looked good in any damn thing, so Bridget knew his attire wouldn't be an issue. After he had taken Maya home that afternoon, he had stopped off at the barber to get a fresh haircut. And he was smelling like new money in the Tom Ford cologne she had gifted him for his birthday. He sure as hell made this look too easy.

Corrine's proposal was still lodged in her mind like a splinter. Again, she debated telling Roman about their conversation, wondering if it would come up tonight or if they would just ignore the elephant in the room. On second thought, she decided to hold off until after they returned home. No sense in both of them being anxious about this little get-together.

It was a simple twenty-minute drive to Corrine's house in Fairburn. Sunday evening had the traffic light with everyone probably at home enjoying family dinner and prepping for a rigorous work week. Bridget spent the ride consumed in her own thoughts, letting the music fill the silence between them while Roman toyed with her fingers across the console.

Fairburn was a nice area; one Bridget had asked Roman to consider before they mutually decided to move to Fayetteville instead. The city was steeped in rich history and culture while embracing the modern revitalization of the future, with diverse shopping, entertainment, and dining that peppered the historical square.

As they rode through, Bridget noted a number of residents sprinkled out on the lawn, all eyes toward the blow-up screen that played some action movie under the twinkle of the night sky.

Corrine's house was much bigger than Bridget expected. She wasn't really sure what the net salary was for a caterer and a mechanic, but the luxurious new construction estate with four-sided brick had her double- and triple-checking the navigation system to make sure they were at the correct address.

Roman pulled up to the plantation-style two-car garage and cut off the engine. Bridget had managed to remain calm the whole ride over, but now the excitement had her nearly bubbling up off the leather seat.

"You good?" Roman asked, lifting an eyebrow.

She stifled an embarrassed smirk, not realizing her eagerness was so evident. She flipped the sun visor down, running her fingers through the few tousled strands that had started to stray. "I'm good," she assured him. "Just do me a favor."

"What's up?"

"Tell me what you think of Corrine."

Roman chuckled. "Babe, I ain't met the woman yet."

"I mean after," she corrected, turning to meet his questioning gaze. "Just be honest and tell me the vibe you get. If you like her."

"Man, I'm more concerned if I like this food, because I'm hungry as hell." Roman shook his head and climbed from the car. "If this chick can't cook, I swear I'm gone say something. Then we going to Waffle House."

Bridget followed her husband up the walkway to the wood double front door. They had no sooner stepped on the covered porch than the porch light flicked on and the door opened wide.

Bridget took the opportunity to size Patrick up again, this time without the eclipse of strobe lights, club ambiance, and cigarette smoke.

He wasn't a bad looking guy. Not quite as clean-cut as Roman, a little bulkier and rougher around the edges. He carried himself like a man used to being in control, and the knuckles of his muscular hands were slightly bruised and discolored. *Probably from working with cars all day*, Bridget deduced.

Patrick glanced at her, and that same something from before flickered in his eyes again. But he was already turning to Roman before Bridget even had time to analyze the look.

"Glad you two could make it," Patrick greeted coolly. He held out his hand. "Pat, Corrine's husband."

Roman accepted the hand. "Roman. And my wife, Bridget."

Pat nodded. "We've met," he said.

Bridget remembered how he had kissed her on the hand in the club and had to purse her lips to keep from chuckling at the thought. The man was definitely a character.

Patrick stood to the side to let them enter. "Corrine's in the kitchen," he said as they stepped into the foyer. "Dinner should be ready soon."

Bridget glanced around, impressed with the immaculate home. They stood between a formal dining room and what looked to be an office conversion turned makeshift Hall-of-Fame room. Numerous shelves and glass cases held trophies and plaques of various types. Even the walls were cluttered with framed certificates and accolades. Bridget noticed a Kobe Bryant basketball jersey in a framed case, complete with the snakeskin material. Roman noticed it, too, because he was already moving forward to get a closer look for himself. The man loved Kobe.

"This is nice, man," he commented.

"'Preciate it. You a Lakers fan?"

"Hell yeah."

"I got some stuff in the basement if you want to check it out."

Roman's eyes seemed to light up, and Bridget knew it was a wrap. Men and their sports. She was already nodding when Roman turned to her.

"I'm going to go find Corrine," she said before he had a chance to speak. "See if she needs some help."

Patrick pointed down the hall, his eyes lingering on Bridget. "Kitchen's back there," he said. "You need anything?"

He seemed to be baiting her, or maybe Bridget was just being way too meticulous given the circumstances. She shook her head. "I'm good, thanks."

Patrick gave her the smallest of smirks before turning back to Roman. He tossed a quick pat on Roman's shoulder in a brotherly gesture. "Come on, man. Let me show you how the king lives. You play video games?" And the two disappeared around a corner.

Bridget was relieved they were already hitting it off. It would definitely make all of this much smoother.

She headed in the direction Patrick had indicated, taking in the beauty of the home. Corrine had certainly put a lot of time into decorating, she noticed. Their minimalist but contemporary furniture combined with the vaulted ceilings boasted lots of airy space with neutral touches of creams and grays. Corrine obviously loved abstract art. Oil paintings and sculptures were in every room, clearly intended to spark deep conversations about art and life's meanings. Again, Bridget couldn't help but internalize the prices, because everything looked and smelled like expensive taste. Maybe she and the woman of the home had more in common than she thought.

Just like Pat said, Corrine was in the kitchen, an apron covering her red cocktail dress, as she maneuvered expertly from stove to sink to oven. An international spread had already been stationed across the island, with pans of braised short ribs, a sweet potato and corn medley, and a pineapple, jicama, and avocado salad, the spices like an exotic fragrance perfuming the air.

"Girl, you got it smelling delicious in here," Bridget commented.

Corrine turned from the oven and set a pan of bread on the counter. "Thank you," she said snatching off the mitts and wiping her hands on the thighs of the apron. "I was thinking this would be good for the party, if you like it."

"I can already tell that I'm going to like it."

Corrine glanced around. "Where's your husband?"

"Patrick took him to the basement. Roman saw the Kobe jersey hanging up, and it was over after that."

Corrine laughed. "Uh oh, girl. Once Pat gets 'em down in the man cave, ain't no coming out." She pulled the apron over her head and tossed it on a nearby barstool.

The dress, and her body, stood out like a siren. Bridget almost felt self-conscious and cursed herself for not changing outfits when she first thought about it.

"You thirsty?" Corrine asked. She was in full-blown host mode, moving about the kitchen as she spoke.

"Yeah."

"You want something strong or a light buzz?"

After last night's rendezvous at Shadow Lounge, Bridget dreaded even the thought of hard liquor. But she knew the liquid courage would take some of the edge off. So far, as comfortable as Patrick seemed, maybe she would be the only one needing to relax a little.

"You got some wine?" she decided.

"I sure do." Corrine turned, a wine bottle in each hand. Her body shook with the gesture, and if Bridget had to guess, she wasn't wearing panties or a bra. "Red or white?" she asked.

"White."

While Corrine busied herself with pouring them each a drink, Bridget let her mind wander to her feelings about Roman having sex with her. She was damn gorgeous, no doubt about it. And by the looks of it, she had been nipped and tucked into a man's walking wet dream. But the fact that she was a sexual goddess didn't make Bridget feel awkward, and she was both surprised and relieved. She knew Roman loved her, never doubted that fact. And all she could see was him being thrilled by the sex, and nothing more. She herself felt like absence would make their hearts grow fonder, and even while she was trying to wrap her mind around sex with Patrick, it would only turn her on more for her husband. And like Corrine had said, she trusted him wholly and completely and taking this . . . what was it? Risk? Opportunity? It would deepen their love, and trust, for each other. Ava's mention of the *soul ties* entered her mind, only briefly, before she dismissed it again.

"Your home is gorgeous," Bridget spoke up after the two had let the silence linger. "I see you love art."

"Not really. But the paintings are my sister's pieces," Corrine said with a proud smile.

"Really? She's very talented."

"I tell her that all the time. But she doesn't want to sell her stuff. Says she just does it as a hobby." Corrine set a glass in front of Bridget. "You have any siblings?"

"Yep, six of them," Bridget said with a sheepish shrug. "I sometimes wished I was an only child, though."

"Oh, damn. Seven kids?"

"Yeah, it was pretty eventful around my house. It was just you two girls growing up? No brothers or other sisters?"

Corrine's smile chilled a few degrees before she turned back to the stove. "Just me and Gina," she said. "We've always been really close."

Bridget detected something heavy in the comment, something almost wistful, but she didn't elaborate.

Corrine cleared her throat and turned around again. She now spoke with renewed energy, and her face had brightened once again. She leaned a hip on the counter. "So you going to follow in your folks' footsteps and have a shit ton of kids running around?"

"Oh, hell no." Bridget hadn't meant to laugh, but even if she wanted kids, she knew damn well seven would be ridiculous. She composed herself, keeping her face neutral. "I can't have kids and ain't trying to, girl. Roman has a daughter and she's more than enough. Maya. She's eight."

"Oh, she's right around the same age as my niece. We should maybe get together for a playdate or something."

Bridget nodded but didn't comment. She wasn't sure if Corrine was serious or just tossing out the suggestion because it sounded good.

Corrine raised her glass a little and nodded to Bridget's, still sitting untouched on the countertop. "You want to toast now or with the fellas?"

"What are we toasting to?"

Corrine paused in thought. "To Shadow Lounge," she said, finally. "May we have a successful and productive event and it opens the door for more . . . opportunities together."

The innuendo was subtle but clear. Bridget lifted her glass. "I'll drink to that," she murmured as the ladies clinked their glasses together and took twin sips.

"Well, what did you think?"

They hadn't even backed out of the driveway before Bridget dove in. She rested her elbow on the middle console and cut her eyes at Roman. Even in the dark, she saw the outline of his profile, his eyes narrowed on the road ahead.

"Think about what?"

"Corrine and Pat. Did they seem nice to you?"

His shrug was nonchalant. "Yeah, they seemed cool. Ole boy is a little . . . I don't know. Quiet. I saw the way he was looking at you," he added with a wink. "His ass is lucky I know my lady is sexy."

Bridget rolled her eyes. "Whatever. And what about Corrine?"

"She's cool. Their vibe is a little off together. Did you feel that at dinner? Like they're awkward."

"I meant, doesn't she look good?" Bridget pressed.

Again, Roman shrugged at the question, a confused frown marring his face. "I mean, yeah, I guess. Why?"

Bridget took a hesitant breath. "When I went to Shadow Lounge," she started, "Corrine and I talked for a while." She conveniently left out the Ecstasy part. He didn't need to know all that.

"Okay, about what?" Roman prompted.

"You ever thought about swinging?" she asked.

"Sleeping with other couples?"

"Yeah." A brief pause, and then Bridget caught the grin that split Roman's face.

"Ah, hell nah," he said. "This that shit Dorian was talking about and you see where he at? Assed out on my couch."

The mention of his friend had Bridget smacking her lips in disgust. "This is different," she insisted. "We actually know and approve of the couple. We're safe, they're safe. No strings attached, because everyone already knows the arrangement. It gives us more control over the whole thing and less variables to fuck up, unlike your boy."

Roman scratched his beard. "So where did this come from?"

"I went to a swingers' club, remember? Of course the thought crossed my mind."

"And is that why you wanted us to do this dinner?" The pieces were beginning to click together. "Corrine and Pat, they're the couple you picked?"

"Basically." Bridget put her chin in her hand, her eyes never leaving Roman's face. He was considering it. He wouldn't have entertained even this much if he wasn't. "It's an adventure, babe," she went on, sweetening the pot. "You know we both like a thrill. Plus, it'll bring us closer together, don't you think?"

Roman frowned. "How?"

"You do you, and I will do me. Completely uninhibited. Plus, we know these people so it's not like cheating. We can come home and fuck each other senseless, because, let's face it, we know how we do when we start missing each other. It'll build trust. And we can see the green grass without leaving our own yard, so it makes you appreciate what you got."

"So," Roman's words were slow, as if he were still trying to process it all, "you and Pat and me and Corrine?"

"Yeah." The more she talked, the more hyped she felt. "Think of it like, you know you got the best car on the lot, right? A Tesla or something. But wouldn't it be nice to drive that Lamborghini one time? It doesn't mean you don't want your Tesla."

Roman laughed. "Hey, that is a good-ass analogy."

"I know."

"How long you been plotting this one, Bri?"

Bridget reached across the console, resting her hand on his thigh. "Does it really matter?" she said. "All I know is, doesn't the idea turn you on?"

Roman snatched the car over to the shoulder, the tires skidding on the gravel where the road met the embankment. She was already pulling her shirt over her head and climbing into the back seat to release the pent-up sexual energy that had been festering all throughout dinner.

Chapter Ten
Corrine

French Twist was known for two things: big personalities and even bigger gossip. The reputation was well-earned, no thanks to the salon's flamboyant owner, Frenchie. Folks who knew Frenchie before she transitioned knew she had adopted the name after the character from *Grease*. But let her tell it, she lived up to the connotation with some kind of French trick she put on her sex partners that kept them coming back for more. "It's like a French kiss," she would boast when asked about it. "But with a twist." It was only fitting the name would stick with the boutique hair salon, and garner just as much curiosity as it did attention.

It was on the Southside of Atlanta in a shopping plaza that had seen better days. Visitors who had frequented the salon as long as Corrine remembered when the adjacent shops had been everything from clothing stores to check cashing spots to wing stands. Now, the plaza had been vacant so long that everyone assumed the entire building belonged to Frenchie, and eventually, she would get around to expanding French Twist.

No matter the day, the place was always packed, and this Saturday was no different. Every dryer and sink was occupied as the steady stream of clientele revolved from station to station for their cosmetic fix. The smell of chemicals and burnt hair infused with an assortment of fruit-flavored body washes hung like a dense fog in the air.

Even though Corrine had made an appointment for early in the day, it had been four hours, and she was just now being moved to the stylist's chair from underneath the dryer. The only reason she bothered to come was because the place was so popular among the LGBTQ community. And if she had to face the facts, Corrine didn't trust anyone else to touch her mane but the boss diva herself. The woman could work miracles on a scalp.

Thankfully, Corrine didn't too much mind the extended time she spent in French Twist, and she had come to know what to expect. Either bring a snack, or make sure to grab something to eat when one of the vendors popped in with plates for sale. Plus, Frenchie and all five of her stylists would keep clients entertained with shit-talking and stories where they were too enthralled to want to leave anyway.

Now was one of those times. Frenchie was deep in a story about her latest sexual conquest, waving the curlers in the air as she spoke. She had everyone's attention. Hell, someone had even paused the music so her voice would carry from corner to corner.

". . . and do you know that joker had the absolute nerve," Frenchie exaggerated the word with a roll of her neck for emphasis, "to ask Miss Frenchie for a golden shower?"

The shop erupted in hollers and laughter as Frenchie tossed her waist-length weave over her shoulder.

"Wait a minute, Miss Frenchie." JJ, the all-around hype man and youngest stylist, put his hand on his hip. Though he should've been using the hot comb on the woman sitting in his chair, he instead used it to gesture to the crowd in the room. "Now you know somma these uppity bitches wanna act like they don't know nothing 'bout no golden shower," he said with a smirk. "Gone head and educate these hoes one time."

In true Frenchie fashion, she smacked her lips and sashayed to the middle of the room where she could be sure everyone saw her. "Oh I know y'all bitches not in here acting brand new," she said, her eyes sweeping all of her patrons. "He wanted me to squat my big ass over his chest and piss on him."

More laughter exploded. Corrine chuckled. She was supposed to be getting ready for the party that night at Shadow Lounge, but she knew she wouldn't be going anywhere now that they had Frenchie on a roll.

"So wait, wait." Another woman spoke up from across the room, lifting up the dryer so she could hear better. "He asked you to pee on him, Miss Frenchie? What did you do?"

Frenchie grinned, taking a dramatic pause for effect. "Shit, what you think?" Despite the six-inch pumps, she bent her knees into a deep squat. "I pissed on that nigga like a prize-winning racehorse at the Kentucky Derby."

And with that, she made her way back to her station to the exuberant cheers of her makeshift fan club.

"Frenchie, your ass needs to write a fiction book," Corrine commented as the woman rolled her around in the chair to finish her hair.

"Girl, ain't nothin' fiction about my stories, okay? You know these men, and women, can't get enough of Frenchie."

"Yeah, I know."

"Speaking of which, where is that fine-ass husband of yours, Boo?"

"He's out getting ready. You know we have that party tonight." Truth was, Corrine didn't know where Pat was. That was her best assumption since he hadn't bothered to return her text messages.

Frenchie nodded, pulling pieces of hair and teasing out some curls with expert precision. "Yeah, you told me you're trying to look extra special for this couple."

Corrine couldn't help the smile that blossomed on her face. "Yeah, I have a feeling tonight is the night." At least she hoped so.

She and Bridget hadn't spoken on a personal level since their little dinner party. Conversations since had been all about the Shadow Lounge party, coordinating logistics and confirming details so it would go off without a hitch. She knew through Marco that Bridget had proceeded to pay the club membership fee, and she had gone back a few times in the daytime for measurements and finalizing the décor.

Corrine had attended at night when Shadow Lounge was in full swing, disappointed when she hadn't seen Bridget there. But then again, she couldn't really blame her after the encounter during her first visit. So Corrine was anticipating tonight would unfold like she wanted. And though it may have seemed premature, she had reserved two VIP rooms: one for Bridget and Pat and one for her and Roman.

Corrine felt her body beginning to quiver at the thought of Bridget's husband. He was everything she had described. Physically, the man was sexy as hell with a body that had her salivating at the prospect of exploring it with her tongue. But sex appeal aside, he was so compassionate, so attentive and loving to Bridget. Exactly as a man should be. The complete opposite of Patrick.

There was a void there. Corrine had already acknowledged that fact. And that night at dinner, watching Roman so freely bestow the same attention she craved, Corrine couldn't help but yearn for the man, in more ways than one.

So tonight was her night. She knew Roman would take his time and breathe life into her again. Not that she needed a man to make her feel alive. But just like a vehicle, nothing like a tune-up to have her running again like a well-oiled machine. Then maybe, just maybe Patrick would recognize the lengths she would go to for him. And it would remind her why she fell in love with him in the first place.

Two more hours and three Frenchie stories later, Corrine had been teased, waxed, clipped, pampered, and primed into bliss.

She headed to the mall to find something to wear. To be honest, she didn't need any new outfits. The closets in her room and two of the guest bedrooms made that abundantly clear. But it was only one-thirty and she didn't have to be at Shadow to set up until seven. A few hours of retail therapy would be just what she needed to take her mind off of her rising anxiety.

Her first stop was the lingerie department, and she made a bee-line for the lace bra and panty sets. Red was her color; she had been told time and time again. So immediately she was thumbing through all the fire-red garments, looking for something that would look good on her skin. Of course, she had plenty of sexy thongs and bras at home, but every time they swung with a new partner, Corrine always purchased something new. It didn't feel right sexing another man in the see-through ensembles she had worn for Patrick.

But Corrine took her time with this search, eyeing the various cutouts and mesh strings until she found the perfect set for Roman. She would pull out all the tricks with him, making this night as unforgettable as possible.

Corrine was at the register when another outfit caught her eye. She zeroed in on the tight sheath with the zip-up back and corset, recognizing it as the exact dress that Bridget had worn when she'd first visited Shadow Lounge.

The *beep* of her purchases being slid across the scanner had her glancing to the cashier momentarily. "Let me get that in a large," she said, nodding toward the dress. At least she knew what she would wear tonight. Hopefully, it would be enough to catch and keep Roman's attention.

"Oh, hunny, you look good enough to eat."

Corrine smirked at Marco's compliment and did a slight twirl to show off the skintight dress. "You think?"

"Oh, yes. I don't know who you're after tonight but you're going to have them eating you up. Literally."

She certainly hoped so. Corrine hadn't thought twice about wearing the dress she knew was identical to the one hanging in Bridget's closet. But part of her did wonder if Bridget would recognize it, or even care, for that matter. If necessary, she could always feign ignorance. But she had one goal, and one goal only in mind when she was pulling it over her curves and tying the accompanying corset in place: to hook Roman Pierce.

She had taken extra care with her makeup, and with Frenchie's magic on her hair, the straightened style and swept bang added some length to her tresses, giving her entire look a sultrier and more enticing aura that she loved. She felt like a vixen. Even Patrick had paused and taken a second look while she was getting dressed, and Corrine's confidence had soared. There was something about her husband being potentially jealous that turned her on and made her that much more determined to sex Roman into oblivion.

"Is Bridget here?" she asked, already knowing the answer.

Marco nodded toward the great room. "Of course. She's getting things up and rolling. It's looking sinful already."

"Just like you like it."

"And you know it." Marco's grin was mischievous as he headed up the stairs to the VIP rooms.

Corrine strutted past the desk rolling her entrees on a food and beverage cart toward the kitchen to begin setting up. Behind her, a few club workers she'd rallied to help followed along, each carrying the rest of her catered dishes in steaming foil pans and covered trays. The overhead lights were on, and she saw decorators were hard at work, hanging mood lights, suspending cages, and draping sheets and themed décor to create the ultimate immersive experience.

Corrine saw Bridget off to one side, clearly delegating with professional vigor as she pointed between the ceiling and a clipboard in her hand. She was dressed to assist, it appeared, with her sweatpants, crop tee, and baseball hat. Corrine couldn't help but wonder what she planned to wear later that night for the festivities.

Shadow Lounge's kitchen was similar to that of a five-star restaurant, both in style and functionality. Marco had kept the residential gourmet aesthetic with its black cabinetry, marble floors, and granite countertops. But knowing it was necessary to accommodate hundreds of people, he'd had industrial stoves and ovens installed, plus two sets of deep double sinks. A walk-in refrigerator was concealed behind a standard door, and tons of counter space gave ample room for the club's diverse dining options.

Corrine transferred her pans from the cart to the center island and began pulling out the ingredients to start a few of her signature sauces.

It was times like these she thrived in the kitchen, her sanctuary. Cooking was her reprieve, and it brought her peace. She loved experimenting with different spices and recipes and bringing dishes to life. Nothing could beat watching someone's face when they sampled her food, or complimented her on the plate's presentation. It was her laying her very essence bare time and time again, and she relished the fact that she could so easily satisfy someone's appetite.

Her sister would always tell her, her knack for the kitchen was a God-given gift. It was refreshing to hear, especially since her parents were so quick to remind her that God had abandoned her long ago. So anytime she heard the sizzles in the pan or smelled the aroma of whatever morsel she let her hands prepare, it was like a security blanket. And the confidence boost, however small, was an indicator of her self-worth. That much she could live with.

"Oh, good, I was hoping I would catch you before everything

started." Nikki swung into the kitchen, her eyes already rounded in anticipation.

Corrine continued stirring the sauce so it didn't stick to the pot, even as the first few bubbles boiled up to simmer at the surface. "Hey, Nikki," she greeted. "Everything okay?"

"Yeah, I just wanted to taste a little of what you had in here. You got it smelling so good, and Bri told me how you had her sample the meal a few nights ago. And by the way," she crossed her arms over her breasts, "why wasn't I invited to this little taste test?"

Corrine had to chuckle to herself. She seriously doubted Bridget was going to divulge their little arrangement to her best friend and business partner. Everybody had secrets. "It was just a last-minute thing," she said with an apologetic smile. "I just needed a second opinion on the menu." Not the complete truth, but not a complete lie, either. The fact that they'd spent the evening vetting each other wasn't worth revealing.

"Uh huh." Nikki lifted the foil to one of the pans and peered inside. "Well, luckily I trust my girl, so I know all of this food is about to be delicious. But I still think I'm due for a sample anyway." Without waiting for permission, Nikki begin to help herself to pieces of the short rib. "So, this is pretty interesting," she was saying as she made her way down the pans in a buffet-style shimmy along the counter, adding small servings to a paper plate.

"What's interesting?"

"This." Nikki gestured in the air with her fork. "This club. I didn't even know they had these types of places around here."

"You'd be surprised."

Nikki leaned back on the counter, forking some corn into her mouth. She rolled her eyes to the ceiling. "You did it again," she said with an approving nod. "Not that I doubted you," she added. "I just like good food. So anyway, how did you find this place?"

"Well, my husband and I are swingers," Corrine admitted, her face coloring a little with the admission. Why did she suddenly feel ashamed?

"Hey, no judgment," Nikki said, shrugging. "Do whatever works for you. I just could never do anything like that. I'm way too selfish."

Corrine recognized the words she had once said herself. For a moment, her mind flickered to her relationship before Shadow Lounge. Before swinging. Just before. When they were happy and all Patrick knew was that she was a woman and he saw her as such. When that was all that mattered. "I get it," Corrine murmured. And she did. This was probably the most unselfish thing she had ever agreed to, and here she was years later still trying to prove her love. If she hadn't been the one in the situation, she would pity herself.

Nikki moved in a little closer and lowered her voice. "Can I ask you a personal question?"

"What is it?"

"No offense or anything, but have you had some work done?"

Corrine froze, frowning at the invasive question. "What do you mean?" she asked, struggling to keep the brewing annoyance out of her voice. This chick was way too nosy for her own damn good.

Nikki tossed her empty plate into a nearby trash can. "I'm just saying," she said, looking Corrine up and down, her eyes narrowed pointedly. "I would pay Jesus Himself for a body like that. I'm trying to get one of those Mommy Makeovers to tighten up in some areas." Nikki lifted her hand to her little belly pudge, and then up to cup her breasts. "My body didn't bounce back like I thought it would, girl, so I'm trying to stop traffic like yours."

Corrine turned back to the stove and, to appear slightly distracted, she went ahead and lifted the pot to pour her sauce in a nearby bowl, though it could've simmered for a bit longer. The question had rubbed her the wrong way, even though she was sure Nikki meant it innocently enough. "I know a few doctors," she said simply and left it at that.

The door swung open, and Corrine smelled his cologne before she even could process he was the one who had entered. She glanced up to confirm and had to keep from cracking a grin at the sight of Roman.

He looked good, even dressed down. Corrine marveled at the toned legs and arms exposed by the basketball shorts and tank top. Bridget must have had him helping set up, and dammit if Corrine didn't appreciate her for it.

"Nikki, Bri is looking for you," he said.

Nikki nodded. "About time to get this party started." She clasped her hands together and tossed a look over her shoulder at Corrine. "You good? You need anything?"

"I'm fine. Just finishing up in here."

"Bridget probably wants to keep everything set up in here and have the servers bring out the food. I'll let you know." And with that, Nikki pushed through the door, leaving Corrine alone with Roman.

Corrine's stomach was suddenly bunched into a knot, and her mouth had gone dry. The chemistry bouncing between them was so strong it was nearly suffocating. Her back remained to Roman, but she felt his eyes dragging up her body, and the intense scrutiny had her legs wanting to quiver under her weight. And her kitty purred to life.

"Smells good," Roman said, breaking the silence.

Corrine dipped her head low to hide the smile. "Thank you. Since you and your wife enjoyed it so much the other night, I figured it would work for the party."

"Yeah, I've been saving my appetite all day," he said, leaning against the counter. He was close, entirely too close for comfort. "You look nice," he commented, his eyes taking in her attire. She wondered if he recognized the dress as a copycat of Bridget's, or if he just appreciated the view.

"Thanks. I certainly hope you're not wearing that tonight," she teased on a laugh.

Roman spread his arms wide. "You don't like the casual look?"

Was she really supposed to answer that? The man looked good enough to devour. Instead of admitting it, she said, "The theme for the night is Cirque du Soleil. I don't think the casual look really goes."

Roman shifted closer, just a little. "I may be able to find something then," he said. He angled his head toward the trays of food. "You got me starving. The least you can do is let me have a taste, Corrine."

Her lips curved at the loaded comment. Right then and there, she wanted nothing more than to strip down to the lace bra and thong to let him feast on her at his leisure. But since it wasn't time, and she didn't know if she would be able to peel herself off of him in time for the party, she merely nodded.

In response, she lifted a nearby serving spoon from the collection of utensils she had brought from home, dipped it in the sauce, and held it out in his direction. "It's a little spicy," she flirted, her eyes twinkling with delight.

"I think I can handle it," he responded.

Oh, he was most certainly potent. It was a wonder how just his presence, hell, his attention had her questioning her own sobriety.

Corrine continued holding the spoon out in Roman's direction, expecting him to take it from her hand. Instead he stepped forward, cupping her hand to lift the spoon to his lips, and opened his mouth to accept the offering.

"Delicious," he said with a wink.

He was not bothering with subtlety. Good. That's how Corrine liked it anyway. And because the invitation was there, she went ahead and lived in the moment. Closing the distance between them, she wrapped her hand around the back of his head and pulled him in for a kiss.

To her surprise, Roman's arm snaked around her waist to press her body against his. Her tongue darted in his mouth, the sauce mingling with the flavor of alcohol that lingered on his tongue. He tasted of ripe, unadulterated lust; sweet and forbidden. Intoxicating. Corrine savored it.

It was Roman who broke the kiss first, gently pulling back and leaving her aching. "Later." He left the one word suspended between them. It wasn't until after he was gone that Corrine braced against the counter to keep from melting like putty.

He had gotten into her mind. It was just a damn kiss, but somehow, he had managed to fuck up her mind. And Corrine wasn't used to being thrown off her game. So, she spent the rest of the prep hours immersed in her food, focusing the best she could on showcasing the spread and not on what she knew was to come later that night. By the time the guests had started arriving, Corrine was feeling somewhat back to normal.

Bridget was nowhere to be found, but it was obvious all of her efforts were paying off. The club had been transformed, and it looked amazing. She had put up mood lights for ambiance, illuminating the black sashes and curtains draped from the walls and ceilings. Two cages had been set up with women in animalistic body paint showing off their flexibility in handstands, splits, and double-jointed motions as fluid as water. Up above, female aerialists were suspended in the air from ribbons; twisting, twirling, and performing acrobatic stunts of their own. Their diamond-studded leotards glittered like stars in the darkened room. The entertainment piece was sensual and definitely mesmerizing.

Corrine found herself relaxing in the atmosphere, not nitpicking over her food like she figured she would. And thanks to the Ecstasy pill she'd popped earlier, Corrine felt like she was drifting on an erotic high, her whole body stimulated with the aura of the club.

About halfway through the evening, the music lowered, and Marco took to the makeshift stage they had set up in the center of the great room. Everyone quieted down as he lifted a microphone into view. "I just want to thank you all for coming tonight to our Member Appreciation Party," he said. "Shadow Lounge would like to especially thank A Brinique Lux Affair for coordinating this wonderful event."

Applause erupted, and a spotlight swept the crowd, finally landing on Bridget and Nikki off to one side. Corrine noticed Bridget had clipped her hair up into a high ponytail, and she wore a tight, black jumpsuit that hung dramatically low in the front to expose her cleavage and the top part of her stomach. Roman leaned over to kiss her cheek as she nodded her appreciation for the announcement. The gesture had Corrine swallowing a brief twinge of jealousy. But still, she clapped and smiled right along with the guests.

When Roman's eyes met hers, his arm still around his wife's waist, Corrine knew it was time. She held his gaze a moment or two. The silent invitation felt like bolts of electricity shooting between them from across the room.

Corrine turned and made her way through the crowd toward the stairs, the remaining part of Marco's speech beginning to fade in the background. She didn't bother looking back. He would follow. That much she was certain.

A guard was manning the staircase, and Corrine paused at the velvet rope, lifting her arm into view. He eyed her black bracelet and looked down to the clipboard in his hand. "I have a guest," she told him, hearing the footsteps approaching from behind. The guard glanced at Roman, zeroed in on his white beaded bracelet, and scribbled something on the paper. Wordlessly, he stepped to the side and unclipped the rope to allow them through.

Room 202 was Corrine's favorite for two reasons: it was massive with floor-to-ceiling windows overlooking the yard. And the signature feature was the rectangular Jacuzzi that was now already bubbling with rose petals on the lip of the tub. A king sleigh bed dominated the room with downturned covers and a sheer black canopy draped on all three sides.

The door closed behind her with a quiet click, the lock echoing as Roman snapped it into place. Without turning, she reached behind her to pull off the corset, then she hooked her thumbs in the top of the dress to roll it down her body like a latex glove.

Corrine didn't hear him approach, but the sudden hands on her waist had her breath catching in her throat. His lips touched her neck, gentle, his tongue like silk on her flaming skin. She closed her eyes and let him have control. She had wanted to take the lead, pull out all the tricks that she knew would have turned him out. But it felt so damn good to be teased and pleasured, the unfamiliarity of this man's lovemaking building suspense until she felt like she would boil over.

She was right. He was gentle, but he stroked her body with a fervency that awakened a fixation she didn't realize she had been craving. Leave it to him to make her feel like a virgin with a whisper and a touch.

To her utter surprise, he hoisted her in the air, startling an erotic gasp from her lips. And when he laid her down on the satin sheets, she exhaled again and again, even after his head disappeared between to her thighs to coax her cream with his tongue.

"Ooohhh." The gibberish was dripping from her lips in a sort of awkward melody as he took his time to explore her very essence. Her mind was a blur, his cologne assaulting her senses until it was his name twirling on her tongue like a chant. He already had her climbing, and he hadn't even entered her yet.

Corrine's body quivered as he stripped naked and, sliding the condom on, positioned himself between her legs. She opened for him, bracing against his massive size. She had always tried to refrain from comparing, but it was hard not to acknowledge the disparity between Roman and her husband. Not just size but girth, and the men were like night and day when it came to sex styles. No wonder Bridget was head-over-heels in love. Roman seemed completely enthralled in satisfying her. When was the last time Patrick had even cared? The thought threatened tears, and Corrine probably would have cried had she not been grappling with the edges of euphoria.

Roman caressed her walls like an expert masseuse, and Corrine felt the next orgasm barreling through, leaving her breathless. "Oh please," she whispered. She didn't even know what the hell she was begging for. But the words seemed appropriate. As if given permission, Roman quickened his pace.

After her fourth orgasm (Corrine couldn't even be sure; she had stopped counting), Roman tightened his grip, a sign of his own impending release.

"Oh, shit, Corrine," he muttered through clenched teeth. Corrine wrapped her legs around his waist to pin his body to hers, even as he convulsed with his orgasm. He collapsed against her and, instinctively, Corrine's arm circled his back to hold him in place.

Intense was an understatement. Corrine's mind cleared, even as it continued to circle in a fuzzy haze. She felt his heartbeat galloping against her breast, and her smile spread slowly. He was all hers.

After a brief moment, Roman pulled himself up on an exhausted sigh. Corrine watched his sculpted body as he stooped down to retrieve his clothes strewn on the floor. She watched him pull his cell phone from his pocket, eye the screen, and place it on the table. Maybe when he took a shower, she could steal his number. Not that she would necessarily use it, but the thought of him being so readily accessible brought her a sense of youthful exuberance. "Headed back so soon?" Corrine couldn't keep the glee out of her voice even if she tried.

"Yeah, I know the party is going on," he said. "But thank you," he added with a smirk. "This was fun."

Corrine rose to her feet and pulled off the shirt he had just yanked over his head. She leaned up to scatter kisses across his neck and collarbone. "I thought we could go a few more rounds," she murmured. "We've got the room for two hours. And I want to try the Jacuzzi."

He didn't readily respond, so she reached down and grabbed his dick, feeling it harden in her grasp. His low moan tickled her ear, and she lowered to her knees to take him in her mouth. Now, she could pull out her tricks.

Chapter Eleven
Bridget

Pafuckingthetic.

Bridget shifted out of Patrick's arms, pulling the sheets with her to cover her naked frame. He didn't so much as stir, and she had to chuckle to herself as he slept on, like he had actually accomplished something worthy of fatigue.

The adjoining bathroom was accented in luxury, having been elegantly decorated in browns and golds. Bridget crossed into it and cut on the shower to wash off her disappointment.

The sex hadn't been anything like she had pictured. Not that Patrick was the most romantic-looking guy. But Bridget, at the very least, expected to get wet for the man. So much for that idea. That could partially have been because he was so damn rough, pawing at her body like he was in heat. Which was strange considering he was married to a woman with a body as sexy as Corrine's.

He hadn't bothered with foreplay, and had immediately flipped Bridget over, insisting on sexing her from behind doggy-style, which was her least favorite position. And to add insult to injury, the man was quicker than a weekend. She swore she counted five pumps before he yelled out in some incoherent language and slumped against her back. Then he had the nerve to turn over and snore like he had really put in some work. A selfish lover. Bridget could've had a V8.

Either way, it was over, that much she was grateful for. She hoped Roman's experience wasn't as discouraging, not after she had hyped him up to do it in the first place. But sex with Pat had definitely served its purpose. She missed her husband like hell and she couldn't wait to hop on him and relieve some of this sexual tension that had been simmering.

By the time Bridget stepped from the bathroom, the terrycloth towel wrapped around her damp body, Patrick was sitting up in bed, scrolling on his cell phone. He glanced up as she began reaching for her clothes.

"Damn, girl," he said, his voice laced with eagerness. "You got some good shit."

"Thanks." Bridget hoped she didn't sound as unenthusiastic as she felt. Expertly keeping her towel in place, she pulled on her thong.

Patrick chuckled at the gesture. "You ain't got to hide from me, babe," he said. "I've seen every inch of that sexy-ass body. In fact," he tossed the sheets from his lap to expose his naked body, massaging his flaccid dick, "I was thinking you needed to come over and show daddy what that mouth do."

By the looks of his expression, Patrick was completely serious, and it took every ounce of willpower not to laugh in the man's face. Bridget turned her back to him to mask her amusement. "I think we're good," she said.

"Corrine reserved both rooms for two hours."

And if he thought his jackrabbit sex was going to persuade her to stay in that room to get another 119 rounds in, he was delusional.

Bridget pulled on her jumpsuit and strolled to the mirror to fix her hair. Downstairs, she heard the party still going strong, and she was more than ready to get back to it. Nikki was handling the hosting just fine, she was sure, but she wanted to oversee everything herself to ensure the night went off nice and smooth. Maybe Roman was finished and she could sneak a mini quickie in one of the closets somewhere. Whether he came or not, her husband knew just what to do to seduce her orgasm every single time.

Since Patrick was still staring at her as if waiting for a response, Bridget turned to face him. "This was cool," she lied. "But I have to get back. Can't have my event going on without me. You understand, right?"

His face slackened, but he nodded anyway. "Yeah, I get it. You know we can make this a permanent thing. I'm sure Corrine and Roman won't mind."

"Let me talk to my husband and I'll let you know." The lies were rolling easily at this point, but she would say anything to wrap this up. And she didn't want to hurt the man's feelings and risk ruining her relationship with Corrine. So for good measure, she blew him a kiss and quickly made her exit.

Cirque du Soleil *Zumanity* was known for its provocative performances, and Bridget had added a number of their acts to the night to encompass the theme. Right now, two women were performing sensual contortions in a bowl of water as everyone watched in silent intrigue. Bridget eased her way through the crowd into the kitchen to check on the food.

Nikki was assisting one of Corrine's assistants, prepping more plates for the servers to take out to the guests. "Bri, where is your girl?" she asked as soon as Bridget pushed through the door. "I can't plate the food as pretty as she can, and I don't want to mess up her whole presentation."

Bridget waved off the question. "She'll be back in a second. Everyone is watching the show anyway, so it can wait a minute."

Nikki shifted a plate to the side and began nibbling on some of the salad. "Okay, good, because I need a break anyway. Good idea on the theme, Bri," she added. "That shit is sexy as hell and perfect for this type of club."

"Yeah, I thought so, too. It's going well."

Nikki paused, looking as if she had something else to say.

"What's up?" Bridget prompted at her continued silence.

Nikki chewed on her bottom lip. "Did you notice what Corrine was wearing?"

Bridget frowned. What *had* she been wearing? "No. Why? What was wrong with it?"

"It was that same dress you bought when we went to Dallas. The one with the corset. Remember, because you couldn't decide if you wanted it in black or red."

"Oh, okay." Bridget shrugged, not following the insinuation. "So?"

"I don't know. Just thought that was a little strange."

"Nik, lots of people have the same outfits. Not like it's one-of-a-kind."

The comment had Nikki relaxing on a relieved giggle. "Yeah, you're right. I'm tripping," she admitted. "But for real. How much do you think she paid for a body like that?"

"How do you figure she paid for it?" Bridget teased.

"Girl, come on, if God was handing out bodies stacked like that, then me and Him need to have a little chitchat."

Bridget shook her head and poured herself a glass of wine. Since Nikki knew Roman's friend Dorian had been a plastic surgeon before he lost his medical license, she said, "If you wanted me to hook you up with Dorian, that's all you had to say." It was a recurring joke between them. In another time, she would have thought the two would make a cute couple. But Nikki sure as hell wasn't having that.

"Anyway." Nikki rolled her eyes at the comment. "Where is Roman? Don't tell me you sent him home already."

"No, he's around here somewhere." Bridget wasn't going to elaborate. Nikki was her best friend, hell, blood couldn't have made them closer, but some marital secrets were just that, secrets. And Bridget planned on keeping it that way.

The door opened and Bridget glanced up, partially hoping it was Roman. She tried to hide her disappointment as Marco glided in with Jonathan close behind.

"Oh, my girls," Marco said, dropping an arm on both Bridget and Nikki's shoulders. "Did I tell you both how absolutely amazing you are?"

"You did. But a tip speaks a whole lot louder," Nikki teased with a wink.

"Oh, I have a tip all right." Marco's eyes flickered to Bridget's with a knowing glint. "I want to hire you both for the year."

Bridget's face split into a grin, her mind already spinning with the possibilities. The steady stream of income was appealing, but the opportunity to work for a little longer at Shadow Lounge Bridget had to admit was even more attractive.

"Oh, my God, thank you," she squealed, grabbing Marco's hand to give it an appreciative shake. "That is amazing. How soon could we get started?"

"As soon as we can get the paperwork drawn up," Jonathan spoke up. "I'm assuming you two would need some kind of re-tainer—"

"Wait a minute," Nikki interrupted, lifting a hand in the air. "This sounds . . . incredible, but Bri and I would need to discuss it first."

Bridget had to look over to her friend to make sure she was se-rious, but the telltale crease of her forehead made it more than obvious she was. What Bridget didn't understand was why Nikki wasn't doing cartwheels over this opportunity. No, they had never done this type of arrangement, but it could be done. Plus, it was guaranteed money. Why the hell would this even be a question?

"Um . . . Nik, Marco and Jonathan are trying to hire us on under a contract." Bridget said the words slowly as if it would make it that much easier to understand.

"I'm not saying we won't accept it," Nikki clarified. "But it's a lot to consider, and we would need to go over the details of the agreement. How many events a month, payments, that kind of thing. Plus, we would need to look at our schedules. We have a few other events already in the works."

The spontaneous side of Bridget wanted to push the issue. But the business side of her, the more sensible side, knew Nikki was partially right. But still, her friend checking her like that was distasteful. She planned to make mention of it when she spoke to Nikki in private.

"We'll get back to you, Marco," Bridget said instead.

"No problem at all." He smiled through the sudden tension. "Just let us know. We want to start doing some things on a bi-weekly or monthly basis."

Nikki had soured her mood, so Bridget merely nodded before heading back out to the living room.

"Great party."

Bridget eyed the man who had approached her, a drink extended in her direction. An older woman was on his arm, and both eyed her with a not-so-subtle gaze that would have turned her on had the two not been old enough to be her grandparents. She recognized him from her last visit when he was flirting at the bar. What was his name? Eddie? Earnest?

The man's lips peeled back into a knowing grin at her continued silence. "Earl," he said, as if reading the confusion on her face. "And this is my wife, Lucille."

"Nice to meet you, Lucille. Thanks for the drink." Bridget

wasn't planning on drinking it, but to be peaceful, she accepted the glass anyway.

"Where is that husband of yours?" Lucille's voice was gushing with excitement. "I can't wait to meet him."

Bridget gestured vaguely. "I'm sure he's around here somewhere."

The woman's enthusiasm was humorous. Bridget knew Roman would probably never forgive her if she arranged for them to swing with this couple. Not that she was set on doing it again, but her poor husband probably wouldn't even get hard for Lucille.

"So do you plan on becoming a permanent member of our fine establishment?" Lucille inquired.

"I'm not sure."

"We would love to have you," Earl said, licking his lips.

Bridget's lips thinned into a polite smile. Could he be any more brazen? And disgustingly so?

She caught Roman out of the corner of her eye and, thankful for the excuse, sidestepped the couple continuing to ravage her like a lamb in the lion's den. "I better get back to my husband," she said. "You two enjoy the party." And with that, she hurried in his direction.

Roman was smiling as she approached. He looked relaxed and freshly showered. Bridget caught the faint whiff of Flowerbomb perfume permeating from his pores under the Axe soap. She easily recognized Corrine's signature fragrance, but other than that, he exhibited no other signs of his recent tryst. Thankfully, neither did she.

Bridget had wondered how she would feel afterward, whether jealousy would come rearing its ugly head and stain their relationship. Surprisingly, she felt completely at ease, even relieved they had gotten it out of the way. And seeing him had lifted her spirits after the little moment in the kitchen with Nikki.

Roman pulled her in for a hungry kiss, and she moaned against his lips. She tasted the longing on his tongue. He missed her, too. The flavor had her smiling; and her kitty creaming.

"You good?" he asked, pulling his lips from hers to stare at her. Bridget nodded. "Yeah," she said. "Horny. Needing my husband."

Roman's smirk was mischievous as he glanced around. "Show me," he dared.

As Bridget grabbed his hand and led him across the room, her eyes caught Patrick's through the crowd. The way he watched her, his gaze unwavering, made her uncomfortable. She quickly pulled Roman into one of the oversize closets and let the door swing shut on Patrick's grinning face.

Chapter Twelve
Corrine

Roman was heavy on her mind before she had opened her eyes. The feel of him, the smell of him, hell, even the taste of him was so strong he might as well have been lying right next to her. It had Corrine's lips curving at the thought. Bridget was a lucky woman to be able to wake up to that every morning.

Corrine shifted in the bed, extending her arm to feel for Patrick. The sheets were cool to the touch, which could only mean he had already left. To where, she didn't know. But he hadn't even bothered to wake her up. She didn't know how she was supposed to feel about that.

The chilled air from the ceiling fan peppered her skin, but rather than turn it off, Corrine folded herself under the satin comforter to mask her dejection. It was Sunday. She and Patrick should have been spending the day together, basking in each other's laziness and making love on repeat.

Last night when he had gone to sleep without so much as touching her, Corrine had brushed it off. It had been late, the party had been wild, and of course, he had been with Bridget. To be honest, after having Roman four times, she was pretty exhausted herself. But surely Patrick wouldn't let the weekend roll by after their swinging without making love to his wife. So she had gone to sleep and, without realizing it, dreamed of Bridget's husband.

But now, the night was over, the sun was up, and it was back to reality. And Corrine's reality was Patrick. So why then, was she waking up to an empty room?

Corrine reached for her phone on the nearby nightstand and started to dial Patrick's number. She stopped short of pressing the *call* button. Without realizing it, her fingers swiped through her contacts, looking for the number she had swiped the previous night while Roman was in the shower.

She doubted he would answer if she tried to call. Probably he was snuggling up to his wife like a good husband. Corrine hesitated for only a moment longer before deciding to break the rules and send him a little text. It was harmless, she figured. And it wasn't like she expected him to respond. **Morning Roman. This is Corrine. Thanks again for a wonderful night! You were amazing.** ☺

The doorbell rang and had Corrine sitting up on a frown. The master bedroom was positioned to overlook the front yard, so Corrine swung her legs over the side of the bed and padded over to the bay window. She wasn't expecting anyone, so if it wasn't a package being dropped off, the visitor would be sorely disappointed.

The familiar Ford Focus sitting in the driveway was enough to have her relaxing into a smile. Of course, expected or unexpected, Gina's visits were always a welcome exception.

"Hey, Sis," Corrine greeted as soon as she pulled open the door. Gina's smile was paper thin, and Corrine immediately noticed her eyes were red rimmed as if she had been crying. "What's wrong?" Corrine pulled her into the foyer, her eyes darting around for her niece. "Where's Vanessa?"

"I dropped her off at the skating rink for a birthday party right

around the corner. Figured I could wait here for a couple hours."
Gina turned then, her sneakers squeaking on the polished hardwood as she led the way toward the kitchen.

"What's wrong, Gina?" Corrine repeated, following her.

"Nothing."

Corrine rolled her eyes. "Gina, seriously. Stop it," she said, gesturing to her sister's tearstained face. "What is it?"

"You wouldn't care."

"Why the hell would you say that? Of course I would. You're my sister and you're hurting."

Gina didn't respond. She was stalling. That much was evident as she busied herself with making some coffee. Corrine watched her brisk movements as she pulled down mugs and opened drawers for silverware, familiar with the kitchen as if it were her own. She didn't want to worry, nor did she want to pressure her sister, but the stretch of silence between them had her uneasy.

Gina made them each a cup of coffee, complete with milk, sugar, and a splash of vanilla like they both preferred. It wasn't until she was finished that she finally spoke. "Mom's sick," she said, her voice quivering with the revelation. "She's dying."

To Corrine's surprise, the loaded statement seemed to echo flat off the walls. Gina had been right. She didn't care. Part of her expected the news to stir up some emotions, some strike of grief or dread to confirm she wasn't completely immune to feelings for her mother. But there were none. Gina might as well had said her mail was late, or they forgot the condiments when she went to get breakfast that morning.

Since her sister was staring so hard, waiting for a response, Corrine lifted the cup to her lips and gingerly took a sip. She winced as the liquid scalded her tongue. Was she wrong not to give a damn? She had felt her mom had died a long time ago.

Corrine couldn't pinpoint at what juncture she actually started hating her mother. Maybe it was a compilation of instances when

Paula would publicly ridicule her, verbally abuse and disrespect her, or turn a blind eye when Corrine's father would take a belt or, worse, his fists, to try and "beat some sense" into her. So the fact of the matter was Corrine didn't give a damn about the woman or what blessed ailment threatened to snatch her off this earth and hopefully send her soul to hell where it belonged. Corrine was more concerned with her sister and how Gina was going to handle the inevitable.

Even when their father died, it was Gina who was emotionally shattered. No matter how much of a low-down, close-minded, misogynistic bully he had been, he was still their father and Gina loved him. She was just as close with Paula, and it broke Corrine to think about the mental and emotional anguish another death would put Gina through. Her and Vanessa.

"I'm sorry," Corrine mumbled, not sure what else to say. Her condolences sounded as if she were referencing a stranger.

Gina shook her head and fought back a fresh bout of tears. "You're not going to say anything else?"

"What do you want me to say?"

"I don't know." Gina threw up her hands in exasperation. "I tell you our mother is dying and the most you can say is 'I'm sorry.' How about 'Oh damn, Gina, from what? How? Let me call her.'"

Corrine bit her tongue to keep from lashing back out at her sister, her best friend. Gina had always worn her heart on her sleeve, and right now, it was shattered open and bleeding, right before Corrine's eyes. She took another sip of her coffee as her mind scanned through the right words. Better to console her with a lie than to hurt her with the truth. "You're right," she relented with a sigh. "What happened? I'm just . . . in shock."

There was a pause before Gina's nod came brisk with relieved understanding. "I'm sorry. I didn't mean . . . it's just a lot to process." She sank to the nearby barstool, a daze marring her face. "It's stage four lung cancer. Shit sucks because she never smoked. Not once. Daddy . . ."

She didn't have to finish. Corrine already knew Mama hadn't so much as touched a cigarette in all of their lives. But Daddy, on the other hand, smoked like a freight train. He probably would have eventually been diagnosed with cancer himself if the heart attack hadn't gotten to him first.

"How long?" Corrine asked.

Gina winced as if the words punctured her throat. "Few months. Maybe less."

"Have you told 'Nessa?"

"I don't even know how. This is going to crush her, Corrine. She's too young to remember Daddy, but how am I supposed to explain to a child that her granny may not be around much longer?"

Corrine didn't have any words. Her heart ached for her family, but she felt hollow.

"Call her," Gina spoke up again, breaking the prolonged quiet.

Corrine shook her head. "She didn't even tell me she was sick."

"She didn't tell me either, Rinny. I found out just by being over there when her doctor called, so it wasn't like she could hide it any longer."

"Still. She didn't even bother to tell me anything. *You* did. Sounds to me like she didn't want me to know." The words left a bitter taste in her mouth. Maybe there was more there than she cared to acknowledge.

Gina walked around the counter toward her and grabbed both of Corrine's hands in hers. She squeezed, almost desperately, and Corrine saw the pleading in her eyes. "I know," she whispered, the comment heavy with unspoken sympathy. A lifetime's worth of pain they both felt in those two measly words. "Talking to her doesn't make you wrong or her right. It doesn't justify anything."

"I think I hate her," Corrine whispered, lowering her eyes in shame. To her surprise, Gina didn't flinch at her admission.

"Tell her," she said, her voice gentle. "Get it all out so it doesn't have to eat at you anymore. Give both of you a chance to heal. Because if not now, when?"

Corrine nodded her head, only because she couldn't verbalize the lie she knew Gina was fishing for.

——⇒•⇐——

She needed some air.

Gina had barely backed out of the driveway before Corrine was showering, throwing on some clothes, and hopping into her own car. Hopefully, a little drive would clear her mind because right now it was too cluttered to even think logically. She shouldn't have been trying to ignore those intrusive thoughts of her mother and her cancer. But still, Corrine found herself taking the expressway on-ramp, headed in the opposite direction of Paula's house.

She recognized the first few prickles of guilt at her actions, but she tried to ignore that as well. She would eventually muster the courage, and the patience, to go see Paula. Just not today. Gina would have to accept that she and Corrine weren't built the same. They dealt with hurt differently. And, hell, not even Gina would ever know the depths of trauma their parents had put Corrine through. She would face her demons when she was ready. She just hoped, for Paula's sake, the woman lived long enough to confront them with her.

Corrine didn't have any particular destination in mind, but she found herself navigating toward Pat's auto shop. Since he wasn't answering his phone to confirm, Corrine could only assume he was working today.

Sure enough, his truck was parked in front of the building, along with a few others. The garage doors were up and music was blaring from inside, though no one was in sight.

Corrine parked and made her way to one of the garage entrances with a Chevy Impala elevated in the air on a vertical lift.

For the briefest of moments, Corrine wondered if Kalem was working today. Then, as if someone had read her mind, she quickly dispelled the thought.

Kalem was Pat's right hand when it came to running the business side of things. He had the stereotypical thug demeanor, with felony convictions, a drug-dealing rap sheet, and a bitter, boujie baby mama whom Corrine had seen strutting around the garage a time or two. But even with all of that, plus zero experience to his name, Pat had brought him onboard and groomed the young man into his protégé. Now, Kalem could manage the shop like it was his own, and Corrine knew Pat trusted him with everything, from the finances to the equipment.

Speaking of which, Corrine stopped short when she saw Kalem come strolling from one of the outside storages, rubbing his hands on an oil-stained cloth. He was easily a couple feet under Corrine, but what he lacked in height, he made up for in muscle. Plus, with his chocolate complexion and short locs, not to mention the scar along his jawline, he was still a little intimidating.

Kalem didn't bother speaking, barely sparing Corrine an absent glance when he noticed her standing there in the garage. The sleeves of his jumpsuit were rolled up to the elbow to reveal a tapestry of tattoos etched in his skin. A blunt was clamped between his lips.

He continued working on the Impala, making it obvious he wasn't going to address her, before she spoke up. "Pat in there?"

"Nah."

Corrine frowned, glancing to the parking lot. Her eyes zeroed in on Pat's truck, glistening in the early afternoon sun.

"He had to run out," Kalem added, noticing her gaze. "Back in a few hours."

Pat had mentioned time and time again how loyal the man was, and it was more than obvious as Kalem stood right there, staring her dead in the eye, and opened his mouth to tell a blatant lie.

Corrine felt it in her gut. But the way Kalem watched her now, almost daring her to rebut his statement, made her feel uneasy.

She nodded, spun on her heel, and hurried back to her car, desperate to create distance between them. Something wasn't right about Kalem, and she didn't care to be in his presence any longer than she needed to be.

Pulling open the door, she caught a glimpse of his reflection in her windshield; his eyes fixated on her retreating backside.

Corrine peeled out of the parking lot, expertly steering out into the midday traffic while using her other hand to dial Pat's number. She was surprised he picked up immediately.

"What's up?" He sounded distant.

"Hey. I was just checking with you," Corrine said. "You left out this morning. I didn't know you had to work."

"Yeah."

Silence.

"Well, what time will you be—"

"Look, babe. It's really busy here at the shop. Let me call you back later."

Corrine listened to the *click* in her ear, her heart picking up speed. No matter how she tried to rationalize it, the pieces didn't fit. But she couldn't—*wouldn't* believe Pat was lying to her, no matter how empty she just saw the mechanic shop just now. There had to be a logical explanation. At least that's what she prayed for.

Between Gina's news that morning, and now the suspicions about Pat, Corrine drove aimlessly, taking turns and streets without purpose or focus.

It wasn't until Southern Regional came into view that Corrine even realized she had come to Roman's job at the hospital. She sat for a moment, eyeing the brick building through the first few splatters of rain drizzling on her windshield. The illuminated red letters spelling *EMERGENCY* were mounted on the portico where vehicles passed through to load and unload passengers.

Right now, one such vehicle was pulled up to the automatic doors while a nurse wheeled out a patient in a wheelchair. She didn't know why she had come. Or what she planned on doing now that she was there.

The minutes ticked by as Corrine sat parked in the lot, drumming her fingers on the steering wheel. It wasn't like she was going to talk to him, she reasoned. It would just be refreshing to see him. Roman had a charm about him; a certain aura that made any woman within his immediate radius feel special. And beautiful.

Corrine couldn't help but grin as her mind flipped back to their night together at Shadow Lounge. Four rounds. She hadn't meant to keep count, but her body had grown appreciatively weaker with each passing orgasm. Just like she had imagined, Roman had been slow and tender, as if relishing every inch of her. And Corrine had felt like it was more than her body erupting, but her mind and soul as well.

Had Patrick ever made her feel like that? It had been so long that Corrine couldn't honestly remember. It would be soothing just to be around Roman, if only for a few moments from afar. With that, Corrine gathered her purse and phone and stepped into the damp afternoon.

The rain had slackened to a light mist by the time she made it to the entrance of the hospital. A dense fog hovered low, carrying with it remnants of a vapor that chilled her skin and had Corrine pulling her jacket tighter. It was a stretch, she knew, even as the doors parted to invite her inside. It would be just her luck that Roman wasn't even on call that day, or he was tied up in surgery, or making rounds with his patients. She had to chuckle at the absurdity of roaming the corridors, peeking in rooms in hopes that she could catch a glimpse of him.

The emergency room wasn't crowded. A few visitors were seated in the plastic lobby chairs scattered around the room. A flat-screen TV was on, the volume low as the images from a local news station played on the monitor. Corrine glanced around before walking up to the desk where a young, dark-skinned nurse was pecking away at the keyboard of her computer.

Corrine opened her mouth to speak, but the woman quickly held up a finger to silence her. "Sign in for me please," the nurse said, her voice laced with weariness of the same old routine.

Corrine hesitated, glancing again toward the double doors that gave way to triage and the rest of the hospital floor. "Is Doctor Pierce in?" she asked.

The nurse finally brought her eyes over to meet Corrine's and gave her a quick once-over. "I can page him for you," she said. "You are?"

"No, don't worry about it. Thanks." As if she had been caught, Corrine turned briskly and headed back toward the hospital entrance. Through the glass door, she saw the parking lot, her safe haven. What the hell was she doing?

She heard his voice then, a light chuckle that floated down the halls and had her neck whipping around to see which direction it was coming from. Be it luck, coincidence, fate—whatever the attribution didn't matter to Corrine. All she knew was the sight of him had her lips curving as he strolled through the double doors at the end of the hall.

Apparently, Roman was off work, because the casual attire of jeans and a polo shirt was indicative he may have just been dropping by the hospital. Another stroke of good fortune. He walked hand-in-hand with a little girl, about five or six. She was the spitting image of him, with beaded ponytails cinched with purple ribbons that bounced off her shoulders with each step. Corrine smiled as she noted the similar features, the similar mannerisms. The girl even held her face in a half smirk, half smile just like Roman did.

His daughter, she deduced. An unbelievably adorable daughter. Something tugged on Corrine's heart. Something that felt warm and silky like honey. *So, the charmer is a doting father.* Corrine suddenly remembered the dinner at her house. Bridget had mentioned *his* daughter, not *their* daughter. She turned her back as they walked past, pretending to be engaged in something on a nearby magazine rack.

"Can we get ice cream?" the little girl asked.

"Let's first go home and see if Miss Bri wants some," Roman answered.

Corrine caught the swift motion out of the corner of her eye. Roman scooped the little girl up into his arms, and she squealed with delight. The gesture sent tiny flutters coursing through her body. A longing sigh touched her lips.

Corrine had always wanted kids. She remembered mentioning the thought to Patrick, but he had been vehemently opposed to it. Adoption, surrogacy, he hadn't given any option so much as a second thought.

"We don't need no damn kids," he had said. And that was that. So Corrine had never mentioned it again, burying her own desires behind submission and complacency. But now, seeing Roman with his precious little one, something was beginning to flicker and grow inside of Corrine. Again, she wondered if Bridget knew how lucky she was to have it all. Did she even appreciate it?

It was coming down a little harder now, and she watched Roman dash off across the parking lot through the sheets of rain, his little twin bobbing off his hip.

Moving on instinct, Corrine took off out of the hospital, the downpour immediately drenching her hair and clothes. She wasn't worried about Roman seeing her. The rainfall was heavy and cloaked her in obscurity. But she kept her eyes on them anyway as Roman quickly jumped into a black Navigator and backed out of the lot. Corrine was in her own vehicle in a matter of seconds, following suit.

It wasn't like she had anything else to do, Corrine reasoned with herself as she caught up to the truck at a traffic light. She was just curious. Patrick had her do enough digging on Bridget and Roman to pique her curiosity, and now she wanted to know more. Where did they stay? What did their house look like? Bridget gave her the impression that she could be a little uppity and materialistic, so it was fair for Corrine to assume their house would reflect their expensive tastes. She was a little nosy; Corrine could admit that about herself. But that's where it ended. She would drive by their place then continue home. She had her own problems to sort through. Satisfied, Corrine kept her eyes trained on Roman's truck and kept a discreet distance as she weaved with him through the Southside city congestion.

When he pulled through the open gate of an upscale community, Bridget trailed behind, happy when the gate remained open to allow her through. She watched him steer into a driveway, and she pulled along the curb across the street, turning the car off. At least it had stopped raining, so she could clearly make out Roman opening the back door for the little girl and helping her hop down from the high position. She took off across the manicured lawn, hitting a sloppy cartwheel, much to Roman's amusement. Even from this distance, Corrine's heart melted, hearing him clap and cheer on his little gymnast.

The garage door opened, and she saw Bridget emerge, crossing her arms over her chest as she looked on at her family. There it was again, that twinge of envy that had Corrine yearning, then feeling guilty. That could have been her. That could have been Pat and their daughter. This should be her life. Didn't she deserve this type of happiness? It wasn't her fault she was born in the wrong body, to the wrong family, with the wrong men and their impure intentions shattering her heart and expectations.

A solitary tear touched her cheek as she watched Roman and Bridget exchange an intimate kiss. Happiness. Was that too much to ask for?

Corrine pulled out her cell phone to take a picture. It was then she noticed the envelope icon at the top of her screen indicating a new text. She swiped her screen to open it, her mood instantly brighter when she saw it was Roman responding from earlier. How had she missed this?

If he asked how she got his number, Corrine was prepared with the lie: Bridget had given it to her, along with Nikki's, in case she needed it for the party. She was pleased to read he hadn't bothered questioning it. His message simply read: **Yeah, last night was fun. ☺**

So he had enjoyed himself just as much as she had. She quickly keyed in another message then turned her eyes to the window to see if he would readily reply. Sure enough, Roman pulled his cell phone from his back pocket, eyed the screen, and began typing. Corrine watched the text pop up on her phone, and her heart inflated like a balloon.

CORRINE: When can I see you again? When are you coming back to Shadow?

ROMAN: Soon.

It wasn't until they had disappeared inside with their daughter, the garage door lowering to close them into their perfect little world, that Corrine cranked her car and pulled away. But that image had been captured like a screenshot, sure to remain impressed on her mind as a glimpse of what she didn't have. But what she planned on experiencing for herself. Just like Roman promised, *soon.*

Corrine was surprised Patrick's truck was in the garage when she pulled into her own driveway an hour later. She was sure his nonsensical lie of overwhelming work would've kept him away until late into the night. She drew in a breath for strength and headed into the house. All the better that he was home. Now she could confront him about what had been playing on her mind the whole ride from Roman's side of town.

The smell of fish had Corrine frowning as she stepped into the mudroom and shrugged out of her damp jacket. She followed the aroma into the kitchen, glancing around at the slew of pots and pans strewn across the counter. Patrick always tended to use every piece of cooking equipment they owned, which was one reason why Corrine preferred for him not to invade her territory. But right now, she was too shocked to be mad at the gesture, all rehearsed script of her argument dissipating into thin air.

"Hey, babe," Patrick said, turning and pecking her gently on the cheek. "Where were you? I thought you would've been home when I got here."

"I didn't know you were coming home so soon," Corrine countered, lifting a questioning eyebrow. "You were so busy at work, remember?"

"Well, I wrapped things up early and wanted to hurry home and do a little something nice for you."

Corrine watched him sprinkle entirely too much seasoning on the salmon. "What's all this?"

"Just because I love you."

"No, really," Corrine said with a roll of her eyes. "You only do shit like this when you want something."

Patrick turned from the sink and handed her a glass of red wine. "I want my wife," he said with a smile. He paused, turning back to a pot boiling with rice. "I was thinking we should have another night with Roman and Bridget," he went on. "It went good the first time, and Bridget was interested in making us their permanent partners."

Corrine paused, the glass halfway to her lips. So that's what the point of all this was.

Patrick kissed her again, trying to pry her lips open with his tongue.

Corrine didn't return the gesture. "I went up to the shop," she said, pulling her face away from his. "I saw your car, but Kalem said you weren't there."

The slightest flicker of something crossed Patrick's face, but just as quickly, it was gone. "Yeah," he said. "So what?"

"Where were you?"

"At the post office. Had to mail off some stuff for parts."

"Then who did you go with?" Corrine pressed. "Your car was still in the parking lot."

Patrick's sigh was thick with agitation as he gripped the side of the counter. Corrine saw the veins in his arms popping with the movement, and she knew she was pushing too hard. "I just wanted to see you," she said instead, her voice more gentle.

Patrick spread his arms wide and gestured to himself. "Well, I'm here now," he said. "And I thought I wanted to see you, too, but not if you're going to start all that bitching."

Does Roman talk to Bridget this way? Do they even have arguments?

Because Patrick was waiting, Corrine swallowed the rest of her argument and opted for her usual, peaceful approach. "I'm sorry," she said. "I didn't mean—"

"Here I am trying to do something nice for your ungrateful ass," Patrick spat, the strained anger lacing each pronounced syllable.

Corrine lowered her head, her eyes downcast. That temper. Lord, she wished he would do something about that damn temper. "I'm sorry," she murmured. "I shouldn't have brought it up. Can we just do what you have planned for this evening? I appreciate you cooking."

The loud motion startled a gasp from her lips as Patrick swept his arm across a few pots and pans, sending them clattering to the hardwood floor. One of the pans banged against her ankle and sent a shooting pain up and down her leg. She hissed, gritting her teeth against the pain.

Patrick turned to the door, and she reached for him. She didn't want him to leave mad. "Babe, I'm so—"

Her words were clipped by him snatching from her out-stretched hand and shoving her shoulder with so much force it knocked her up against the wall. Her back hit first, letting loose another raw jolt of pain that pierced clean through to the bone.

"Nigga, don't fuckin' touch me," Pat snapped, jabbing a pointed finger into Corrine's chest. He only reverted to the n-word when he was beyond pissed, which she hated. He knew the word was offensive. But once Pat was mad, all semblance of compassion was out the window. He left then, and this time, Corrine didn't stop him.

Alone in the kitchen massaging her bruised shoulder, her mind shifted, once again, to Roman and Bridget. Her life could be perfect. A fresh round of tears wet her lashes. If God didn't see fit to allow her a little happiness, she was determined to make her own. No matter the cost.

Chapter Thirteen
Bridget

The car had been following her for the last twenty minutes.

At first, Bridget hadn't given much thought to the black Cadillac with blacked-out rims and tinted windows. In fact, the vehicle initially caught her attention because of the glistening paint job, which had the color looking showroom new. Then a few exits up from Stonecrest Mall, she'd just so happened to glance in the rearview mirror and see the same Cadillac, strategically positioned about three cars behind her.

Bridget decided to take a detour and turned on one of the Lithonia access roads. Sure enough, the car turned as well, still maintaining a safe distance behind her. She gripped the wheel with both hands, her mind flipping over when she first noticed the vehicle. *Had it been outside of her home? Her neighborhood?* She really hadn't been paying attention, having been consumed with the little brief disagreement with Roman before she left the house.

It hadn't been one particular thing that had pissed her off, so much as it had been a combination of things. First, Roman had mentioned Maya staying with them for a few months. Apparently, her mother, April, had lost her job and was struggling to keep them afloat along with her other two kids by her first baby daddy. Roman's child support alone wasn't cutting it, so it made the most financial sense for his daughter to come stay. But Bridget didn't give a damn about what made sense or April's money issues. A full-time mother? That was sure as hell not what she had signed up for. Especially with no definite end in sight.

"How long is this arrangement for?" Bridget had asked. She hadn't meant to come off as insensitive, but, hell, she needed to know. April could still be "trying to get on her feet" when Maya graduated high school. Plus, Roman was a doctor, and his unpredictable work schedule warranted Bridget to always be available to look after Maya; be it pick her up from school, take her to cheerleading practice, or pick up her asthma medicine, because her forgetful-ass mama kept her priorities out of sorts. Bridget couldn't make him understand that when Maya was around, she wasn't just his responsibility but hers, too. He didn't seem to recognize the inconvenience, and tying up Bridget's schedule was something she wasn't jumping for joy to give up; even if did mean Roman could take better care of his baby girl.

He had given her this funny look like he'd bit into something sour, and Bridget knew she probably should've kept her mouth shut. Maybe she was tripping, but she couldn't help the disappointment radiating to her core. And if she wasn't still a little pissed with Nikki, Bridget would have called and let out some of her frustrations. But much like she usually did with her husband when it came to his daughter, Bridget put her feelings to the side.

That had been yesterday morning, and the unspoken tension had the two going through the day exchanging only a few cordial words.

Then last night, Bridget had decided to go with Nikki's suggestion and had sat down to write her book. Something about the success of her event with Shadow Lounge had a burst of inspiration striking, and she'd pulled open her laptop and let the words flow.

She had managed to write an entire chapter and showed it to Roman, all but bursting with a nervous excitement. He hadn't cared. Well, maybe she shouldn't say that, Bridget reconsidered with a frown. He hadn't *seemed* to care. He was too enthralled with the movie he was watching with Maya and had spared the computer an absent glance. Perhaps he was still upset about their previous contentiousness, but still his brazen nonchalance had hurt. She wasn't an author by any means, and dabbling in this unfamiliar territory had her questioning her own expertise. So at the very least, she was relying on Roman's encouragement to give her a little boost of confidence. But it was clear. Even through her success, Roman still didn't support her like she craved.

She had asked him about it before they went to bed, and he again had brushed it off. "Bri, why are you even doing that?" he had said. "You don't know anything about writing. That's just going to be more time invested in something you don't even need to be worried about. You work a lot as it is. Besides," he had added, "that's more time you can devote to me, Maya, and to little RJ."

It had been said in jest, but that shit had pissed her off even more. Without a response, Bridget had gone down to her office to do some more work. Then when she was positive Roman had fallen asleep, she went to camp out in the guest bedroom for the night.

Nikki had texted her that morning about meeting at the mall to chat about the offer with Shadow Lounge, and Bridget was glad she had initiated the conversation. Not only could they get everything cleared up, but she didn't have to spend the day pacifying and tiptoeing around Roman. Sleep had done nothing to soften her attitude, and she knew she was going to have to address it sooner rather than later. Because their arguments about this were becoming more and more frequent. Or maybe her tolerance for the subject was becoming less and less.

Bridget pulled into the parking lot of Stonecrest Mall and took another look in the rearview mirror; satisfied when she still didn't see the black Cadillac anymore. She grabbed her purse and started inside, heading straight for the food court.

This was her and Nikki's little hang-out spot, if one could call knocking back barbecue and people-watching "hanging out." The mall had once been more of an upscale caliber before gentrification took over. Now it was barely hanging on to its reputable distinction as more shops opened to accommodate the urban culture.

It was early, so the typical mall activity was minimal, which was how Bridget liked it. Knowing her girl would be late as usual, Bridget took the longer route to the food court, stopping to peer in a few stores on her way.

"Bri?"

The voice had her turning from the Forever 21 window display to see who had called her name. A surprised smile touched her lips as Corrine waved. A Macy's shopping bag dangled from her wrist.

"Hey, Corrine. What are you doing here?"

Without hesitation, Corrine pulled her in for a friendly hug. "Just needed to do a little shopping," she said brightly. "Pat's birthday is coming up, so figured I could catch some of these sales."

Bridget started to comment on how far Corrine was from Fairburn to have come across town to shop, but quickly dismissed the thought. That would have been the pot calling the kettle black.

"Well, what did you get him?" Bridget asked as she gestured to the bag in her hand.

"Oh, that's for me," Corrine quickly corrected with a guilty grin. "I'm still trying to decide what to get him. What have you gotten Roman before? I need some ideas."

The ladies easily fell into step with each other as they resumed their leisurely walk. "Girl, everything," Bridget said with a chuckle. "A watch, cologne, shoes, luggage, basketball game tickets . . . Roman's pretty easy, but the thing is, you have to get a little creative with your man's gift so it's not too generic."

"Creative how?"

"Like one birthday, I bought him a glass chessboard, and I had it customized with his name, birthday, and a nice little freaky quote. He loved it."

Corrine nodded absently. "Oh, okay, he plays chess?"

"Girl, yes. Loves it. I can't really get into it, though."

"Yeah, me neither. Pat doesn't really play games like that, so I'll have to come up with something creative, like you said."

They paused at the entrance to the food court. Immediately, Bridget scanned the lines of people, confirming Nikki still hadn't arrived.

"You want to grab something to eat while we're here?" Corrine asked.

"Actually, I'm meeting Nikki, but of course, she's late," Bridget said on a laugh. "Do you want to join us? We usually go to the little barbecue spot in the back."

Corrine smiled at the invitation. "That sounds good."

They took a seat at one of the high-top tables, and Bridget sent a quick text to Nikki to let her know where she could find her.

"So, Marco and Jonathan told me about their proposal," Corrine started, shrugging out of her jacket. "Congratulations."

"Thanks. I'm excited about it."

"You should be. Marco doesn't just extend that kind of offer lightly. He's very possessive of his club and everything that goes on in it."

"Yeah, I'm appreciative of the opportunity. Just got to get Nikki onboard."

The smallest of frowns flitted across Corrine's lips. "What do you mean? Nikki doesn't want to do it?"

"It's not that she doesn't want to do it," Bridget clarified, her voice laced with apprehension. "I think she just wanted some more details first before we just jump in this thing headfirst. It's a big commitment."

Corrine's shoulder lifted and fell in a shrug. "I guess so," she said. "But hopefully she sees how good this will be for business and doesn't hold you back."

The words were said casually but still, something else resonated with Bridget; something she didn't particularly like. "It's not that she's trying to hold us back," she corrected, marinating on the thought as she tried to affirm her own uncertainty. "You have to know Nikki's ways. Some things, she can go with the flow. Other times she can be a little more analytical. It's like she has a personality type right between A and B."

"I got it. A and a half."

Bridget laughed. "Yeah, that's a way to think of it. We usually balance each other out pretty good, so I'm sure when we get everything ironed out, she'll want in."

"I hope you're right," Corrine said. "I would hate you two to fall out over something minor like this."

Bridget couldn't tell if the comments were intentionally triggering or if she was just taking them out of context. She hated that Roman had her out of sorts that day. Now she was feeling hypersensitive to every damn thing.

She opened her mouth to rebut the last comment, insist that "falling out" was the last thing on either her or Nikki's mind, when something caught her eye.

It was only because of Corrine's posture that Bridget even saw the bruise. Any other angle, and the shirt wouldn't have shifted up her arm to expose the red discoloring the smooth brown skin of her wrist. The markings were strategically positioned and oddly reminiscent of fingertips, as if someone had been grabbing her arm a little too tight. They appeared to be on the end stages of the healing process, and even though she had attempted to cover the discoloration with makeup, the bruising was still visible.

She hadn't meant to stare, but Corrine's expression let her know she was doing just that. Corrine dropped her eyes to catch what had captured Bridget's attention, and she quickly gasped, covering her arm with her hand and pulling her sleeve down a little to conceal her skin from view.

Neither one bothered speaking at first; Bridget was unsure what to say and Corrine, knowing whatever justification she came up with would probably sound like a lie, kept her mouth shut, too.

It was a bruise, no question about it. And with nothing else logical to go on, Bridget was already concluding Patrick was the culprit. No, he didn't give the impression that he was the abusive type. But controlling? Very much so. Bridget had made that assumption that night when they exchanged partners in Shadow Lounge. His mannerisms, the way he spoke—the abusive conclusion wasn't too far-fetched. Now Bridget wondered if she should actually speak on it, or would she be again overstepping her bounds. But what kind of friend would she be to sit back and let Corrine suffer domestic abuse? She wasn't even sure if she could consider the woman a friend, but still. She had seen the bruises plain as day. To not say anything was as good as giving Pat—or whomever—permission to continue. And didn't that make Bridget just as accountable?

"Corrine, is there something going on?" Bridget asked cautiously.

Corrine was already shaking her head before she even got the full question out. "No."

"Oh, yeah. What's with your arm?" Bridget struggled to keep her voice from rising.

Corrine's eyes narrowed into slits. "What are you insinuating?"

"I'm not insinuating anything," she said. "I'm just asking you a question."

"Girl, you are tripping." Corrine tried to lighten the mood with a laugh. "It's not what you think."

"Tell me what to think, then." Bridget tried to keep her voice calm, even as she felt the anger building at the obvious reason for the woman's pain.

"Please don't make this into a big deal." Corrine lifted her eyes, and they were glassy with the beginnings of tears. "It was just a one-time thing, I swear."

Bridget frowned. "Did Patrick put his hands on you?"

Corrine averted her eyes even as her lips remained pursed together, a silent verification of the truth in the statement.

"I can't believe you let him do this to you," she said, her voice elevated into a full-fledged scream. "How can you, Corrine? You're not stupid."

"I'm not." Corrine's voice shook. "That's why I'm trying to deal with it. Patrick is a wonderful guy."

"Oh, wonderful, huh? Is that before or after the abuse?" Bridget snapped back.

"Stop being so dramatic, Bri. Abuse? Really?"

"Well, what do you call it?" Bridget gestured wildly toward Corrine's arm. "Please tell me what to make of it, because I'm utterly confused why you're taking up for the bastard."

Silent tension settled between them. Neither woman spoke as their eyes pierced each other's; Bridget's pure disgust and Corrine's heavy with a plea for understanding. Finally, Corrine sighed in exasperation. "Look," she said. "I don't expect you to understand. I love him. You're in a relationship, so you know about the sacrifices and compromises it takes to make one work. I just need you to promise not to say anything," Corrine went on. "Please. I can handle this."

The more she spoke, the more Bridget couldn't help but feel like Corrine sounded just like those battered women on the Lifetime movies. The words were eerily familiar, putting the blame on themselves rather than the men who caused their hurt.

"Bri." Corrine pulled Bridget's attention back to her as she reached across the table. "Promise me you'll drop it. I need you to do this for me."

Bridget didn't say anything. She really didn't know what to make of the situation. Part of her wanted to address Patrick herself and make sure he regretted ever touching Corrine. Or maybe she could talk to Roman. But she seriously didn't want to get him involved. Especially given the circumstances. So, for now, she would respect Corrine's wishes. And pray like hell she wouldn't end up regretting the decision.

Abruptly, as if desperate for a reprieve, Corrine pushed back from the table and swung her purse over her shoulder in one fluid motion. "Let me use the restroom," she said and hurried away, scissoring her legs around the congested scatter of plastic tables and chairs.

Bridget watched her until she disappeared, her mind already working in overdrive about what she had, mistakenly, been exposed to.

"Hey, girl." Nikki's greeting interrupted Bridget's thoughts. She carried a collection of shopping bags in both hands, which she plopped down on the floor.

"Wasting time?" Bridget motioned to the bags with a nod of her head. "You had us waiting while you went shopping, Nik."

"First off, I was getting some new things for Dennis, thank you very much." Nikki's eyes darted around the table. "And what do you mean 'we'?" she asked, but her eyes were already landing on Corrine's jacket hanging across the back of a nearby chair.

"Corrine," Bridget answered her questioning glance. "I ran into her and invited her along."

Something that resembled annoyance flickered over Nikki's face as she sighed.

Bridget frowned at the reaction. "What was that for?" Her friend was off for some reason. She couldn't quite put her finger on it, but her entire demeanor had changed.

"Okay, let me be honest with you." Nikki lowered her voice. "And I'm only saying this as your friend. I don't know how I feel about Corrine."

"What do you mean, you don't know how you feel about her?"

Nikki shrugged. "I don't really trust her. Doesn't she seem a little . . . attached to you?"

Bridget had to chuckle at the ridiculous question. "Why? Because she's shopping at the same mall as us?" Bridget tossed a pointed look to the bags at their feet, and Nikki brushed off the comment with a wave of her hand.

"She's just suddenly always around. Is she bisexual?"

"What?"

Nikki lifted her hands in defense. "Just hear me out. She's married but she probably swings both ways. I see the way she looks at you."

Bridget shook her head. She'd had enough. Especially after what she had just witnessed with the bruising on Corrine's arm. Nikki's little . . . what was this? Jealousy? Yeah, that would have to wait. Besides, Bridget was ready to address the elephant in the room.

"Listen, Nik, about the Shadow Lounge thing—"

"Hold up. Here she comes."

Corrine appeared at the side of the table and took a seat. Bridget noticed she looked completely refreshed. She exuded confidence, and she carried herself as such. No one would suspect anything amiss, especially any type of domestic violence. Her being able to disguise it so well made Bridget that much more sympathetic. She lowered her eyes to Corrine's arm. Sure enough, the sleeves were pulled down low to cover any exposed skin on her wrist.

"Hey, Nikki," she greeted brightly. "I hope you don't mind. Bri said it would be okay if I joined you ladies."

Nikki's smile was thin. "Of course not," she said. "Whatever *Bri* says certainly works for me."

Her words dripped with sarcasm, and even across the table, Bridget caught the excessive phoniness in her statement. *What the hell was her problem with Corrine?*

Rather than dwell on it and risk further frustrating herself, Bridget changed the subject. "We need to talk about the Shadow Lounge deal," she said. "I wanted to go over some things Marco proposed so we can really assess if this is a good move."

"I don't think we need to discuss business in front of Corrine," Nikki said through tight lips.

Corrine waved her hands. "Oh, please don't let me stop you. But if you want my opinion," she added with a wink, "it's a dope-ass offer. And Marco takes very good care of his people."

"See, Nik?" Bridget said, satisfied she had an ally. Even Corrine knew the opportunity was worth jumping on. So why, then, was Nikki so damn opposed?

"Bri, we'll talk about this later," Nikki insisted. "I'm not saying we can't or won't do it. I just want to go over some more details."

Her stubbornness was pissing Bridget off. Nikki wasn't really one to be this damn defiant, especially over more business. Which, Bridget could only assume, was because of Corrine. And it was a damn shame she was letting whatever personal and unsubstantiated feelings against the woman interfere with business. Shit was immature.

Bridget sat back and crossed her arms over her breasts. She didn't want to admit it, but maybe Corrine was right. Best friend or no best friend, she wasn't about to let Nikki be the downfall of her enterprise. They would have to split up first.

Her mother had warned her years ago that she should be careful going into business with her best friend. Sooner or later, it would either destroy their friendship, their company, or both, Vernita had said. Of course, Bridget hadn't believed her. But now it was clear. And she didn't like seeing Nikki's true colors.

"I'm going to go ahead and grab something to eat," Corrine

said, standing up. She turned her eyes first to Nikki, then Bridget. "You two want anything?"

Bridget opened her mouth to respond, but Nikki spoke up first. "Nah, we're good," she said quickly. "You go ahead."

Corrine nodded and, grabbing her jacket, turned to head toward one of the food vendors.

Bridget waited until she was out of earshot before she spoke. "Nik, what the hell—"

"Did you see that?" Nikki interrupted, gesturing toward Corrine standing in line across the room.

"See what?"

"Your girl's new tattoo," Nikki said with triumph. "She's got the same tattoo on the back of her neck, just like you."

Bridget turned to eye Corrine, her exasperation slowly dissolving into discomfort. And then, fear.

<hr/>

"Bri, we need to talk."

Bridget didn't bother turning from the computer, instead continuing to peck away on the keys. She figured Roman would come into her office sooner or later, especially after she came home from the mall and completely ignored him. Part of it was because she was still pissed at him. The other part, the part she was still grappling with, was what Nikki had brought to her attention about Corrine's new tattoos; tattoos that were completely identical to Bridget's.

The monochromatic butterfly tattoos on the back of her neck were symbolic for her. They represented her freedom. Coming out from under her parents' thumb, Bridget had found herself at Mercer University, discovering her love for event planning, having her first heartbreak, losing her virginity. She felt like she actually began to live.

So she hadn't hesitated when her roommate suggested they

visit the tattoo parlor right off the college campus one night. It was painful, and Bridget had gritted through the needle for a grueling hour. But in the end, she loved the artwork and what it represented for her.

So now to have Nikki point out that Corrine had gone out to get a duplicate tattoo, well, Bridget had to admit the shit was freaky. She had caught a glimpse of it herself when Corrine had returned to the table, but she couldn't bring herself to address it. Not right then. To take her mind off it, Bridget had come home, burrowed herself in her office, and began working on her book.

Roman interrupting her concentration was only a mild annoyance on top of the day's stresses. Bridget felt him behind her, his hands suddenly on her shoulders to massage her muscles.

"What are you working on?" he asked.

Still riding on her attitude, Bridget lifted her arms to shrug off his hands. Rather than tell him the truth, she merely answered, "Working." No use in telling him more about her book and risking his discouragement. She didn't need that right now. "What did you want to talk about?"

"Earlier." Roman took a seat on the leather ottoman. "Look, is it a problem for Maya to stay with us?"

Bridget kept her face neutral. "Of course not," she lied. "Why would it be a problem?"

"It shouldn't. At least I hope it's not." Roman met her gaze, his face pained at the possibility. "Earlier it just seemed like you had an issue when I mentioned it."

"Nope." Bridget let the one word hang suspended between them. When Roman just continued to stare, she went on. "Anything else?"

"You sure you been good lately?" A deep-set frown creased his face. It was obvious he was struggling to read his wife, and she wasn't making it easy for him.

Bridget nodded and rolled her chair back around to face her desk. She thought of telling him about the car following her that morning to the mall, then quickly put it out of her mind. And surely there wasn't a point in mentioning her growing suspicions of Corrine. Nor the trivial drama with Nikki.

"I'm good," she said, her voice dismissive. "I don't know why you keep asking me that."

"Well, look, I'm sorry if you felt I didn't care about your work," he said. "You know I love and support you, babe."

Do I? Roman's apathy about her book reminded her of when she first told him she was starting a business. Hell, it had taken him a while to actually start calling it a "business" and not her "little hobby."

She caught Roman's movements out of the corner of her eye; saw him turning to glance out of the window. "What is it?" she asked.

Roman stepped closer and pulled the curtains to the side, peering through the glass into the darkened night. Even from her position across the room, she could see the worry lines on his face's reflection against the pane.

"Just thought I saw something," he murmured absently. He stood there a moment longer before pulling the curtains closed.

It crossed Bridget's mind again about the black Cadillac from earlier tailing her clear across town. "Roman, I wanted to tell you—"

The shrill ring of the cell phone at Roman's hip cut her off, and she pursed her lips. She knew what that meant.

Roman sighed, but he was already moving to grab his stuff to head to the hospital for work. "Babe, you mind watching Maya? She's in her room watching TV."

Again, Bridget turned back to her desk, swallowing the disappointment. She didn't respond, but of course Roman took the silence as compliance.

"What did you want to tell me, babe?" he called from the bathroom.

"Nothing," she mumbled to herself. "Not a damn thing, obviously."

Bridget had just begun to type again, trying to pick up her prior groove with this particular chapter, when a gentle knock on the door broke her train of thought. She struggled to keep the irritation out of her voice. "Come in."

The door opened, and Maya crept in, a Princess Tiana jean suit adorning her tiny frame. "Miss Bri, is my daddy here?"

Bridget's smile was small. "Yes, sweetie, but he's about to go to work."

"I'm hungry."

Roman emerged from the bathroom, his work bag slung over his arm. "Well, Miss Bri can get you something to eat. Maybe you two can go grab a pizza and some ice cream." He turned to Bridget with a wink. "What do you think, babe?"

"Oh, yay!" Maya's eyes brightened with the idea, even as Bridget's face fell.

In one swift motion, she clicked the *exit* button on her Word document to close out of the page she had been writing. So much for her own plans.

Chapter Fourteen
Corrine

She felt like a woman obsessed.

Corrine pulled into the parking lot of the Walmart, taking care to park a few spaces down from Roman's truck. She hadn't meant to follow him. In fact, she had just swung by his house that day on her way home from picking up her niece, only because it was on her route. But when she had caught his truck backing out of the garage, her curiosity had gotten the best of her.

Peering through the windshield, Corrine watched him help the little girl from the back seat before scooping her up in his arms. For a moment she wondered where Bridget was, then quickly brushed off the thought. If she would rather not spend time with her husband, so be it. That had nothing to do with Corrine.

She didn't move until they had crossed the parking lot toward the store. Then she turned around to Vanessa sitting patiently in the back seat, immersed in some handheld video game.

"Let's go get something to cook for dinner," she suggested.

"Okay," Vanessa said, clicking off her seat belt.

Corrine dropped her arm around the little girl as they breezed past the automatic doors of the store. Her eyes swept the crowded checkout counters, pleased when she saw Roman headed toward the grocery section. "So, what do you want to eat?" she asked, steering Vanessa in the same direction.

"I don't know. Lasagna?"

Corrine considered the meal, thought of the large freezer aisle with boxed Italian dinners. "Lasagna it is, then."

"I like when you babysit me, Auntie," Vanessa said with a gap-toothed grin. "You let me eat whatever I want."

Corrine couldn't help but smile back. She loved it, too. It didn't take much to please her niece. A little cookie dough ice cream and a Disney movie, and she was having the time of her life. So it helped when Gina had to pull overtime at the restaurant where she worked, because Corrine did enjoy bonding with Vanessa.

Corrine grabbed a buggy and wheeled it through the throng of customers toward the freezer section. She kept her eyes peeled for Roman as they walked. She didn't have any kind of plan but maybe "running into" him for a little idle conversation.

They had only texted a handful of times since Shadow Lounge; a little harmless flirting here and there. But Corrine had to admit her disappointment when days, then weeks, had gone by and neither he, nor Bridget, had returned to the club. It had been a stroke of sheer luck to see Bridget in Stonecrest Mall that other day. Well, maybe that wasn't entirely true. "Sheer luck" meaning she had followed the woman out there, hoping to run into Roman. All that would change soon once Bridget took Marco up on his offer. Then hopefully she, and her husband, would be regular patrons, and Corrine wouldn't have to go stalking them like some desperate madwoman.

They'd had a connection, she and Roman. And right now she was yearning for that, especially given Patrick's frequent absences and his lack of affection when he was around. He was opening up another garage soon, Corrine knew that much. And though she didn't necessarily agree, or believe, for that matter, he was spending all of his free time working, it was easier to go along with the story to keep the peace. And her sanity. Besides, she wouldn't have time to worry about Patrick if her and Roman's friendship blossomed like she hoped.

"Can we get some cookie dough ice cream, Auntie?" Vanessa asked.

"Of course." Corrine reached through one of the freezers and pulled the carton of ice cream from the shelf. She heard Roman's voice before she actually saw him.

"I've got more work to do first," he was saying. Corrine straightened, glancing both ways down the empty aisle. She caught him walking by, still holding the little girl. He was following a young lady pushing a cart full of food.

Corrine didn't know why the frown came first. Before she realized what she was doing, she had turned the buggy and wheeled it after him. She didn't know what she was going to say or even why she was doing it, but her feet seemed to be moving on their own.

Roman was following a young woman who was most certainly not Bridget. She was rattling on about something, and Corrine immediately noticed she was way too scantily clad for casual grocery shopping. The ripped jean shorts stopped just shy of her ass cheeks, and the tummy pudge from the yellow crop top was indicative of the woman's wistfulness for the body she used to have. Waist-length braids were pulled up into a high ponytail and exposed gold earrings dripping from each ear. She spoke, making exaggerative gestures with her hand, the gold bangles on her wrist jingling with each movement.

"You're not fooling no damn body," she was saying, her voice oozing with the flirtation. "You just wanted to see me. Otherwise, you would've just given me the money."

Roman chuckled and shook his head, shifting the little girl to his other hip. "Yeah, if you say so."

"I do say so." The woman paused long enough to let Roman catch up to her, and to Corrine's shock, she watched her sneak a squeeze on his butt. "Bridget will kill your ass if she knew you were up here. But you still came. Don't forget, I've known you much longer. You miss all of this, don't you?"

Roman stepped to the side to break the contact and quickly glanced around. "Girl, you need to chill," he said. "Maya is right here."

"So?" The woman laughed, obviously unbothered by his comment. "I'm sure Maya would love if Mommy and Daddy got back together. Wouldn't you, baby? One big happy family."

Corrine almost didn't recognize the envy that snaked through her at the realization. His baby mother. Why, then, was he meeting up with her at the Walmart? And for the woman to mention it, obviously Bridget didn't know. What the hell was Roman up to?

"Auntie, can I—"

"Hold on, sweetie. Ssshhh." Corrine hushed Vanessa with an absent wave.

Roman stopped at a shelf to eye the soda that was on sale. The sudden movement had Corrine pulling the buggy to a halt and Vanessa colliding into her backside.

Roman turned at the slight commotion, and Corrine sucked in an embarrassed breath as she watched his eyes register.

"Hey," she said and had to curse herself at the exaggerated excitement in her voice. So much for being subtle. "Long time no see, Roman."

"Yeah, I know. Been a minute. How you been?"

"Good, good. Just working. The usual."

"Yeah, same here."

Corrine cleared her throat and shifted uncomfortably under his scrutiny. She couldn't tell if he was suspicious of her presence, but she didn't expect the awkward tension between them.

"So, uh . . ." She gestured vaguely to the produce section. "Out shopping?"

"Is that the best you can do, Corrine?" His face cracked into an amused smirk that had embarrassment burning her cheeks.

It was different speaking to him in person as opposed to over the phone. At least through the text messages she could hide her shyness and insecurities. "I didn't really know what else to say," she admitted.

"Yeah, I get it. You know, after . . ." He trailed off with a shrug. "How is Patrick doing?"

"He's good. He's about to open another garage down in Mc-Donough."

"Oh, that's what's up. Tell him I said congrats on that."

Corrine smiled. She was loving just talking to him, even if it was about their spouses. "I sure will," she said. "And what about Bridget? How is she? I saw her the other day at the mall."

"She's good. Been a little busier lately with the book."

Corrine had no idea what he was referencing, nor why his voice had a hint of annoyance at the mention of that. But rather than ask, she just nodded along. "Do you know if she and Nikki decided what to do?"

"About what?" Confusion crossed his face.

"Roman, I thought you were getting some lettuce?" the woman interrupted as she appeared at Roman's side.

Corrine swallowed the bout of annoyance when the woman eyed her up and down while hooking a casual arm through his. "Oh, my bad. I didn't know you were over here talking. Who's this?"

"Corrine." Then suddenly remembering, she grabbed her niece's hand and added, "And this is my niece, Vanessa."

"Corrine, this is April," Roman introduced. "And my daughter, Maya."

"*Our* daughter," April corrected, placing a hand on her hip.

She was still eyeing Corrine, her eyebrow raised in suspicion. "How do you two know each other?" she asked boldly.

Corrine didn't know how to respond and, thankfully, Roman didn't allow her to. He lowered his daughter to her feet. "April, can you go finish shopping? I'll catch up. Go with Mommy for me, baby girl," he said to Maya.

April was visibly upset about the dismissal, but obediently she grabbed her daughter's hand and pushed the buggy away, her hips switching extra hard as she walked.

Any other time, Corrine would have been tempted to laugh at the blatant cry for attention.

"Sorry about that," Roman said with a chuckle once the two had disappeared down another aisle. "She's a mess."

Corrine waved it off. "It's no problem. I get it. Your daughter is beautiful."

"Thank you," he said, beaming with pride. "So is your niece."

Corrine paused, deciding to verbalize the thought she had been tossing around ever since she first saw Roman's daughter. "We should maybe let them play together one day," she said, her voice innocent. "Vanessa doesn't have anyone to play with when she visits with me. I'm sure I bore her to death."

As if on cue, Vanessa piped up. "No, you don't, Auntie."

Corrine ignored her, making up the lies as she went. Anything to take advantage of the opportunity. She could barely breathe, let alone think clearly, with all the excitement bubbling up in her gut. "I was actually thinking of swinging by the park on our way home. Do you and Maya want to join us?" She held her breath as she watched Roman consider the suggestion.

"Yeah," he agreed. "I wanted to talk to you about something anyway."

⟶•◦•⟵

Kenwood Park was a signature in Fayette County. The outdoor recreation available included sporting activities from basketball and track to soccer and tennis along with playgrounds that kept children of all ages entertained. Corrine had been there once before when she and Pat had first moved to the area. She had been meaning to bring Vanessa back but never seemed to remember.

Now, as she parked next to one of the pavilions and Vanessa nearly jumped from the car, she was happy they had made the spontaneous trip. Especially with Roman and his daughter.

A small breeze rustled the excessive greenery that flanked the playground, and somewhere in the distance the soothing melody of water could be heard. Off to one side, a paved trail twined through a thicket of spring foliage, the beautifully wooded paths Corrine remembered leading back to flowing creeks. She inhaled the ripe fragrance of woods, flowers, and musk, the smell eliciting fond memories of her own childhood; when she and Gina would go for hikes in the woods behind their home, and Corrine would come home riddled in mosquito bites while her sister didn't have a mark on her. Corrine used to joke that even the bugs hated her, and she would give a bitter laugh to cloak the painful truth in her own comment.

"Girls, be careful," Roman called as both Maya and Vanessa took off toward the playground at top speed, their braids dancing in the air. Corrine's chuckle was wistful.

"What?" Roman asked, breaking her gaze from the children as they jumped on the swing set. "What is it that's got you smiling like that?" he clarified at her puzzled frown.

Had she been smiling? She didn't even realize it. Corrine motioned toward the playground, the goofy grin she now felt still in place. "Just love watching Vanessa," she had to admit. "Kids, you know. Especially girls. They're special."

"For sure." Roman shoved his hands into his pockets. "When Maya came along, it changed me. I grew up."

Corrine led the way to one of the wooden picnic tables and took a seat on the bench. Roman sat beside her. A somewhat safe distance, she noticed.

"Do you have kids?" he asked.

Corrine winced, having already expected the question, though it still didn't make it any less of a sting.

"No, just Vanessa," she answered. "I usually help my sister out with her."

"Yeah, Maya is our only for now. We're trying for another one."

Funny. She vividly remembered Bridget saying she couldn't and wasn't having any kids. Clearly her husband hadn't gotten the memo.

Corrine was tempted to ask more about his baby mother, April. She hadn't been too happy when she and Roman had parted ways in the Walmart parking lot. Corrine just sat in her car and waited while watching April toss disgusted looks in her direction. Eventually, she turned and stalked off to her own car but not before flipping Corrine the middle finger when she didn't think anyone was watching. It was obvious that, despite Roman's marriage, she wanted her old flame back. Too bad.

For a while, the two just sat in silence watching the girls play, their shrill laughter carrying across the short distance. Corrine tried her best not to concentrate on his delicious smell, or the heat radiating from his body that threatened to awaken every fiber in her being. Instead, she shifted just slightly to eye him from the side. She could all but see the gears turning in his mind. His jaw was tightened, and she was tempted to lean forward and run her tongue along the tense skin.

It would be nice to soothe him, relieve all of the stresses that played across his face like a motion picture.

When he turned with eyes narrowed in concentration, he was looking in her direction but rather through her to something in the distance. Whatever it was had him in his own little world. And his troubled expression tugged on her heart strings.

"What is it?" she asked at his continued silence.

He gave a weighted sigh, his eyes finally focusing on hers.

"Nothing," he lied. "What were you going to tell me in the store? Something about an offer with the club?"

"Yeah. The club owner, Marco, offered Bridget and Nikki a chance to work with him permanently. Be the sole source of planning events for Shadow Lounge."

Roman nodded, as if struggling to understand. "And what did Bridget say?"

"She wanted to do it," Corrine admitted. "Nikki . . . well . . . not so much. The two just haven't been seeing eye-to-eye about this, so I know it has got Bri a little stressed."

Roman paused, his lips turned down in a contemplating frown. "She didn't mention it to me," he mumbled, almost to himself. "She told me she was going to take it easy a bit. Not work so much."

Corrine hadn't meant to instigate, but it felt so good to talk to Roman, to comfort him, to be there for him in a way his wife wasn't right now. Maybe she was using Roman as her own crutch, since lately it was as if she were a single wife when it came to her marriage with Patrick.

The words were almost tumbling out without her knowledge or permission. "Well, it would be more work for sure," she exaggerated a little. "And Bri seemed pretty adamant on taking the job. I told her I just hoped this didn't make things awkward with business with Nikki."

"Yeah."

She felt him seething, could almost taste it as he lapsed into more silence. Yearning to touch him, Corrine placed her hand on his, their contact sending tiny tingling sensations piercing up her arm. Even she was surprised how sensitive she was to this man. "Hey, everything okay?"

Roman shook his head in disbelief. "She didn't even tell me. Just not sure at what point we got off. That's all."

Imagine what else she's keeping from you, Corrine wanted to

say. For a moment, she allowed herself to indulge in the fantasy. If she were his girl, she would be completely transparent with him. A man like Roman would appreciate the open honesty. She could tell when he looked at her that he saw her for her truth. When he touched her, it was like he touched her soul. And it made her feel utterly and completely pure.

A thought crossed Corrine's mind and she stood up, her smile blooming. "Come on," she said, grabbing Roman's hand and pulling him to his feet.

"What?"

"Let's do something fun." She was both surprised and thrilled when he didn't immediately drop her hand as she led him to the outdoor pieces of the jumbo-size chess board.

Roman stopped once he saw the game and lifted his eyebrow. "You play chess?" he asked. "You don't strike me as the chess type of woman."

Corrine giggled as she grabbed pieces to begin setting up the board. "That's because I don't play," she boasted. "I dominate."

His laugh was like music to her ears. "Oh, okay, so you like to talk shit, too."

"Shut me up then." It was a loaded comment dripping with seduction. Roman didn't seem to notice. Or if he did, he didn't let on.

All it took was a few moves in the first game before it was painstakingly obvious Corrine had overhyped her skills. Sure, she knew how the pieces moved, but her lack of strategy had her in a checkmate in fewer than seven moves. But even though she couldn't play worth a damn, she had to admit it was fun watching Roman gloat after his victory.

"If that's the way you dominate," he teased as they reset the pieces, "then I'd hate to see you suck."

"Well, teach me," Corrine suggested. "I've always wanted to learn the game."

So he did. They spent games two and three walking through various openers and strategic moves. By game four, Corrine still sucked, but not as bad. And she'd never thought she would actually care, but chess was a lot more interesting than she thought.

"You catch on pretty quick," he commented. "I'm impressed."

"I'll get the hang of it one day."

The girls had found some other kids and were now engaged in a game of dodgeball, so Corrine and Roman moseyed over to a nearby bench to keep an eye on them.

Somewhere on the other side of the park, a dog barked, and the courts were becoming more populated with teenagers getting a basketball game started. Corrine didn't want to leave but she felt their time winding down. She suddenly remembered the frozen lasagna in her car, knowing now it would probably be no good. Vanessa would have to settle with grabbing a pizza instead. She wondered if it would be too forward to invite Roman and Maya.

They sat closer this time, their legs bumping companionably against each other. From a distance, Corrine was sure no one could tell if they were old friends or rekindled lovers. Or both. The thought turned her on.

At that point, Corrine put all rational thought out of her mind. No more thinking. Only feeling. And right then the chemistry between them was ripe and strong, almost magnetic. She caught them both by surprise when she leaned in closer, and she knew he saw her intentions. Yet, he didn't bother stopping her. His lips parted in a welcome expectation. She cupped the back of his head and stopped a breath away from his lips, her eyes a passionate request for permission. On a smile, Corrine closed the distance between them, pressing her lips gently against his.

Desire. She was all but licking it from his tongue. Despite the urgency she felt on his lips, they remained tender, coaxing, like whispers on her skin. It was driving her wild, and she leaned into him more, begging for the bottled aggression she sensed. She poured everything into the kiss, desperate for him to taste every emotion he ignited. He returned her passion, swallowing her moans, massaging her tongue with his. He trailed his tongue down the corner of her mouth, down to suck on her neck, and she shivered. Ignoring everything around them, Corrine deepened the kiss. No one had made her want this much. So much she was aching.

Just as quickly as they started, Roman snatched back, startling a gasp from Corrine. Embarrassment slapped her in an instant. What was wrong with her? Here she was in the middle of the park feasting on someone's husband like a starved bear. She had allowed him to open her up. Show her vulnerability. She couldn't muster any other emotions other than raw lust, so she leaned back on the bench and waited for her breathing to steady. Good thing was, the same passion she felt was reflected in his eyes as he stared, first with confusion and then with regret.

"We can't do this." He was mumbling. Yearning had deepened his voice so much it wasn't even recognizable. That shit was erotic and turned her on even more. To hell with all the rules.

"Roman, we've already done this," she said. "Don't you want it again?"

He shook his head and spoke with more urgency, desperate to rationalize their indiscretions. "No, this isn't the same."

"How much I need you is the same. Then and now." Corrine scooted closer, keeping her mouth an inch away; just enough to feel his rapid pants caress her face. "I just want to please you, Roman," she whispered.

He shifted, and Corrine was soaring in the fact he was going to kiss her again. But instead, Roman climbed to his feet, his movements abrupt, and trudged off toward the standalone restroom building.

She should've felt bad, but she didn't. In fact, it was quite the opposite. Corrine felt more alive than she had in a long time. Her lips, still warm from his, curved at their spontaneous intimacy, right there in the middle of the park in broad daylight. The only regret she had was teasing them both with that kiss. Because now she was hungry for more.

Corrine rose, and with one quick look to the playground to confirm the children were still occupied, she headed up the hill to follow him.

Roman stood over the sink almost frozen in place when Corrine entered the men's restroom. She paused at the entryway, taking in his backside, the bunch of muscles somewhat prevalent underneath his white T-shirt. She didn't move until his eyes lifted to meet hers in the mirror. In her mind, the gesture was the non-verbal permission she was waiting for. She risked taking a step forward, keeping her gaze level with his.

Roman kept his back to her, though he watched her very slow, very meticulous movements in their reflection. She pressed her breasts on his back, her arms circling his waist to fiddle with the belt buckle on his jeans.

"Corrine . . ." His voice was hoarse. And weak. Still he made no move to stop her. Corrine turned him around to face her and lowered herself to her knees, replacing her hands with her lips. Instinct had his hand gripping the back of her head, urging her to take him in deep. That was all she needed.

She worked him slowly with her hands and mouth fluctuating in harmonious strokes, coating him with enough spit to have it dribbling down her chin. His girth had her gagging, and she loved every minute of it. When she felt him tighten in her cheeks, his orgasm threatening to erupt and fill her mouth, he pulled her up, snatching her leggings down the length of her legs. With strength she hadn't even realized he possessed, Roman lifted her on the sink and immediately she spread like an eagle to welcome him. She had known it was only a matter of time before he was all hers for good. Thank God that time was now.

When he ripped his lips from hers to savor the smooth column of her throat, Corrine moaned her pleasure. "I love you," she whispered.

It was like a switch, and suddenly Roman was stumbling backward as if she were poison. He leaned over to fumble with pulling his pants up. Still dazed, Corrine shook her head to make sense of what had just happened.

"Wait, Roman. What's wrong?" She eased down from the sink, watching him avert his eyes.

"We can't do this."

"What are you talking about? Why?"

"Look, Corrine." His gentle response was sympathetic. "You're a beautiful woman, but I love my wife."

Corrine pulled her pants up as she shook her head to deny his statement. Deny the truth. There was no way. Not when he made her feel like he did.

"You must love both of us, then," she said with a nervous chuckle.

"I don't."

"I'm every bit as much a woman as she is," Corrine shot back.

Confusion had Roman pausing. "I never said you weren't," he said. "But no matter what clothes you wear or how you wear your hair, you are not Bridget."

She couldn't take the rejection. It did something to her, snaking through her like a viper coiling around her heart to constrict. Yet again, she gave up herself to be what she thought this man wanted. What he needed. And it wasn't enough. She could almost hear Patrick's condescending laughter echo through the trees.

Roman was turning again, reaching for the door to put as much distance as possible between them; to close her out of his world and away from him.

"She's not better for you than me," Corrine tossed to his retreating back. "She can't even have kids with you, Roman!" She immediately repented the words after they left her lips, especially when he spun around, his face ashen. And because his eyes were searching hers as if seeking confirmation in her statement, she quickly pushed past him with enough force to knock him out of the way and dashed for the playground to get Vanessa. *What the hell had she done?*

Chapter Fifteen
Bridget

She had counted twelve calls so far.

Bridget watched her phone ring from the unknown number, already familiar with the routine that would happen if she decided to answer it. Whoever the person was would just hold the phone, not responding; their heavy breathing roaring in her ear as they listened to her repeated greetings. This was the third day in a row she'd been dealing with this mess. Bridget was well past the point of confusion; beyond the anger that had her streaming a slew of choice curses to the dead air as the silence wore on. She was now afraid.

It was clear someone was fucking with her, their merriment obvious the more they played on her rising anxiety. And the fact that Bridget was a pawn in the anonymous scheme for some nameless, voiceless, faceless amusement—it honestly frightened her more than she cared to admit even to herself.

The vibrating stopped and within seconds started up again. The *Unknown Caller* identifier displayed on the screen was taunting her. Bridget rejected the call, put her phone on silent, and placed the device in her purse. She wouldn't let the foolishness ruin her night, so she would just try her best not to dwell on it. She turned her attention back to the task at hand.

No, she wasn't at all in the mood to chaperone Nikki and her new boyfriend, Dennis. She would have preferred to spend her evening relaxing or writing as opposed to the scheduled double date. And even though she and Nikki still weren't on the best of terms, she had promised her she would check out this man, if only for Nikki's best interest.

Plus, tonight she would use the opportunity to let her friend and business partner know that she'd already made the executive decision to move forward with Marco's offer. The deal had been finalized, contracts had been inked, and he'd even given her a three-month retainer to start.

This was the first time Bridget had made a move for the company without Nikki's consent. Her ambition was making her feel a little guilty, though. But Nikki had been dragging her feet about making the decision, and the shit was really pissing Bridget off. So, what was done was done. Hopefully, it would make things a lot easier to digest when Bridget passed her half of that fat-ass check over the dinner table tonight.

Roman entered from the bathroom, buttoning up his shirt as he crossed to the dresser. He didn't speak. She didn't, either.

Bridget continued applying her makeup as he too moved about the room to finish getting ready.

It had been like this for about a week now. She didn't know what had them in their little funk, but it seemed that Roman didn't care to divulge more than a few short answers when she inquired about the tension. Sure, he was working more hours at the hospital, but, hell, she was having to do triple duty herself between working, writing her book, and now being a full-time mommy to Maya. She felt her stress compounding daily, which was another reason she was partially appreciative for the date night, however strained. Her sister Ava would be coming over to babysit Maya for a few hours, so Bridget was going to make the best of her night on the town.

The doorbell rang, and Bridget glanced to Roman. He didn't move or respond. She rolled her eyes and pushed back from the vanity with a huff. "Damn, I'll get it," she grumbled and headed downstairs.

Bridget pulled open the front door with the greeting for her sister already on her tongue. To her surprise, the stoop was empty, a solitary porch light casting an eerie yellow glow against the night sky. She felt her heartbeat quickening. "Ava?" she called on a shaky breath. With the exception of the hum of crickets serenading the darkness, it was dead silent.

She took a single step outside, craning her neck to peer at the driveway for Ava's car. The air was still, the driveway empty. A chill crawled up her spine, and Bridget couldn't help but feel like eyes were on her, studying her every move. She closed the door, quickly flipping the locks into place.

"What's wrong?"

Bridget yelped at the voice, spinning around to face Roman with her hand over her palpitating heart.

He frowned at her reaction, no doubt thinking his wife had gone crazy. "What's wrong?" he repeated as he flicked a quick gaze to the door. "Where's Ava?"

"No one was at the door." The words trembled off her tongue. She was failing miserably at trying to keep calm.

Roman's frown deepened. "So, someone just rang the doorbell and ran? Kids still do that these days?"

Bridget was already shaking her head in rebuttal. If only it were that simple. "I think it's something else."

"Like what?"

A stalker, she wanted to say. First the car following her to the mall. Then the strange phone calls from the unknown number.

And now this. Shit wasn't adding up. But who the hell would want to stalk her? And why?

The doorbell rang again, having Bridget clamp her lips on her response. She stepped back, putting as much distance between her and the door as possible. She was grateful when Roman passed her, unlocked the door, and snatched it open.

She breathed a sigh of relief when her sister stood on the porch, illuminated in the yellow wash of light.

Ava carried a vase of orange roses in her hands and immediately held them out as she stepped into the foyer. "Here," she said, passing them off to Roman. "These were sitting by the garage when I pulled up."

The arrangement boasted her favorite color with its orange roses, yellow lilies, and bronze mums in a chic clear vase. They were beautiful and surprisingly so Bridget.

She and Roman exchanged questioning gazes, the other already knowing the truth. She knew Roman didn't give her the flowers, and even if he did, he sure as hell wouldn't leave them outside by the garage. Which could only mean they had been hand-delivered by someone. The person had gone so far as to ring the doorbell and then leave. Did that mean her feelings were substantiated and someone was out there earlier, hidden in the shadows observing her as she stood at the door? That would explain why she felt she was being watched.

"Who are they from?" Ava addressed the question on everyone's mind. She was already sifting through the bouquet for a card, shaking her head when there was none.

"Throw them away," Bridget said, even as she crossed to Roman and snatched the flowers from his hands herself. She walked briskly to the kitchen, her sister and husband following, inquiring into her hasty actions. Now someone was sending flowers to her house. She didn't care how crazy she looked. The shit made her uncomfortable. Bridget tossed the arrangement, vase and all, in the trash and moved to the sink to wash her hands.

"What the hell is going on?" Roman asked at her back.

Bridget had to turn up her lips at the irony. Now he wanted to care when he hadn't said more than three words to her all week. As shaken up as she was, her stubbornness now outweighed her fear. Now, he would have to wallow in his confusion, because she wasn't in the mood to talk about it. Besides, they were already late for the double date with Nikki. They would deal with it later. Even still, Bridget was already making a plan to get to the police station to file a report. Whoever this stalker was had hit too close to home.

"You want to tell me what is going on with you?"

Roman didn't bother looking at Bridget, instead continuing to focus on the road ahead. They had already been riding for twenty minutes in silence. Not even the rain beating against the windshield could calm Bridget's nerves or ease the tension between them.

"What are you talking about?"

His apathy only heightened her irritation. "You've had a damn attitude all week," she snapped.

"You know I've been working doubles like crazy. Shit, I'm tired."

"Oh, really? Is that all it is?"

"What the hell else would it be?"

Bridget didn't know, and that was what pissed her off. Of course Roman worked shit hours. Such was the doctor's life. But it was something else, something she couldn't quite put her finger on. It was bad enough he wasn't there and she felt like a single mother and wife. But, hell, even when he was around, he seemed . . . distracted. Like something weighed heavy on his mind. And when she questioned him, he would merely give that same stupid-ass excuse. He was fine, he was tired. As if she weren't battling her own lethargy from working and parenting his child.

If Bridget had to put an label to it, she would have to say she felt neglected. Roman was so wrapped up in Roman right now, he didn't bother to ask how she was doing, how business was going, hell, how she was feeling mentally. And frankly, she was crumbling under it all. Added to that she had some sick stalker watching her every move, and now sending her flowers. The added stressors were liable to make any sane person crazy. To put it simply, she was not okay. And Roman was too "tired" or busy or whatever to actually see that.

Bridget sighed. Thankfully, it was dark, so Roman couldn't see the tears glistening like pearls on her lashes. Ava had suggested a getaway was what she needed, whether alone, with her sisters, or with Roman. Either way, a change of scenery to clear the chaos and put her back in a peaceful headspace. The idea was sounding more and more glorious.

"Maybe we should go somewhere," Bridget said, turning hopeful eyes to her husband's side profile. "A little getaway. What do you think?" She thought she felt Roman tense at the suggestion, which had her already shaking her head. "Forget it," she mumbled.

"Nah," he grumbled. "I'm not leaving Maya."

Of course. Never mind her or the time she wanted to spend with her husband. They had to work around a schedule now.

"How about we all do something," she suggested. She would rather have gone somewhere as a couple, but she figured her idea about some family shit would appeal to him. "Disney World or the beach. What do you think?"

"Oh, now you're interested in being a fucking family?"

She blinked in shock at his snide comment. Then anger took over. "What the hell do you mean by that?"

"Man, whatever," he muttered, not bothering to stifle the attitude.

"No, say what you got to say. What is that supposed to mean?" Radio silence. And it was raking across her nerves how he just tuned her out so effortlessly.

"Fine, fuck you then," she mumbled under her breath. She was sick of it, but she surely couldn't communicate that. Bridget had to bite her tongue to keep from saying something she knew she would not regret but would probably be detrimental to her marriage. So instead, she just shook her head, turning back to the window to watch the city speed past. Maybe a solo vacation was a better idea after all.

It was during these times that Bridget began to wonder about their compatibility. She knew it was fast how they had gotten together, and everyone doubted the genuineness of their whirlwind romance. But, dammit, she loved this man and all of his faults and baggage. She had to, in order to put up with some of the things that would have sent her running in the other direction. When all was good, Roman was pure perfection, and sexually, she couldn't have asked for a better lover. But when things were bad, Bridget was ready to pack her shit and disappear. Her sister once said her passion was a blessing and a curse; Bridget loved and hated hard, and that often clouded her better judgment. And coupled with her spontaneous nature, Bridget did what "felt right" in that moment, whether that was her professional or personal life.

She cut her eyes once more at Roman, a sense of dread settling over her spirit. Unfortunately, she didn't like what had been "feeling right" lately.

Café Milano was a quaint Italian restaurant nestled in a Conyers shopping plaza. The food was deliciously authentic while the low-level mood lighting and piano and accordion background music contributed to the ambiance. It always made Bridget feel as if she had stepped right into the city of Milan.

Nikki was from Conyers, so naturally the spot was one of her favorites. So Bridget wasn't at all surprised when she had insisted that they meet her and Dennis there at eight o'clock.

She and Roman didn't pull up until closer to eight-thirty. They were late, which Bridget couldn't stand. On top of that, she expected to feel a little more at ease since the thirty-minute ride had afforded them an opportunity to talk. But they had spent the majority of the time in silence. Plus, Roman still seemed upset about whatever was on his mind and hadn't even bothered initiating further dialogue after their brief argument. Which was just fine with Bridget. She was too busy sorting out her own thoughts to care about the silent treatment.

The host led them to a booth toward the back of the restaurant, where Nikki was already waiting with a white, blond-haired gentleman at her side. She didn't immediately rise as Bridget approached, instead just sitting there with a polite smile planted on her face. Usually, she would be quick to greet Bridget with a hug or something, so it was obvious their friendship had become significantly strained. Bridget didn't know how she felt about that.

"Hey, y'all," Nikki said, her voice crisp and stoic. "We were waiting to order until you got here." She grabbed Dennis's hand and Bridget saw she gave it a little squeeze. "Bri, Roman, this is Dennis. Dennis, these are my friends."

Dennis turned kind brown eyes to Bridget, a warm smile gracing his handsome face. He looked nice enough, but in no way did he look like Nikki's type. Even in college, her girl wasn't seen without some saggy-pants, no-job-having, twenty-baby-mama-having, tatted-up corner boy. The fact that she had made the switch to Brad Pitt was still something Bridget would have to get used to.

Dennis rose, his hand extended in Bridget's direction. "A pleasure to finally meet you," he greeted as dimples winked in each cheek. "I've heard so much about you."

Bridget nodded and accepted his hand on a light shake. He turned and did the same to Roman before they all eased into the booth.

She noticed Nikki had taken extra care with her makeup and cropped hair. She looked like she had lost weight, and the navy-blue halter dress accentuated her now slender frame. The fact was, she did look extremely happy. Much happier than Bridget was.

For a brief moment, a little twinge of envy tried to creep in as she watched the new couple sneak coy grins at each other in the candlelight. Meanwhile, Roman made sure to sit an exaggerated distance from her, and he hadn't even looked up from his menu. It was going to be an interesting evening.

"Dennis is an IT manager." Nikki addressed them, but her eyes were fixated lovingly on her man. "And he loves to travel; no kids but he loves my daughter."

"Oh, yes, Jordan is amazing," he gushed, toying with Nikki's fingers on the white linen table.

The validation had Nikki giggling like a schoolgirl, and Bridget rolled her eyes. All this lovey-dovey shit was damn near nauseating. Maybe this hadn't been such a good idea. Especially when she and her own husband weren't reciprocating the endearment.

Dennis ordered appetizers and a bottle of Riesling for the table, and once the waitress brought baskets of bread, the group settled into light-hearted conversation. Dennis's boyish good looks were deceiving, because Bridget wouldn't have pegged him as ten years her senior at forty years old.

The two seemed polar opposites; he had no kids while Nikki had one, he was calm and laid back while Nikki was loud and boisterous. Bridget sat and listened while he humbly downplayed his privilege. Meanwhile Nikki gloated and bragged on everything like his personal sales associate; from his summa cum laude honors at Georgetown to his exemplary tennis techniques. Hell, Bridget didn't even know Nikki was interested in tennis, much less played. Apparently, a new boo begot new interests, which would explain why Nikki had been so inaccessible for the past few weeks. More power to her and her little *Get Out* romance.

Roman managed to dodge any interaction with her, expertly guiding the conversation back to Dennis. Bridget wondered if the three even realized she was not as engaged. She took that as a blessing and just sat, sipping her white wine while the discussion swirled around her.

"So, Bri," Dennis said, turning his attention to Bridget. "May I call you Bri?"

No. She smiled and lied with a nod of her head, putting the glass to her lips to stifle her intended response.

"Nikki tells me you two own an event planning business," he went on.

"That's right."

"I was telling her I would love to have you both coordinate an event my company is hosting in a couple of months. Nikki said you two could handle that easily."

Of course, she would say that. Bridget felt the first few flickers of anger heat her face. It started first at the base of her neck and snaked around to incinerate the last little bit of restraint she had. Nikki had no problem voicing her opposition to the Shadow Lounge opportunity, insisting they had to talk about it first. At the same time, she could commit to a gig with her precious boyfriend and didn't feel it was worth the same type of preliminary consultation. How ironic.

"I'm sure it would be fun," Bridget said. "But Nikki and I would have to talk about it first."

If looks could kill. Nikki's eyes had narrowed into deadly slits at the recognition of Bridget's words. Even Roman was tossing her the side-eye.

"I just figured we had a little more time now," Nikki spoke through lips tightened in embarrassment.

"Well, not really. We have the Shadow Lounge deal."

"*We* haven't agreed to anything," Nikki snapped, not bothering anymore with subtlety.

Bridget reached into her purse and pulled out the neatly folded check from Marco. She held it across the table.

Nikki just looked at the paper. "What the hell is this?" she said.

"It's your half of the retainer."

"For what?"

"From Marco."

Nikki stood with such frenzy that she bumped the table and had her wine sloshing over the lip of her glass. "Bitch, you had the nerve to sign that deal without me?" She was all but yelling, her words puncturing the smothering tension like a blade. Immediately, all surrounding noises ceased, and heads whipped around in their direction to see what was going on.

Bridget's eyes rounded at the reaction before her own anger took over. She rose as well, throwing the check on the table. "I did what we needed to do. But you can't see that because your head is so far up Dennis's ass."

"You fucking bitch." Nikki snatched up the check and ripped it to shreds, throwing the pieces back in Bridget's direction. "You know what? Fuck you, fuck that raggedy-ass swingers' club you seem so obsessed with, and fuck this company. I'm out."

Nikki snatched up her coat and, shimmying out of the booth, stormed toward the exit. Dennis, clearly unsure of how to react, quickly fished in his pocket for his wallet.

"I better go with her," he said as he tossed a few bills onto the table. "So sorry about all of this." And he was gone just as quickly.

Bridget sighed at the night's events. She couldn't believe Nikki's reaction. And what did she mean she was out? Out of the company? And for what? Because Bridget had made a savvy business move, bringing in consistent work and income? White dick had definitely messed with Nikki's head, because she wasn't being smart. Maybe it was better if they did sever professional ties so they could salvage some sort of friendship. If that was even possible.

Bridget didn't realize her fury had her trembling, and she took a breath, then two, to try and calm down. By her side, Roman quietly sipped his wine. He still hadn't acknowledged the incident, the bastard.

The server approached with eyes filled with apprehension. She glanced from Bridget to Roman, then the seats their tablemates had left vacant. "Is everything okay?" she asked, her voice timid.

"Yeah," Roman answered. "Sorry about that. We're headed out." He waited until the server had scurried away in relief before he turned a weary gaze to his wife. "You ready to go?"

"You're not going to say anything, Roman?" Bridget hadn't meant for the angry tears to blanket her voice.

"What do you want me to say? How wrong you were? How you were completely out of line for not only making the decision without Nikki, but also bringing it up tonight? You don't want to hear that shit."

"You're right. I don't want to hear that shit." Bridget jumped to her feet. "Let's go." She started for the door not knowing, or caring, if Roman followed.

She had made it past a few tables when she saw them sitting at a booth in the corner. They, like everyone else in the restaurant, were watching her, probably in disbelief of the scene she had just caused. Bridget didn't give a damn about that. More importantly, she wanted to know what the hell they were doing there.

Corrine smiled as Bridget approached their table, her eyes bouncing back and forth between her and Patrick. "Hey, Bri," she greeted. "Everything okay?"

Bridget ignored the question. Instead, she was too focused on Corrine's new hairdo; a style that looked suspiciously similar to hers. "What are you two doing here?"

Corrine's eyes slid to her husband as her brows lifted in surprise. "We're just having dinner."

"Here? Now? What are the odds of that?" Bridget turned to Patrick, who sat in silence. If she didn't know any better, she would say he was entirely too damn calm and too damn smug, which pissed her off even more. "Why are you two always around?" she went on.

"Bridget, I don't know what you're insinuating, but we're having dinner just like you," Corrine said, her words slow. "We saw you over there with Nikki, and we were going to come speak, but we didn't want to disturb you all."

Bridget shook her head, overwhelmed with confusion. "Nah, I don't believe it," she hurled back. "It's too much of a coincidence."

"Bri—"

"No!" Bridget pointed to Patrick first, then Corrine. "You two need to stay the hell away from me. Do you hear me? Stay away from me." She turned and stalked toward the door, pushing out into the night.

Bridget sucked in a greedy breath, almost desperate for oxygen. Everything about the night had gone completely left, but seeing Corrine and Patrick had been disturbing enough on top of the chaos.

She spun around when she heard the door open and sighed in relief when it was just Roman. He looked as exhausted as she felt. "What was that about?" he questioned. "First, you pop off on Nikki and then Corrine and Patrick?"

"Roman, I don't know what it is, but I don't like them."

"Oh, really? Was that before or after we fucked them? Because a while back you liked them just fine."

"It's not that." All of the anger had drained. Her tone was now singed with fear. "Corrine is always around," she said. "Don't you think something is weird about that? Think about it."

Roman remained quiet, and for a moment, it looked like he was actually considering what probably sounded like paranoia. Bridget couldn't be concerned with his perception at the moment. She knew there was some truth in her words. "Look," she tried again, keeping her voice level. "I want to go to the police."

"Now you're doing too much, Bri."

"No, I'm not. Corrine is stalking me."

Roman's lips turned down in a doubtful frown. "All because she just so happened to be at the same restaurant as you tonight?"

"No, just everything." Bridget's mind flipped over the past few instances, the pieces falling into place like dominoes. "She *coincidentally* was at the women's conference. She *coincidentally* was at the mall the other day. She *coincidentally* is here at dinner. She's worn clothes like mine, she went out and got a tattoo like mine, and now look at her." Bridget gestured vaguely in the direction of the restaurant for emphasis. "Her fucking hair is like mine."

Roman sighed in the cool air, a pillar of fog seeping from his lips. "Look, let's just get home—"

Bridget caught his arm before he could turn around. "There's something else," she added. "Someone has been following me."

That elicited the effect she had expected. Roman's frown deepened, and the vein bulged at his temple. "What do you mean, following you? When? Why the hell didn't you tell me?"

"I know. I'm sorry. I've been getting random phone calls, too. Someone keeps calling and hanging up. And then the flowers earlier . . ." Bridget gave him a pleading look. Maybe she was wrong for not telling Roman sooner. But now, she hoped he saw the severity in the situation. Because she sure did.

To her relief, communicating everything to him had her feeling as if a weight had been lifted from her shoulders. She let herself be led to the car and waited as Roman opened her door. She paused before sliding into the seat and cast a leery gaze back toward the restaurant. She wondered if Corrine had seen the entire interaction just now. Had she heard everything? Just because the thought played on her mind, she had to ask. "Has Corrine ever approached you?"

Roman shook his head. "No," he answered, his tone clipped.

Bridget nodded, mulling over the bizarre situation. So Corrine was obsessed with her. Nikki had been right. The question now was why.

Roman started the drive back, and Bridget reached for his hand on the middle console. "Thank you," she said with a small smile.

"For what?"

"For believing me with this whole Corrine shit. It sounds crazy, I know, but—"

"Why don't you want a baby?"

The unexpected question had Bridget stammering. "Wha— what are you—"

"Don't lie to me," Roman pushed on. "Why don't you want a baby?"

"Who says I don't want a baby?"

"Stop avoiding the damn question, Bri!" Roman hit his fist against the steering wheel and had Bridget jumping in response. Where the hell was this temper coming from? "Can you have kids? Yes or no?"

She didn't know whether to be angry or afraid, so she shook her head in response. "Who told you that?"

Roman cut his eyes at her, and even in the darkened car, his gaze cut through like daggers. Bridget could only blink back in shock.

"Where is this coming from?" she tried again. Her thoughts were spinning out of control and she couldn't keep up. She didn't know which would hurt worse, a lie or the truth.

"Does it matter? You're a fucking liar."

"I never lied to you!"

"Well, why the hell didn't you tell me you couldn't have kids?" He swerved, narrowly missing the shoulder, and Bridget sucked in a fearful breath as she clutched her seat belt. "You knew I wanted to have kids," he barked. "You knew! And you never mentioned you couldn't have kids!"

The truth was probably better, she decided. Whoever his source was had him convinced, so there was no turning back now. "It was before I met you," she started.

"But that was one of the things we talked about when we started dating, Bri. Tell me I'm lying if it's not."

Under the rage, she detected the first few trickles of pain. She squeezed her eyes shut and released a shuddering breath. "You're not lying," she affirmed. "I just never knew how to tell you that I had the surgery. I got it right when I hit twenty-five because I knew I never wanted kids. And then we met and . . ."

"You just didn't know how to stop lying," Roman finished with a pathetic shake of his head. "Fucking figures."

"Wait a minute, I didn't lie to you," she retorted. "Okay, yes, I should've told you the moment we started dating, but it all happened so fast and then you proposed—"

"A big fucking mistake," he mumbled. "I can't believe this shit."

It was easier to match anger for anger. She would be damned if this man weakened her. "After everything I do for you," she snapped through clenched teeth. "I take care of you, your house, your kid, and what do I get in return, huh? You don't support me, my dreams, or anything I do. You don't give a shit about me or anyone that's not kissing Roman's ass!"

Roman shook his head. "You're right. I don't give a shit about a lying bitch."

His disrespect had Bridget's mouth dropping open. She waited, thinking Roman would immediately retract his statement once he realized what he had said. An apology had to follow, because he had never stooped so low about her. He did neither.

Bridget closed her mouth, opened it, then closed it again, deciding there was nothing more to say. Unable to do anything else, she turned to the window, the anger between them simmering like pollution, threatening to suffocate them both. The more she thought about it, the angrier she got. Until finally, the only thought on Bridget's mind was cussing out the two-timing bitch that could have blabbed to Roman about her secret: Nikki.

Chapter Sixteen
Corrine

Corrine was losing herself. Somewhere along the way, she was getting so far removed from her normal, and she hadn't even realized it. So, when she got a call about catering a baby shower, she jumped at the chance. Even though the family's budget was a little tighter than what she was used to, the simplistic dishes would keep her mind, and hands, occupied for a few hours. Maybe then she wouldn't revert back to her stalking regimen and could begin to focus on what was important.

Corrine lifted the Crock-Pot lid on the meatballs, the sweet aroma of the barbecue sauce and grape jelly wafting up to assault her nostrils. Satisfied, she dipped a serving spoon in the sauce and begin transferring the meatballs to the foil tray she would use to transport them. She then turned to the stove to finish her Ro*Tel dip.

When Patrick entered the kitchen, she had finished prepping the requested entrees, meatballs, dip, and wings, along with potato salad and mac 'n cheese cups. She had made sure to go to the farmer's market for fresh fruit, which she had cut and cubed into bite-sized pieces and threaded onto kabob skewers. And since baby showers, well, baby anything, always put Corrine in a jovial spirit, she had thrown in a little key lime cake, adorned with green and yellow macaroons and baby footprints made out of fondant. Maybe one day, she could do a similar one for her own little one.

Patrick plucked one of the skewers from the neat arrangement and scanned the various dishes she had scattered across the counter. "Don't you think you went a little overboard?" he mused, nibbling on the bits of fruit.

Corrine quietly reconfigured the skewer arrangement to cover the one he had stolen. "It's what they asked for," she replied.

"Yeah, but all this for a baby party? Hell, she could lose the damn thing any day. You know that shit happens."

Corrine cringed but decided to hide her disgust by ignoring his flagrant insensitivity. Instead, she asked, "What are your plans for the day?"

Patrick polished off the skewer, leaving the wooden stick on the counter. "I don't know. Probably just watch TV. Kalem may come over later."

Corrine was surprised. This was certainly a first in quite a while. The new garage was coming along and set to open in a couple months, so usually Pat was tied up with work. Now, she wished she hadn't committed to catering this little function. It would've been nice to spend a free Saturday afternoon with her husband. She wondered why he hadn't communicated his open schedule for the day.

When Patrick breezed by her on his way to the refrigerator, Corrine caught his arm to stop him. Wordlessly she wrapped her arms around his waist and rested her head on his chest. She needed him then, especially after the big episode at Café Milano.

It had been her idea to follow them to dinner after she had left the flowers at the house for Roman. At first, she had been hesitant, thinking it was too obvious. But after mentioning it to Pat, his insistence corroborated her determination. It would be nice to see Roman again. He hadn't been responding to her text messages after their little affair. Plus, she knew Patrick had been dying to get to Bridget. No matter how she emulated the woman's hair, makeup, and wardrobe, Corrine just wasn't her.

Going inside the restaurant had been an impulsive last-minute decision. It was bold. Perhaps too bold. Neither she nor Patrick figured Bridget would actually catch them there. And fueled on the adrenaline from her argument with Nikki, she had freaked out. It did look suspicious. But for Corrine, desperation was overshadowing rationality.

Never did she suspect Bridget would not want to see her again. And when she'd blown up at the table, Corrine could only curse herself for going too far. Now, it seemed she had messed up a good thing, but she was determined to fix it. She had been rejected too damn much: first her parents, then men, Patrick. She couldn't bear the notion that Bridget was rejecting her, too. And that would mean Roman would follow suit. For real this time.

So she stood motionless in Patrick's arms, yearning for a little reassurance, however slight. Patrick lifted a light arm to touch his wife's shoulder. The gesture was his only outward display of affection.

"Maybe I can finish up early," Corrine said, lifting her head to meet his gaze. "Come home and we can play a little."

Patrick shrugged before pulling out of her grasp. "I'm probably going to Shadow Lounge a little later," he said coolly. Corrine frowned at his back as he grabbed a beer from the fridge. His exclusive verbiage was troubling. Not *we*, but *I*.

He disappeared from the kitchen and she sighed, turning back to the food to begin covering the trays with tinfoil. She didn't want him to go back Shadow Lounge. Dammit, why couldn't the man just love her? Why did he have to go searching for something that was right in his face?

Corrine checked her phone for the time, and instinct had her scrolling to her messages to see if Roman had texted her. Nothing, with the exception of the numerous pleading messages she had sent him that now sat on *read* with zero replies.

She paused for a moment and then dialed Bridget's number. It went straight to voice mail. She hung up, shoving the phone in her pocket. No use worrying about it right now. She had work to do. But she would make a point to go by their house later. Just to see.

The city of Decatur was the best of both worlds: the traditional small-town atmosphere coupled with the benefits of inner-city living. Local residents knew it was a prime hub for the creative community, with its numerous festivals and eclectic homage to modern-day art and vintage in the indie boutiques along Little Five Points.

Corrine hadn't been to this side of town in a while, since she went to her support group sessions off of Ponce de Leon. She navigated through the bustling tree-lined streets, steering her vehicle while following the GPS instructions.

Corrine pulled into the parking lot of the Decatur Conference Center and saw they had already started decorating the exterior in yellow, white, and silver streamers wrapped around brick columns. Gold foil balloons that spelled out "Oh Baby" were suspended from a huge balloon arch in the entryway. A few guests were unloading more décor and other shower additives from their trunks.

Inside, everyone was pitching in to drape linens over the tables and add centerpieces to bring the theme to life in the banquet hall. Corrine carried her trays over to what appeared to be the food and dessert tables off to one side, where an older woman, looking to be in her fifties, was placing tabletop decorations and scattering confetti. She glanced up as Corrine approached.

"The caterer, right?" she asked, her eyes dropping to the trays Corrine carried.

"Yes, I am."

"Oh, good, sugar. So glad you could handle this for us. I'm Bernadette." The woman held out her hand and then, noting the food in Corrine's hands, pulled it back with an apologetic smile. "Sorry about that. You can just put all that stuff down here."

Corrine made several trips from the car, transporting dishes and spreading them out across the beautifully decorated table in a buffet-style arrangement. Bernadette, who was the mother of the mother-to-be, introduced Corrine around to a few other guests and insisted she stay for the duration of the shower. Corrine would have much rather set up the food and left the family to their festivities, but it didn't seem like Bernadette was going to take no for an answer. Besides, Pat had made it obvious he wasn't exactly rushing to have her back home. So Corrine made herself comfortable at one of the round tables in the back and watched everyone mingling from her little perch.

At one point, a young, light-skinned woman entered the hall, pivoting expertly on red-bottom stilettos as she canvassed the room. She wore a short, cropped 'do that fell in casual layers around her face, leggings that accentuated her petite frame, and a white cold-shoulder top. Corrine had to double-take as the woman waved politely before making her away across the room to deposit the wrapped box in her hand with the other presents adorning the gift table. She looked vaguely familiar, but for the life of Corrine, she could not place her.

Her eyes followed the woman's effortless movements as she shifted next to the food table and spooned some punch from the bowl into one of the plastic cups. When the woman turned, their eyes met briefly. That's when a huge grin split the woman's face and the light bulb went off like a trigger.

Excited recognition had Corrine rising, and the woman was across the room in a few quick strides. "Oh my God, Corrine!" she squealed, immediately pulling her into a warm, familiar hug.

Tangie, her friend she met in the support group all those years ago. The woman that Patrick had accused her of cheating with, and, reluctantly, Corrine had had to make the difficult decision to let Tangie, and the group, go for the sake of having peace in her marriage. Hindsight was twenty/twenty, because that sure as hell hadn't helped a thing.

"Tangie, I can't believe that's you." Corrine stepped back, spreading the woman's arms wide so she could get a better view of the complete transition. Her old friend looked absolutely stunning, and the transformation in her seemed to radiate from the inside out. She was glowing. It warmed Corrine's heart that Tangie had finally been able to afford the surgery she had been saving up for.

They sat down together, and Tangie scooted her chair closer so they could lower their voices to speak in private. "So how have you been? What are you doing here?" Tangie gushed, giving Corrine's hand a longing squeeze.

"I catered the meal and they invited me to stay. I wasn't going to, but now I'm so glad I did. What about you?"

"Ariella is a makeup artist I've worked with," Tangie revealed, making mention of the mother-to-be. "We met when I started my modeling career."

Corrine nodded, her own pride beaming. She just hated that she hadn't been there for her in the way she should have been. And, damn, she had missed her. The two had gotten extremely close in the few months Corrine was attending the support group sessions. Tangie had been more than just a friend. She was like a little sister.

The thought brought a wave of regret, and shards of lingering guilt had Corrine's smile dropping a few degrees. "Look," she said getting serious. "I am so sorry, Tangie."

She frowned. "For what?"

"For us. For everything. I was wrong for just cutting off all communication with you. It wasn't fair to you. Or to me."

Tangie smiled, her eyes reddening with the threat of tears. "You don't have to apologize, babes." She leaned in to Corrine, and the two embraced once more. "I know it was tough with your husband," she murmured against Corrine's shoulder. "But just know I missed you like crazy. Would it be okay for us to be friends now?"

"Girl, yes. You don't know how bad I need your friendship." Corrine didn't give a damn about Patrick's feelings on the matter this time. She wasn't losing Tangie again.

——◇——

Corrine was surprised to find Patrick in bed when she entered the bedroom a few hours later. He was under the sheets, not snoring like he usually did, but the steady rise and fall of his chest indicated he must've recently fallen asleep. Corrine was somewhat happy he was still at home and had decided against going to Shadow Lounge like he mentioned. Maybe they could snuggle in for the evening, watch a movie, order a pizza or something, and just enjoy each other's company.

Corrine stripped out of her clothes, making sure to stay as quiet as possible as she moved about the room so as not to wake him. She was still reeling at seeing Tangie again after all of these years. God must have known she was who Corrine needed in her life right now, with all the other turmoil that had been going on. Her spirit was unsettled, and it felt so good to just sit, talk, and *be*. Tangie had always been a great listener, and her advice was on point, whether Corrine had wanted to hear it or not. But this time, she would not tell her husband about Tangie. She sure as hell wouldn't make that mistake again. It had cost her too much before.

The steam from the shower caught her attention first, followed by the fogged mirror. Corrine opened the glass door, surveying the stall still soaking wet from an apparent fresh bathing. She paused, her head craning to the towel rack. Sure enough, two towels were draped over the bar, one for her and one for Patrick. She zeroed in on the three face cloths, one of them also wet and bunched from its recent use.

Quietly, Corrine closed the shower stall door, reaching for her robe as she headed back into the bedroom. She stood for a moment longer, her eyes sweeping across the huge master. Nothing looked out of place, but still, she *felt* something. Patrick hadn't moved from his position in the bed, but other than his subtle breathing, all was quiet.

She approached the side of their king sleigh bed with eyes narrowed in scrutiny. Sure enough, Patrick's skin was dry as a bone as were the sheets where he was now snuggled. No type of indication he had just showered.

Fury had her snatching off the covers to expose Patrick's naked body. "Get your ass up," she yelled.

Just like she expected, Patrick exaggerated a yawn, rolling over and rubbing his eyes like he had really been pulled from a deep slumber. "What are you doing?" he groaned.

"Where is she?" Corrine whirled then, her head whipping around for the most plausible hiding spaces.

Patrick rolled his eyes. "Man, what are you talking about? Don't start this shit again."

Corrine ignored him. Even as her heart cried and pleaded with her head to forget what she knew, she couldn't just brush this off as a mistake. Not this time. She dropped to her knees with enough force to have crisp pain stinging her kneecaps. Still, she was holding her breath as her eyes skimmed over shoe boxes and the bins of winter clothes they stored underneath the bed.

Patrick grabbed her shoulders, pulling her to her feet. "Corrine, calm down," he was saying. She noticed that he was now, conveniently, wide awake.

"Where is she, Patrick?" she said again, trying to keep the quiver out of her voice.

"Where is who?"

"Don't play with me."

Patrick tried to pull her into his arms for a hug, and she pushed him away. "No," she snapped. "Who was in the shower?"

"I was."

"Stop lying to me!" Her hands were itching to slap him, punch something, throw something, or all of the above.

Corrine turned to the closet and ran almost blindly to the door, already seeing what was about to unfold. The woman would be shorter than her, sexier, with longer hair. She would have a dazzling smile and a body to die for. But most importantly, she would be a cisgender woman, since that was apparently all Patrick had eyes for.

She grasped the doorknob with trembling fingers and flung open the closet door, the gasp ripping from her lips.

"It's not what it looks like." Kalem's eyes were guilt-ridden as he lifted his hands in the air. The robe he wore, *Patrick's* robe, drew open with the gesture to reveal his naked body still damp from the shower. Everything about the situation was indicative that it was *exactly* what it looked like.

Corrine felt light-headed. She stumbled backward, her arms flinging out to grab something, anything, to brace against before she tumbled to the floor.

"Corrine." It was Patrick this time. He was amazingly calm given the circumstances.

Corrine felt like a zombie as she turned to face him with a

pleading stare. "How could you?" she whispered. Her voice cracked, and she allowed her legs to give way. Tears were futile. Yet still they came in a steady stream that left her face drenched with sorrow. She had done everything she knew for this man. Cheating she had always suspected, but never in a million years . . .

A sound erupted; somewhere between a scream and a wail. It was almost primal as it bubbled up from her belly, stabbing her throat as it coursed to gush from her lips like molten lava. Both men froze, not able to do anything but stare at the fractured woman crumbling in the middle of the floor.

She heard Kalem's feet shuffle by before fading out of the room. Patrick, still unsure what to do, sank to the bed with his head in his hands.

Once she was sure the bile had settled, Corrine risked lifting her eyes to her husband, this complete stranger. "How long?" she managed.

"Corrine, it's not—"

"How long, Patrick?"

He didn't respond, just shook his head as if that were answer enough.

She could only chuckle at the hypocrisy. "That long, huh?" Silence. "Figures. You beat my ass when I told you I was transgender. You ranted and raved about you weren't gay even though I told you that wasn't the case."

She probably should've stopped right there. Especially when she saw Patrick's fist clench at his side. It was too late. She was letting loose all the pain and anger this man had put her through over the years. The overpowering emotion had her sobbing the words. "I gave you everything, Pat! Every fucking thing! And not only do you cheat on me, you cheat with Kalem. But you want to demean and disrespect me. All this time, you were just trying to cover up that you really wanted to be with a man."

"You fucking bitch." He lunged across the bed and narrowly missed Corrine as she dove to the floor. Not missing a beat, she scrambled to her feet and grabbed her purse as she flew past the dresser. Her breath roared in her ears. If he caught her, she knew he would beat the living daylights out of her. Just like before. She didn't hear him, only her own panting and heartbeat galloping against her chest. She wasn't going to hang around long enough to give him a chance.

Corrine's bare feet slapped the cement in the garage as she jumped in the car and immediately locked the doors. The garage door was achingly slow to lift, but she flipped the car in reverse, skidding backward with enough urgency for the door to clip the roof of her car. But she didn't care. As long as she got to safety.

When she was completely certain Patrick hadn't followed her, Corrine risked slowing down, but she remained attentive to the rearview mirror, just in case. Thankfully, her keys and phone were in the purse she managed to grab on her mad dash out of the house. But other than that, she was ass-naked with merely a robe on.

Her first thought was to go to Gina's house, but her sister would ask too many questions she wasn't prepared to answer. Better to leave her out of it for her own sanity.

Corrine pulled over into a gas station and scrolled through her phone. It brought on a ripple of depression when she realized how slim her contacts were. No one to call and no one she could trust to not make her feel like a complete fool for even allowing it to get this far. Except . . .

Corrine eyed the number she had just saved before pressing *send* to connect the call. It wasn't even worth trying to hide her pain, so she listened to the ringing, allowing the tears to flow freely. Corrine didn't even give her time to speak before she sobbed into the phone. "May I please come over?"

<hr>

Tangie lived in some luxury apartments right in the heart of Midtown. It was a rewarding indicator of how far she'd come since Corrine last saw her. Tangie had been struggling before, barely making ends meet as a bartender and server at a little family-owned restaurant. The last time Corrine visited her, she stayed in a slum apartment not more than 500 square feet with more roaches than furniture. But she had been trying, and Corrine hadn't hesitated to help her out with a few months of rent on numerous occasions. Now, how ironic how the tables had turned, and it was Corrine needing the help.

Corrine pulled up to the gated entrance and rolled down her window to reach the call box. Tangie had instructed her to enter the four-digit passcode and drive to the third building past the pool. She hadn't even hesitated to rattle off her address, and Corrine was grateful she hadn't asked for an explanation. She just needed a place to regroup for now. And, as much as it pained her to admit, she had nowhere else to go.

"Oh my God, Corrine!" Tangie was already running to the car before Corrine had placed the car in park. To Corrine's surprise, she had a bundle of clothes in her arms. "Are you okay?"

"I'm fine."

Tangie shoved the clothes at her and closed the driver's door. "Here, put these on first," she said before pointing to one of the apartments. "Come to 4112. Let me go check on dinner." And with that, she ran back inside.

Obediently, Corrine shrugged out of the robe and put on the sweatpants, T-shirt and flip-flops Tangie had brought out. The outfit was a little too short for her given their significant height difference, but she was appreciative just the same.

The smell of sauteed onions fragranced the apartment as she pushed open the door. Tangie was in the kitchen amidst a cloud of smoke, her hum light underneath the sizzle of meat on the grill.

Corrine hadn't realized until that moment how hungry she

was. "You sure you know what you're doing in there?" she teased as she took a seat at the bar.

Tangie flipped the burger patties, sending a fresh cloud wafting into the air. "Of course, I never claimed to be a gourmet chef like you," she said, plopping squares of cheese onto each patty. "But I can do a little something."

A stretch of silence followed, and Corrine turned her attention to the spacious loft apartment. The contemporary aesthetic was fitting, with its exposed beams and brick accent wall. Tangie's modeling career was lucrative, evident by the collection of world-wide trinkets she had on display around the place. And she was especially proud of her new body because her model-esque photos were on wall-to-wall display: Tangie in designer clothes, lingerie, or nothing at all.

Tangie turned with a paper plate for each of them, piled high with the cheeseburger with all the fixings and a spread of sour cream and onion potato chips. "Here we are," she said with a cheerful grin. She then poured two glasses of wine and took a seat next to her at the bar.

Corrine took a greedy bite into her burger and sighed in contentment. A headache was beginning to brew, and sleep was starting to sneak up on her. It was early, but with everything that had taken place, it felt much later than the 6:32 p.m. time shown on the wall clock.

"Stay over as long as you need to," Tangie said, her quiet voice breaking their comfortable silence. "You can have the bed and I'll take the—"

"Patrick is cheating on me." The admission came out in a staggering breath.

"Oh, Corrine, I'm so sorry!"

"He's on the down-low," she went on. Better to get it all out in the open while she had the strength. "I think what hurts the most is how stupid I was."

"You are not stupid."

"I knew, Tangie." The words were acidic, the truth even more so. "I knew he had to be having an affair. All the working late, ignoring my calls, the lack of affection . . . I knew it had to be someone else. I should've paid attention to the red flags." The rub on her back was gentle and comforting. Corrine hadn't realized how much she needed the condolence.

"It's not your fault," Tangie insisted. "That fuck bastard doesn't deserve a woman as wonderful as you. So, let this be your sign. Divorce his ass. There is someone out there that is so much better for you."

Corrine wished she had her friend's strength. Even now after what she had experienced, the thought of permanently severing ties with her husband had fear snaking through her body. And if she had to admit it to herself, part of her still yearned for his love, even if it was poisonous.

"I want you to come to a group therapy session with me," Tangie spoke up again. "I know before, Patrick didn't like you going. But I promise you, Rinny, the amount of support there for people like us can really pull you through even the darkest of places." She sighed, as if the next comment was taking all of her strength. "After you and I stopped talking, I got really, really depressed. I felt you were the only person in this world that actually cared for me, and when you left . . ." A single tear streaked down her cheek. "I tried to commit suicide. Twice."

"Tangie . . ." The apology quivered on her tongue.

"No, no. I'm not telling you for you to feel bad," Tangie clarified, swiping at the tear with her knuckle. "I'm telling you I didn't realize how much our friendship had an impact on my life, until you were gone. And I'm sorry I never told you how much I appreciate you." The hand that squeezed Corrine's was strong with reassurance. "And this therapy group really helped me. I want them to help you. *I* want to help you."

Grateful, Corrine collapsed into Tangie's embrace. Maybe God hadn't completely abandoned her just yet.

"Girl, now you got me looking a mess." Tangie laughed as she rubbed her face to fix her makeup. "And you know this is my moneymaker. I can't be out here looking any kind of way."

Corrine couldn't help but laugh as Tangie jumped to her feet. "You're still gorgeous, Boo."

"I know this." Tangie headed toward the staircase for her loft bedroom. "Let me fix my face and get you some towels and sheets. You're staying with me for a while. Understood?"

"Thank you, Tangie. For everything."

Tangie winked, blew a kiss, and disappeared upstairs.

Corrine rose to begin cleaning up their mess when she heard her phone ring. She paused in midair, her heart racing once again. Maybe that was Patrick. But what the hell could he possibly say after all that he had done? She hated the internal struggle with herself. Part of her wanted to completely ignore him and head straight for the courts first thing in the morning to file her divorce papers. But the other part, the part that was still tied to him, wanted to cuss him the fuck out. Well, maybe hear him out first, then cuss him out. But she didn't even know if she trusted herself. Patrick had a way of roping her back in where she almost felt guilty for even thinking about leaving. Damn him.

The phone stopped, then immediately started that incessant ringing once again. After only another moment's hesitation, Corrine dug in her purse and pulled out her cell. Not Patrick, she realized in both relief and disappointment. Gina. Probably had come by the house looking for her. Corrine didn't even know what, if anything, she should relay without revealing too much.

Suddenly unsure, she let it ring in her hand until it went to voice mail. Just as fast, the text message notification popped up on her screen. Her sister's persistence had Corrine frowning as she tapped on the envelope icon to open it. She didn't know if her eyes were playing tricks on her, but then again, she knew Gina wouldn't play like that. So she reread the message again, the two words hollow and heavy like lead: **Ma died.**

Chapter Seventeen
Bridget

Bridget was doing two things that would probably piss Roman off even more. But at that point, she really didn't give a damn. In fact, that was her intention after the way he had treated her.

She drove with a purpose, the suitcases stuffed with tropical beachwear knocking against each other on her back seat. She hadn't bothered telling Róman she was going on vacation, but after much thought, the solo trip to Cancún was just what she needed. And right then, she had to do what was best for her. Which was why she was making a few pitstops before she headed to the airport later that evening.

The crowded precinct was abuzz with typical police activity. With the exception of paying her speeding tickets, Bridget had never needed to visit a police station. And she sure as hell hadn't thought she would ever have to file a complaint. Though she figured Corrine was harmless outside of her spontaneous pop-ups, the fact was still true: the woman was a stalker. And Bridget didn't know what lengths she was liable to go to.

Roman thought she was going too far, but of course that was

easy for him to say. He wasn't the one subjected to the constant monitoring and looking over his shoulder. Thankfully, since the restaurant incident, she hadn't seen Corrine or had any more run-ins with the black Cadillac or prank phone calls. Still, she went against her husband's wishes and opted to pursue the matter herself. It was better to err on the side of caution.

Bridget made her way through the throng of officers and visitors to the front desk, where a female was keying on the computer. "Excuse me," she greeted. "How do I file a complaint for harassment?"

The woman glanced up through a pair of glasses, the mundane stresses of her job causing her to cast a bored look in Bridget's direction. "Let me guess. Your husband?" she asked.

"Um no, she's . . ." Bridget trailed off, questioning her own situation. What the hell was she? "Someone else," she finished. "Is there some paperwork or something I need to fill out?"

The officer didn't seem to care for the interruption, but she rummaged through a nearby drawer and produced the papers anyway. "Here," she stated simply, sliding the clipboard across the desk.

The officer's attitude was off-putting, but rather than address it, Bridget grabbed the papers and headed to a nearby chair.

The first few questions she had to complete were pretty standard; name, address, and phone number. She jotted down her contact details with a hasty scribble before moving down the paper. It was when Bridget read the next bit of information that she had to pause. *What is your relationship to the person you are filing against?* The tip of her ballpoint pen hovered over the checkbox that read *Other intimate relationship* as she pondered.

All of this bullshit started after she and Roman had entered the swinging relationship with Corrine and Patrick. She had opened the door and let the devil in their home, and now she was suffering the consequences. She thought back to their conversation at

Shadow Lounge. Corrine had assured her all parties involved knew and played by the rules. Bridget wondered at what point the rules changed.

She finished the document and returned it to the officer, who looked it over with a half-hearted glance.

"Now what?" Bridget asked when the woman made no move to speak.

"We'll investigate this."

"Well, do I need to get a restraining order or something?"

The officer's lips tightened with annoyance. "I guess if you want to. Up to you. But you'll have to go through the courts for that."

Bridget rolled her eyes. "Okay. How long will the investigation take?"

"Depends," the officer said with a careless shrug. "A week, two weeks, few months. It just depends on the officer."

"And what am I supposed to do in the meantime?"

Bridget watched the woman's eyes sweep over the paper once more, pausing at one particular part. By the way her lips curved in a slight, patronizing smirk, she probably had read about Bridget and Corrine's relationship. She put the paper facedown to the side and looked up at Bridget, her eyebrows lifted.

"If you happen to see the woman anywhere *other* than your bedroom, I suggest you give us a call, okay, hun?"

Ashamed, Bridget spun on her heel and stormed from the precinct. The bitch was right. She had brought this foolishness on herself. But, damn, that didn't mean it was *her* fault that she was being stalked. She was scared, and her anxiety had skyrocketed. Roman thought she was exaggerating, and the police thought the shit was comical. What would Corrine have to do to get everyone to see the severity? Physically harm her? Would she even go that far?

The phone ringing snatched her from her thoughts. Bridget

glanced at the caller ID and had to stifle a groan. Marco. He had been calling off and on for a week now. She hadn't intended to duck and dodge his calls, but frankly she really wasn't sure what to tell him. He probably was wanting to go ahead and set his next event in motion. But after Nikki's blow-up during the double date, and now with her egregious betrayal, Bridget wasn't even sure if she still had a company to plan an event.

They had both split the start-up costs, including legal expenses, software, certifications, and marketing. Of course, they had each shouldered the load in planning some events for free just to build up their portfolio and clientele. What Bridget could appreciate was, though the business had been her passion project initially, Nikki had taken on an equal amount of the responsibilities, and the rewards. Everything was divided among them. So, if she was really serious about wanting out, Bridget would have to buy her out or dissolve the company in its entirety to start over from scratch. Which would be detrimental to the business connections they had already cultivated. And what then would become of their friendship? The last thought tugged on Bridget's heart, only momentarily. Her thoughts turned to the argument with Roman. How the hell could Nikki tell her husband the one thing she'd sworn she wouldn't? What would she have to gain? It didn't make any sense, but Nikki was the only one who knew, so all roads led back to her two-faced *ex*–best friend.

Nikki had been down for her since the freshman dorm at Georgia Southern. She hated to think a decade-long friendship could be over so easily. Or worse, they would become competitors in the industry that had brought them together. But at this juncture, both end scenarios were entirely plausible. Neither of which Bridget was prepared for.

She sent Marco to voice mail and immediately dialed Nikki's number. Both of them had been riding on stubbornness and hadn't spoken in a week. The way Bridget saw it, it was time they got everything out in the open. Their little grudge was beginning to affect business. Plus, it was time Bridget confronted her disloyal ass.

"Please leave a message for Dominique Parks . . ."

Bridget hung up on a sigh as she pulled into her parents' driveway. She knew Nikki was still pissed, but part of her had actually expected her friend to put the childish shit aside. Hell, Bridget had more of a reason to be upset anyway.

The phone rang right when she hung up, and Bridget quickly put the device to her ear. She was glad Nikki mirrored her sentiments. More than friends, they were business partners. They should at least be able to keep their professional and personal matters separate.

"Hey, Nik," she greeted coolly. "We need to—"

"Good afternoon, Bridget."

She heard the Spanish accent and could only curse under her breath. Dammit, she should have checked the ID again. "Hey, Marco," she said, trying to put more enthusiasm into her voice than she felt.

"I've been looking for you. Is everything okay?"

"Yes," she lied. "Sorry about that. It has been a little crazy. And I'm about to leave town for the weekend, so I was going to call you when I returned."

"Well, I was hoping we could go ahead and get to work," he said with disappointment. "I will be leaving town myself tomorrow on business, but I'll be gone for about a week or two. Is there any way your partner can meet with me so we can get started?"

Highly unlikely, but she couldn't very well tell him that. Nor could she stall any more than she already had. Instead, she said, "I'll tell you what. Can I chat with her and give you a call back later?"

"You're going to call me back, right?" Marco sounded doubtful.

"Yes, definitely."

"Okay, please do. I would hate any miscommunication to have a negative effect on Brinique Lux Affair. You ladies were exceptional with our first event, and I want to continue raving about my positive experience." His message was crystal clear. If they kept messing up, he would drag them through the gutter. Duly noted.

"Don't worry," she assured him. "We take great pride in offering you exceptional service every time. Again, my apologies for the slight delay in getting back to you. It won't happen again."

"That's what I like to hear. Talk to you later."

Evidently, she had said everything he needed to hear, because Marco's excitement was evident by the time they had hung up the phone. But after the damage control, Bridget, on the other hand, felt conflicted. And what made matters worse was that she and Nikki were still at odds.

Bridget had been sitting in the car outside of her parents' house for the duration of the call with Marco. It was supposed to be a quick stop-in to see her folks and Ava to waste a little time before she left for the airport. But now, she didn't even want to go inside.

Luckily, she didn't have to. Her father, Kirk, stepped onto the wraparound porch and leaned against the bannister. Because he waved, Bridget cut off the engine and opened the door. It would be nice to see him anyway.

Easing into his golden years, Kirk Hall was a laid-back type of guy. He had to be to deal with a woman like Bridget's mother, Vernita, plus seven kids. And the graying hair beginning to thin at his temples was evidence enough of his tolerance. His handsome good looks had made him a huge threat back in the day, but despite the rumors, everyone who knew Kirk knew he was a family man above all else. And his pride and joy was Bridget.

Even now as she stepped from the car, Kirk grinned, flashing a beautiful set of white teeth between his black stubble of a beard and mustache. His brilliant gray eyes lit with affection as he stepped down from the porch to meet Bridget on the walkway. "There's my girl," he greeted, welcoming his youngest daughter with a hug.

Bridget's smile was one of adoration. "Hey, Daddy," she said as she relaxed in his comforting embrace. Her eyes wandered to the cigar he had clamped between his stubby fingers. "What did Mama tell you about those?"

Kirk sneered. "I'm a grown man and don't no woman tell me what to do," he boasted. Still, he glanced uneasily at the doorway, just in case Vernita was nearby.

Bridget remembered her previous conversation with her mother about her dad's alleged extramarital affairs. "You moved back home, huh?"

Kirk rolled his eyes. "I never left. You know how your mother is."

She figured as much. But something else registered in his eyes. Something that had Bridget frowning. "She said some wild stuff, Daddy. Some stuff I didn't want to believe."

Kirk looked out into the yard, putting the cigar to his lips, and taking a deep drag. He exhaled the smoke into the air through lips tight with hesitancy. "Things change sometimes, sweetie," he said with a quiet voice. "You know in the beginning, everything is new and fresh, so you're liable to overlook certain red flags. Or mistake them for something else. But the longer you're with someone, the more you'll see their true colors. No one can play the role forever."

The conversation was making Bridget uneasy. She didn't know if he was talking about himself or her mother, but it sounded eerily close to her own relationship. And the parallel was uncomfortable.

The mood had shifted between them, and Kirk suddenly brightened as he switched topics. "How is Roman? And Maya? How is she? You don't bring her around anymore."

"Everyone is good," Bridget said, navigating away from that subject just as expertly as her father. "I've just been pretty busy."

"Busy is good. Business going well?"

"Sure is." She hesitated. No one else but Roman knew about her newest venture. She was thankful her dad was her biggest champion. "I'm writing a book."

"A book, huh?" Surprised jubilance had Kirk's eyebrows lifting. "Wow, that's great! What's it about?"

"It's an entrepreneur book specifically for black women," she said. "Just sharing my journey and providing some motivation to others who want to start their own business."

"Well, congratulations on that." Kirk beamed with pride. "I can't wait to read it."

Bridget smiled, the supportive comment immediately lifting her spirits. "Well, I have to finish it first," she said. "But it's getting there."

"I know it's going to be good because my baby wrote it."

Bridget certainly hoped so. Procrastination was getting the best of her. With the way she had been feeling lately, her head hadn't been in the project as much as she would've liked.

A black car turned onto the street and slowed to a crawl as it approached the house. Bridget's eyes widened. She didn't want to believe it. Had Corrine followed her to her parents' house? The girl was truly sick.

When the car eased into the driveway, fear had Bridget backing up to the door, her eyes turning to her dad for help. She let out the breath she had been holding when Kirk lifted his hand to greet the visitor.

"Hey, Jeff," he called out to the car.

The window rolled down, and a man poked his head out. Bridget felt like an idiot.

"You and Vernita come through later, man. We're putting some meat on the grill," the man yelled back.

"I'll let her know. 'Preciate that."

Jeff reversed the car and headed on down the street.

Bridget sank back into the chair, struggling to calm her racing heart.

"What's wrong?" Kirk's voice was filled with concern.

Bridget debated telling him about Corrine, but that was a subject she wasn't entirely prepared to get into. Especially given the circumstances under which they even met. And she certainly didn't want her father to know about her marital troubles with Roman. Or the crumbling business, and friendship, with Nikki.

"Just work," Bridget answered simply.

"Uh huh." Kirk ran his fingers over his beard in consideration. "You sure that's all?"

Wordlessly, Bridget lowered herself into one of the rocking chairs. "I mean it's a lot of stuff," she admitted. "But mostly work-related, I guess you could say."

"You know, I was proud as hell when you started that company, Bri. Damn proud. You saw what you wanted and went after it. You get that from your mother. But," he added, "it's okay if it's not everything you thought it would be. No one's going to judge you if you need to pause for a minute and reset."

Bridget frowned at how accurate her dad's words were for the circumstances. "Are you still talking about my job?" she asked.

Kirk shrugged, putting the cigar to his lips to take another puff. "That too," he said. Blowing more smoke into the air, he took a seat in the rocking chair next to his daughter. "Let me tell you something," he said. "I once knew a girl that had it all together, right? The whole modern woman thing that everyone expected. Real nice lady. She actually reminds me of you. So anyway, she has the husband, the house and cars, the career; everything. So outside looking in, she had the perfect, successful American dream." He leaned in and lowered his voice for dramatic effect. "But they were wrong, Bri. She was lost and confused. So, she divorced her husband, left her job, and went in search of her happiness. Started traveling, eating, getting in touch with her spirituality, and ended up falling in love. And it was on this path of self-discovery that she was truly happy. You get what I'm saying to you?"

Bridget's forehead creased at the narrative. "Daddy, did Mama have you watching *Eat, Pray, Love?*"

Kirk paused to think for a minute. "Good movie," he reflected with a nod. "Makes you think. But either way, you get the point I'm trying to make?"

"Yeah, I get it, Daddy." And she did. But did that necessarily mean that was what she was supposed to do? Hell, she thought she was happy when she married Roman. But had she been blinded all of this time? Well, maybe this little spontaneous solo trip to Cancún was her own eat-pray-love derivative. She certainly had a lot of soul-searching to do.

"Get the fuck away from my apartment."

Bridget caught the door as Nikki attempted to slam it in her face. "Really, Nik? You have the nerve to be mad after what you did?"

Nikki snatched the door open wide again, her face contorted in sheer bewilderment. "What *I* did? Are you fucking serious right now?" Her voice ricocheted down the hall and had Bridget's head darting around. None of Nikki's nosy neighbors had come outside to see what was going on. But Bridget could tell when the blinds shifted in the apartment next door that folks were listening. The last thing she wanted to look like was a stereotypical ratchet chick putting her business all in the street.

Bridget lowered her voice. "Look," she said with controlled calm. "Can we just go inside and talk about this?"

"No, we can't go inside," Nikki snapped just as loud. "No, we can't talk about this. You can go back in your car and go back to wherever the fuck you came from!"

Again, she tried to slam the door. Again, Bridget pressed her hand against the wood to keep it from snapping back on her face. "Nikki, stop it. You're being really childish and really petty right now. So, do you want to act like we did in college or do you want to handle this like *grown* women?"

Nikki's eyes narrowed at the insult. Bridget had struck a nerve. She knew it would.

Abruptly, Nikki stepped back from the door, allowing Bridget to swing it open to enter. "You're one to talk about childish," she snapped as Bridget shut the door behind her. "Hell, the way you were acting the other day at dinner, I thought I was watching an episode of *Rugrats*."

Bridget rolled her eyes, crossing her arms over her breast. "Oh, if I recall, you were the one that ripped up a fifteen-thousand-dollar check. Now who was being childish?"

"You went behind my back and committed us to a business contract without even consulting me! You don't do that to your partner." Nikki threw up her hands and turned, storming into the kitchen.

"Okay, I get it, you're mad," Bridget said as she followed right on her heels. "But I didn't understand what the big damn deal was. Weren't you the one talking about us doing so well with business and you were trying to get a Tesla and all that shit? I saw a once-in-a-lifetime opportunity and I jumped on it. Not only is it good for business, but it's lucrative. Marco is overpaying us for the actual work he wants us to do. Why the hell would you turn that down?"

"Because,"—frustration had Nikki whirling around to face her—"I don't think we need to make ourselves exclusive to one place. That takes us out the running for any other opportunities that may come up. That's not smart. And besides," she went on, "I don't trust that place. Membership applications, background checks, and all the hush-hush shit that goes on 'in the shadows.' I don't like it, I don't want to be associated with it, and I don't think it's a good look for Brinique. But," she barreled on, throwing up her hands, "God forbid I stand in the way of you and your precious Shadow Lounge. So, *you* go do whatever you want, Bridget. Just like you've been doing. I don't want to have shit to do with it. Period!"

Nikki turned back to the stove, where she was in the middle of cooking something. Bridget watched her friend's back, no longer angry. In fact, the argument had hurt more than anything. She thought she heard Nikki sniff. Was she crying?

Bridget leaned against the counter and stared down at her sandals. Maybe she was right. She hadn't at all thought about any associated connotations with attaching their brand to the club, or any potential opportunities they could miss as a result of the exclusivity. She just wished they had discussed it earlier. For a while, an exhausted silence lulled between them.

Bridget spoke up first. "Why didn't you tell me all of this before, Nik?" she asked.

"I kept telling you we needed to talk about it," Nikki said, her voice low with sorrow. "We always talk about our decisions. I didn't think you would go do something so drastic without us being on the same page." Nikki finally looked up, her cheeks wet with tears. Evidence of her friend's pain broke Bridget's heart, and she felt like a fool.

"I'm sorry, Nikki," she said, folding her friend into a hug. "Damn, you're right. I'm so, so sorry. Shit, I wasn't thinking about that."

Nikki sighed before pulling back a little to look Bridget square in the eye. "I'm not trying to stand in your way, Bri. I swear. We decided to go into business together because we both have the same passion, mindset, and goals. If we're not in this together, we need to just part ways. I would never want to hold you back from doing—"

Bridget was shaking her head to stop Nikki's words. "No. It's not that important," she insisted. "If it means I lose you, I don't want to do it. We're in this together."

Nikki nodded, but her smile was more relieved than anything.

"And here I was thinking you didn't want to do the deal because of Corrine."

"What? Corrine? No." Nikki turned up her nose at the thought. "I mean, don't get me wrong. I don't like her, but that's personal. This is business."

Bridget started to relax, but something was still eating at her. She watched Nikki stir whatever she had simmering in the pot. "So, if this is business and not personal, why would you tell Roman about my surgery?"

Confusion marred her face as she tossed Bridget a sideways glance. "Tell Roman about what surgery?" she asked.

"Come on, Nikki. About me getting my tubes tied because I didn't want kids," Bridget clarified, the thought upsetting her once again. "I told you that shit in confidence, and you really went back and told him after you swore that would stay between us?"

"Whoa, whoa. That wasn't me." Nikki shook her head to reaffirm her declaration. "I didn't even know Roman knew. You know I would never betray you like that, girl, come on." The look on Nikki's face told Bridget everything. Her girl was genuinely ignorant about Roman's knowledge of their secret. She had clearly kept her word.

"Did he say I told him?" Nikki inquired, her face still creased in confusion.

Bridget shook her head on a sigh. "No, he didn't tell me who told him. Just that he knew."

"Well, who else did you tell?"

Bridget thought back, flipping through possibilities and previous conversations. Other than Nikki, the only other person who may have known was . . . Her eyes ballooned as the realization struck like a Mack truck. *Corrine!* And if Corrine told Roman, then that meant he had spoken to her. And if he had spoken to her, that meant the bastard had lied to her face. The thought had Bridget clenching her jaw shut to keep from spewing a slew of curses about her lying-ass husband.

"Well?" Nikki asked again at Bridget's continued silence. "Who else did you tell?"

Bridget shook her head. The last thing Nikki needed was more ammunition against Corrine. "I'll figure it out," she said instead. Bridget would just deal with the woman, and Roman, her damn self.

Chapter Eighteen
Corrine

Corrine was dreading the next few hours. She hadn't been back to Great Haven Baptist since she was a kid. Her parents had her and Gina in church faithfully every Sunday morning. If anything, Corrine knew their frequent visits weren't for the actual Word, but to "fix him," as their dad had once said in reference to her.

So she had to go and tolerate hours of the judgmental stares and discreet conviction from Pastor Franklin as he spoke to the congregation with those laser eyes pointed on her for the whole sermon. Corrine would sit in silence in the stiff brown suit and clip-on tie and have to nod and respond respectively as people would refer to *Christopher* being such a shy *boy* and *he* is so *handsome*. Then as the years wore on and the rumors started, the not-so-discreet whispers would shift to "Jeremy and Paula's gay son" with lifted brows, amused stares, and mocking hand gestures to symbolize homosexuality.

Even worse, the kids in the Youth Center would adopt the same sentiments, and their willful ignorance kept Corrine from addressing it at all. She hated to be the constant topic of conversation and the subject of public ridicule. But their Christian tongues kept wagging with the gossip for years. What was supposed to be her place of peace and acceptance was the root of her misery.

Corrine remembered one girl in particular, Kita, who made it her business to torment Corrine every Sunday. The girl's harassment was as religious as Bible study. At first, Corrine had thought she was trying to be her friend when she started asking so many questions. Corrine had made the mistake of confiding in Kita about feeling more like a girl than a boy. The next Sunday, Kita had passed around drawings of Corrine sucking a dick with the words "call Chris for a good time" scribbled across the top with his phone number.

Corrine had mentioned it once to Gina, and Gina, trying to help, had shared it with their mother. Paula's answer was a nonchalant shrug. "Tell him to stop acting like that and they will stop messing with him," she had said simply and turned back to washing dishes. That was the first time Corrine had attempted suicide.

Now, being in the sanctuary again brought back all of the malicious memories and once more put Corrine under a microscope like some foreign science project. And the fact that it was her mother's funeral only heightened the scrutiny.

The church was thick with mourners. People stood in clusters, speaking in hushed whispers, and dabbing at their cheeks with soiled tissues. Corrine didn't even remember this many people at her dad's funeral. But then again, Paula had been the religious advocate in the family, pushing her skewed Christian ideology on anyone who bothered to listen. Corrine recognized a few faithful members of the congregation that she had assumed had gone on to be with the Lord they alleged to love but contradicted so much.

A single coffin rested at the front of the church, angled in a sharp diagonal from the altar. A picture of Paula sat in a frame on top of the powder-blue stainless steel. Corrine felt eyes on her as she walked down the aisle behind Gina and slid into one of the front pews. Part of her had thought that being present, seeing the casket, feeling everyone's emotions, would ignite the grief. Yet still, she felt as void of life as her mother. If it had been left up to her, she would have sat in the back. Or even better, not come at all. Yet her attendance wasn't a choice but more of a familial obligation. She had to support her sister. Gina couldn't go through this alone.

As soon as they sat down, Corrine draped her arm across her sister's slumped shoulders as she continued to cry in restrained silence. She was taking it hard, and Corrine could only sit by and try to relay comfort that she didn't feel. She heard whispers and tried her best to ignore them. Instead, Corrine focused on an enlarged picture of Paula propped on an easel off to one side.

Corrine remembered the photo vividly. Easter 2017. She had taken it herself when Paula had made the family accompany the church on a fundraiser at the park. The lens had captured something quite different than the woman Corrine knew. That Paula looked warm, loving, compassionate; everything she was not. Corrine supposed she wasn't the only one in the family that had been wearing a mask all those years.

Once everyone was seated, Pastor Franklin walked to the front and stood in all his classist grandeur. He was adorned in a cream-and-purple robe with evidence of the years outlined in his face and salt-and-pepper hair.

He signaled the musician to lower the music, and all eyes turned to him, eager for reassurance. "Good afternoon." His greeting was met with a few solemn murmurs. Corrine heard Gina's breath catch in her throat. "We are here today to seek and receive comfort," he went on. "A wonderful soul has been called home to be with the Lord, and though our hearts ache, we must find peace in trusting and relying heavily on God. Not just in this time of need, but always. Proverbs 3:5 says, 'Trust in the LORD with all thine heart and lean not unto thine own understanding.' We are going to move past the tears, the questions, and the doubt. For God does not make mistakes. And the Holy Spirit is here today to comfort and strengthen each of our hearts. And He will continue to be with us as we continue to live for God."

The pastor quoted a few more scriptures, then someone belted a tear-jerking rendition of Yolanda Adams's song "I'm Gonna Be Ready" that had a mass of sobs erupting:

> *Sight beyond what I see*
> *You know what's best for me*
> *Prepare my mind, prepare my heart*
> *For whatever comes, I'm gonna be ready . . .*

Even as the woman trailed on the last note, the instrumentals continued to play. Gina slid from the pew like butter, her body weakened with grief. Corrine eased to the floor to hold her sister as she rocked in her angst.

"Now," the pastor continued with the ceremony, "we'll have a few words from Paula's only daughter, Gina Crenshaw."

Corrine shut her eyes against the sting of the words. That had been intentional. And knowing her mother, she had instructed Pastor Franklin not to make mention at all of Corrine.

Gina was able to climb to her feet with no assistance, and she shuffled to the front. It appeared to take every ounce of energy for her to stutter through each painful word of the eulogy.

When she was done, Gina looked down at the open casket then back to Corrine with a staggering sigh. "And one more thing," she murmured, her voice cracking through the podium microphone. "I am Paula's *eldest* daughter. Not her only." A hush fell over the congregation, and even in the midst of everyone's pain, Corrine felt her lips curve upward into a triumphant smirk at her mother's thwarted strategy. *Take that, bitch!*

———•———

By the time the procession had migrated to the cemetery, the rain had slackened to a gentle mist. And with the clouds still hanging overcast, it definitely accentuated the gloomy disposition of the entire service.

Corrine kept her distance, but she stood watch as they lowered her mother's coffin into the moist soil. Gina sat on one of the fold-out chairs closest to the plot. Patrick had to work, so it was just her for her sister to lean on for support.

Surprise etched her face when she noticed Kita mixed in the crowd. What the hell was she doing there? She couldn't help but notice she was dressed like she was straight out of Hollywood; complete with a black birdcage veil and satin gloves that spanned the length of her arm. All the memories of her childhood came tumbling back in a wave of disgust and anger. Kita looked her way, her face creased in an amused smile. Corrine rolled her eyes.

When the crowd began to disperse, Corrine started to make her way to Gina when she caught Kita headed in her direction. She turned her back on the approaching woman and silently prayed for strength.

"Christopher."

Corrine cringed but didn't bother looking to the voice.

Kita stepped directly in front of her and placed her hand on Corrine's shoulder to draw her attention. "Christopher, is that you? Oh, wow, I didn't even recognize you."

If they had been anywhere else, Corrine would've slapped the glee off of her face. Instead, she said, "It's not Christopher. It's Corrine."

"Oh, right, I forgot with the whole dress thing." Kita gestured vaguely to Corrine's body as if she were an object, as opposed to a person. "So anyway, I'm sorry about your mom. I know you and Gina are pretty hurt by her death." Funny. She sounded anything but apologetic.

"No, not really," Corrine corrected.

The comment was offhand and completely unexpected, she knew. Kita's face wrinkled in revulsion. "Well, that's quite the shitty thing to say. But then again," she paused, tossing her hair over her shoulder, "I guess I shouldn't have expected decency and respect from you."

Even though her sister was across the yard accepting condolences, Corrine could almost hear her pleas not to act up. So, because she knew whooping Kita's ass and tossing her in one of the open graves would be an embarrassment, she bit her tongue to keep from responding.

"Who did all that work on you?" Kita went on, sliding a hand on her hip.

"Why? Looks like you've had enough," Corrine retorted.

Now it was Kita's turn to roll her eyes. "You always have been jealous of me," she said. "And it's pathetic. Cute, but pathetic. Get a life, Christopher."

And with that, she sauntered off, looping her arm around a gentleman who looked to be three times her age. Corrine watched her lean in and whisper something to the gentleman, who tossed a curious look over his shoulder. And just to make sure Corrine knew they were talking about her, Kita went as far as to lift her hand in the air and wiggle her fingers in a little taunt that had Corrine looking away from the couple. It was a shame. Kita would have been a beautiful woman had she not been so damn ugly.

Paula's site was empty now with flowers scattered around and inside the plot. Corrine stood at the opening and looked down into the hole. She halfway expected to see her mother's face below, looking back at her with that frown she usually did. Gina had been harboring a little attitude since the woman had passed; giving Corrine that "I told you so" speech to try and make her feel guilty about never going to see Paula when she knew she was sick. Corrine hadn't felt a shred of regret. Cancer or no cancer, she hadn't wanted to hear whatever justification Paula had for her actions. It wouldn't make a difference. Gina had insisted it would help her heal. But some wounds were permanent. Corrine was living proof of that.

The pressure began building up in her chest as she spoke. "I loved you," she started. "And you hated me for who I was. For something that you didn't care to understand. Something that wasn't my fault. You were supposed to protect me from the evils of this world. But you were the evil of this world. I am much better off without you. So, thank you, Paula. For finally giving me something to make me happy. Peace."

———

Corrine went back and forth with Gina, but she finally relented and went to pick up Vanessa to take them both home. If it were left up to her, she would've taken her niece to her house to give her sister time to properly grieve. But she obeyed and dropped them back at their apartment anyway.

Afterward, Corrine went home alone and immediately washed the stench of death off her body. She changed into something more comfortable, a maxi dress and jean jacket, and, not wanting to spend the rest of her evening cooped up in that big old house by herself, she headed out with nowhere in particular in mind.

It was a stretch to assume Roman was at home. But after first checking the hospital and confirming he wasn't working that day, it was the only other place she figured he would be.

Corrine glanced in the rearview mirror for the tenth time and let out a relieved sigh when she saw the steady flow of cars passing by. No one seemed to notice her car parked against the curb or her hunched down in the driver's seat watching the house. She still hadn't heard from him, and the lack of contact was playing on her psyche. Now, an hour into her stakeout, she didn't know if she was happy or disappointed that she hadn't seen any type of activity.

Finally, as the sun began to set, Corrine stepped from her car and crossed the street to the Pierce household. She didn't know what she was expecting or what her reasoning would be for her presence. Maybe something dealing with Vanessa and his daughter, Maya. They did mention getting the girls together again to play. Maybe she could suggest another park date. She rang the doorbell and waited.

To her slight surprise, it wasn't Roman who opened the door. Or even Bridget. It was another guy altogether whom she had never seen before. Corrine glanced to the doorframe to ensure she had the correct house number.

The man looked rough in his dingy sweatpants and stained T-shirt; like he hadn't bathed in years, and the smell just added to the proof. He leaned against the doorjamb and took her in. His face remained neutral.

"Um, I'm looking for . . ."—which one should she say?— "Bridget," she decided. "I work with her on events."

"She's out of town," he said.

That was news to her. She wondered where Bridget went, and with whom? Were she and Roman doing the little couple getaway thing? Is that why he wasn't answering?

"Okay," she pushed with a hesitant smile. "What about Roman?"

"He went out."

She didn't like the way he was looking at her. Like he saw right through her. Corrine lowered her head. "Okay thanks."

She turned to leave and heard the door close at her back. The guy was especially rude. But maybe that was for the best. She had already made Bridget uncomfortable. The last thing she wanted to do was freak him out, too.

Corrine must've spoken him up because she hadn't even made it out the driveway when she was startled by the garage creaking open. Sure enough, Roman's truck was coming up the street. Corrine stepped onto the manicured lawn to let him pass through, eyeing the tinted window as the vehicle pulled up and parked.

"What are you doing here?" he snapped, tossing open the door.

His attitude caught Corrine off guard. She hadn't necessarily expected him to be welcoming, but she thought the anger was a bit of an overreaction.

"Um, I was looking for Bridget," she answered.

Roman slammed the door. "She's not here," he said. "And just in case you didn't know yet, she went to the police about you."

Corrine frowned at that. "The police? Why?"

Roman lifted his arm in a sweeping gesture around his property. "Look at you," he said. "What the hell are you doing here, Corrine?"

"I—I wanted to check on you," she sputtered, still reeling from the shock of his abrasiveness. "You haven't returned my calls."

"Yeah, I know." Roman leaned back in his car and pulled out a plastic bag with two Styrofoam to-go boxes of food. "Is there anything else?"

"Roman, why are you acting like this?"

"I'm not acting like anything. You just need to leave."

He bumped his door closed and walked by, headed into the house. Why was he hurting her like this? What had Bridget said to him?

"Okay, okay, look," she said, her words heavy with desperation. "Can I be honest with you?" He stopped, and she didn't wait for a reply before rushing on. "I . . . missed you, Roman. I'm going through some personal things right now. Some things I can't handle, and I just know how you made me forget my stress. You listen to me. And you don't put me down or make me feel like shit. And I appreciate that." She heard his sigh as he lowered his head. "Roman, please," she went on at his continued silence. Maybe appealing to his compassionate side would work. "We just buried my mom today. I . . . I really need someone to talk to right now."

"Corrine, we can't do this anymore," he said, turning to face her again. "I'm sorry about your mom and what you're going through, but we are both married. What happened between us was a one-time exception and you know it—"

"And what about the park?"

She didn't like what she saw reflected in his face. More than anger was pity. It was answer enough, and she was mortified.

Corrine didn't hear the man come out of the house, but suddenly he was beside Roman, taking the plastic to-go bag from his hand.

"What are you still doing here?" the guy asked with a frown.

Corrine rolled her eyes. Who *was* this bum?

Roman glanced between them. "You two know each other?"

"Nah, bruh. She was here before you got here. Saw her watching the house for a while and then she walked up asking for Bridget," the guy remarked.

Roman looked to Corrine for answers, but she was already stepping back. The man was talking too damn much. She just needed to go.

"You're the one that dropped off some flowers, too," the guy went on with a raised eyebrow. "I watched you drop them off and run away in a hurry. Hell, you've been watching the house a few times when they're not home."

Corrine shook her head fiercely to deny the truth, even as Roman's forehead wrinkled with skepticism. "Roman knows I work with Bridget, dude," she retorted, her lip curling in irritation. "Who are you anyway?"

"Dorian."

"Okay, *Dorian,* you need to mind your own fucking business." Corrine smacked her lips and turned to stalk off to her car. The whole visit was a complete waste of time, and the disaster had her riding high on her disappointment. She had to focus to keep from breaking out in a run, but she knew she needed to get the hell away from Roman and his big-mouth friend.

Just then, Dorian's words sliced through the air and had her knees buckling underneath her. "Hey, who did your transition surgery?"

Corrine's breath caught so sharply in her lungs it burned her chest. A mix between anger and fear had her spinning on her heel so fast she nearly lost her balance. "What the hell did you say to me?" she spat with venom.

Dorian's head tilted in consideration. "You transitioned, right?" he pushed, obviously not giving a damn about his probing. "I was a cosmetic surgeon, so trying to see who hooked you up."

Shame had Corrine averting her eyes. She wouldn't—couldn't dare look Roman's way. So she did the only thing she knew to do. She ran back to her car, jumped in, and sped away in a surge of humiliated agony.

Chapter Nineteen
Bridget

Bridget felt completely revitalized.

She stepped off the plane with a little extra pep in her step and sashayed to baggage claim. Mexico had done wonders for her physical and mental health. Her skin was a golden bronze, glowing from the tan she had received during her many hours on the beach. The endless alcohol at the all-inclusive, adults-only resort had her mind in a tranquil haze that had kept her mood on high for the entire five days. Her dad had been right about his little eat-pray-love comparison. She had eaten well, slept long, and most importantly, finished her book.

A rewarding grin crossed Bridget's face as she clutched her laptop case even tighter. She still couldn't believe it, but clearing her mind of all the clutter and bullshit she had left back in Atlanta had allowed the words to flow like water.

Sixteen chapters later, Bridget had put everything on paper, and she damn near wanted to cry. It was probably a shitty first draft and for all she knew, it might not even go further than her Word document. People might not even care to read it. But at that point, she was too ecstatic to care about the negatives. For now, she would just relish her first accomplishment. On top of that, she was still in shock about her stroke of good luck while on the beach.

Bridget had been lying on the lounge chair, her keyboard balanced on her lap as she typed away, when the young white lady in the lounge chair next to her had lifted her sunglasses to strike up a conversation. The first thing Bridget had noticed was the woman's eyes were the same icy blue as the ocean. She spoke with a bold pleasantness as her dusty blond hair blew wildly in the tropical breeze.

"Hey, I don't mean to be in your business," she had said with an apologetic chuckle. "But I couldn't help but notice you're going at it on that computer. The way you're typing, I know it must be something good."

Bridget had been in a groove, and she paused only briefly to eye the woman as she reached for the cranberry mimosa resting on a nearby table. "I'm writing a book," she revealed with a delighted grin.

The woman's eyes rounded, and she flicked a glance to marvel at the computer screen, shielding her view from the harsh glare of the sun. "Oh, wow, talk about fate."

"What do you mean?"

The woman held out her hand. "I'm Allison Daniels. I'm actually a literary agent." She let out an amused chuckle. "And here I was thinking I was taking a vacation from work, and look at work following me to the beach."

Bridget shook the woman's hand, maybe a little too excitedly. The woman was right. Utter fate.

The two had spent the rest of the afternoon bouncing between topics of work and personal life. While Bridget had admittedly traveled alone, Allison was on an anniversary trip with her husband from New York. The discussion had turned back to Bridget's book and she, quite shyly at first, revealed a little about the subject matter. Allison was interested and had even suggested she add some extra bonus material to make the book interactive, such as worksheets, business resources, goal calendars, and things to really make the content fun and engaging.

"I see why you're in your line of work," Bridget had said, appreciating the great ideas.

"That's why I'm good at what I do," Allison bragged with a wink. "When you get back home, why don't you give me a call?"

Bridget patted her purse where she had tucked Allison's business card. And just for good measure, she had gone ahead and saved the woman's number in her cell phone. Could never be too cautious.

Bridget waited until she had made it back to her car before she bothered powering on her cell phone. She had intentionally turned it off and left it off the moment they departed from Hartsfield Jackson. She had wanted to make the most of her vacation with no distractions and no bullshit. Her phone hadn't been on but a few seconds before it started *ping*ing with numerous incoming notifications. Bridget sat in the car, absently scrolling through various messages and missed calls to make sure there was nothing of importance. Thankfully, she and Nikki had made up prior to her leaving, so she had asked her friend to notify her parents of her absence and to email her if an emergency arose.

First things first, she sent Nikki a text message to let her know she was back and was headed to the house. Her friend's response came through almost immediately: **Missed you Boo! Everything was fine while you were gone. Headed out with Dennis so call me later so we can chat about all the fun you had.** Bridget smirked, keying in her reply before she moved on to see who else had been looking for her.

Marco hadn't called, but she saw some missed calls from his husband, Jonathan. Bridget had expected as much, especially after she left the message on Marco's voicemail right before takeoff. She had apologized profusely and requested to terminate the contract after a discussion with her business partner. She then indicated she would return the money first thing Tuesday morning. She was uneasy, looking at the numerous calls from Jonathan in her call log, but at that point she would have to take whatever negative backlash came from her brash decision to sign with them. The good thing was that Nikki was 100 percent in her corner.

"Girl, don't even worry about it," she insisted after they had talked it out and Bridget divulged her concerns. "Whatever happens, happens. If these people try to bring us down, we will hire a damn good PR person to fix it."

Bridget appreciated Nikki sticking with her, and most of all, sticking with their company. She had no doubt they could've both gone their separate ways and made little subsidiaries from Brinique. But nothing would've been as strong as what they had already built together.

She made a mental note to return Jonathan's call. Later. Now, she was too exhausted to talk business. She just needed a hot shower to wash the travel off and to lie in her own bed. The hotel suite was luxurious, but she certainly missed the comforts of home.

Speaking of which, Bridget didn't bother checking the numerous calls and messages from Roman. She really didn't give a damn what he had to say. Their last argument had cut her deep, and when she wasn't writing, she had spent a lot of time reflecting on her relationship. She still hadn't come to any kind of resolution, but she doubted she was supposed to without her husband's input. Now that she'd had a chance to clear her mind, she hoped to approach him with a level head. No more secrets, no more disrespect. And no more arguing, because she was damn sick of it. Who knows, if the stars were aligned, they might be able to come through the discussion with a marriage still intact. And if not . . . Well, she said she wouldn't harp on the negatives. She wasn't trying to fuck up her good mood.

Roman's car was not in the garage when she arrived. Bridget had to admit it was the tiniest bit of a reprieve. It would be nice to have a little more freedom to unwind before he got home. Like the calm before the storm.

Bridget entered from the garage and nearly tripped over a few boxes cluttering the kitchen floor. She frowned, stooping to open one of the flaps and peer inside.

Sweaters and jeans had been folded and stacked neatly. Sitting on top was a framed picture of Dorian, and a woman Bridget knew was his ex-wife, Shantae. It was one of those professional photographs taken on a beach somewhere, against an ocean backdrop with the sun glistening like a jewel overhead. For some reason, the smiling couple in the picture made her think of Roman. They, too, had once been happy.

"Hey."

Bridget jumped at the voice and glanced up as Dorian stepped into the kitchen, a tote bag slung over his shoulder. He had shaved, showered, and put on fresh clothes, which was a shocker.

"Hey," she greeted, watching him drag another suitcase across the floor to put with the rest of his boxes. "Moving out, finally?"

"Yeah, I figured it was time."

Been time, she wanted to assert, but decided it was best to just bask in the good luck that had swung her way. "I'm glad you cleaned up," she said. "But you were really owning the whole homeless look."

"Ha ha." Dorian looked her up and down, noting her radiance. "I'm glad you had fun on your vacation."

"Thanks, I did."

"Roman has been worried about you."

Bridget shrugged her shoulders. "I'll talk to him when he gets home." She hadn't meant to sound so indifferent, but she honestly couldn't care less about Roman or his precious feelings. Any other time, that probably would have prompted her to check herself as a wife. Now was not that time.

"He went to drop off Maya," Dorian volunteered when Bridget didn't ask. "And by the way, your girl dropped by."

Bridget frowned. "What girl?"

"The transgender."

Her frown deepened as she sifted through her mental Rolodex. Who did she know that was trans?

"Corrine, or something?"

"Wait." Bridget shook her head at the revelation. "Corrine is trans?"

"Yeah, shit, you can't tell? Her surgeon worked his ass off, that's for damn sure."

Bridget could only stand there in shock, images of Corrine flashing through her mind. She would never have known. Corrine walked, talked, and acted like a woman. "Oh, wow," she murmured simply.

"Appreciate you letting me stay," Dorian was saying as he opened the door. "I know you couldn't stand my black ass."

"Still can't," Bridget said with a smirk. "But you're welcome."

She turned then and left him to finish his moveout process. That bath was now long overdue.

> ⇒●⬌

Bridget emerged from the Jacuzzi tub, her body feeling like satin. She was ready to lather herself up in some scented lotion and lie naked in her sheets until she passed out.

Her mind wandered to Corrine, and Bridget was suddenly curious why she had come by looking for her. The police may have already started the investigation. Still, Bridget took out her cell phone and scrolled to Corrine's number. The coming by unannounced, the stalking . . . investigation or no investigation, it was time to end this shit once and for all.

"*You have reached Corrine. Please leave a—*"

Bridget hung up without leaving a message on a shake of her head. Interesting how she was always around, but when Bridget was looking for her, she was suddenly a ghost.

The garage door creaked open, and all of the relaxation Bridget had savored suddenly extinguished into gripping tension that had her muscles aching. She braced herself for the shit show that was going to happen as soon as Roman came up the stairs. She was sure he had plenty to say about her just up and dashing out of the country with only a text message indicating she was in travel status. As far as she was concerned, they had more important things to discuss. And by the time she heard the door slam and his brisk, heavy footsteps all but running through the house and up the stairs, she was ready for him.

"Where the hell have you been?" Roman's frame blocked the doorway as he frowned at Bridget. He looked threatening.

Bridget turned her back to him, not wanting to let on that he was making her slightly uncomfortable. "I told you I was going out of town," she said, her voice light.

"To where?" He didn't miss a beat. "Dammit, Bridget, you were gone for four days. I was fucking calling you and you couldn't even pick up your phone!"

"Obviously, I didn't want to be bothered."

Her lack of concern was only fueling his fury, she knew. A sudden clatter of her perfume and lotion bottles had her flinching. She whirled on him as he hovered over the mess he had knocked across the floor.

"What the fuck is your problem?" she screamed.

"You! You are my fucking problem." Roman grabbed his head as if trying to hold it steady on his shoulders. He began to pace like a caged tiger. "First, you lie to me about the kid shit. You've been dropping little slick shit about Maya. You throw your little bitch fit and just leave to wherever you go, without giving a damn about your husband, and oh yeah, your grimy ass sets me up with a transgender!"

Bridget started to object, but the last comment had her clamping her mouth closed on her instinctive retort. "Wait, what the hell does Corrine have to do with this?"

He was still pacing, his steps nearly burning a hole through the carpet. "I'm not fucking gay," he yelled.

"Hold up, we have all of these problems and you have the nerve to be bitching about Corrine right now?"

Bridget watched as he swiped at the table lamp, sending it shattering to the floor. "Roman, stop it!"

He spun around then, jabbing a finger in Bridget's direction. "Fuck you, bitch," he said with a laugh. "Fuck you and fuck your bitch, Corrine. You knew he was a dude and you set me up with that swinging shit."

He was close now, and Bridget could smell the wrath on his breath. For the first time, she took a good look at him. A really close look. His appearance was rough and disheveled, his clothes tattered. His hands, in particular his knuckles, were red with bloody bruising. At that moment, she would have felt more stable had she been hit with a brick.

"Roman, where have you been?" Her voice came out in a whisper.

"Oh, now you want to act so fucking concerned!"

"Roman," she tried again, her voice pleading. "Where were you just now? What did you do?"

She watched his jaw tighten, his eyebrows drawn so close and low, his eyes nearly got lost in them. He kept his mouth shut as waves of indignation swept across his crinkled face.

"I-I'm calling the police," she stammered and reached for her cell.

Before she even had a good grip on the phone, Roman slapped her hand, sending the device flying across the room. Bridget watched the metal crack against the plaster, her skin stinging from the hasty blow on her hand. She froze. He was deranged, and she was afraid of her husband.

With one last menacing look, Roman turned and stomped out of the room. Bridget didn't move until she was sure he was gone. It wasn't until she heard the car engine fading as he drove away that she risked releasing the breath she had been holding. She felt like she was hyperventilating. The tears flowed next as Bridget's legs gave out and she collapsed to the floor.

She barely heard the phone ringing over her own deafening breaths that sounded like thunder in her ears. Praying it wasn't Roman, she crawled to her phone, or the part that hadn't cracked, and put it to her ear. "Hello?"

"Bridget?"

The unfamiliar voice had Bridget pulling the phone into view, squinting to see the screen. The damn thing was black, broken by Roman's temper tantrum. Bridget angled it back to her face.

"This is Bridget," she said.

"Hi, this is Gina, Corrine's sister."

Bridget took another breath, already prepared to tell the woman they needed to talk another time. She didn't know what it was about, but nothing could be more important than what she had just experienced.

"Okay, Gina—"

"I saw you just called looking for Corrine," she rushed on, muffling a sniff. "She's in the hospital. There's been a terrible accident . . ."

Chapter Twenty
Corrine

His eyes. She would never forget those damn eyes. They bored into hers with enough hatred to chill her blood clean through to the bone. Her terror was palpable. She lay frozen in the middle of the floor, the begging trembling on her lips as she cowered under him. She looked up, watching his every move through eyes nearly swollen shut with his brutal beating. But even through her bloated lids, she could still make out the rapid succession of emotions that played on his face like a motion picture: fury, confusion, hate, and, most pronounced, disgust. If she could just make him understand, just make him see . . .

"You conniving, manipulative bitch. You deceived me into fucking you. I'm not fucking gay!"

In Corrine's mind, she wanted to scream out that's not how this works, that's not how any of this works. That she was a woman, the same woman he had made love to and had feelings for. She was no different than any other woman he had dated. That she didn't mean to seem deceptive, but full disclosure in the beginning often resulted in an onslaught of disgusting insults and anti-trans bigotry.

She couldn't bear that from him. She loved him too much. And Corrine hadn't wanted to play any kind of games or be seen as deceptive. Her heart had longed for him to see her for what she was, a woman. Not a label.

But of course, that's not how he saw it. In his mind, she was delusional, a liar, deceiver, and any wretched connotation he hadn't hesitated to spew out like bile. But more than his hurtful comments, or his death stare that had the whites of his eyes tainted red with unbridled rage, was the knife clamped firmly in his steady hand that had her own words frozen on her tongue.

He was bigger than her, stronger, and with the way he towered over her now broken body, he looked completely unhinged. Was this how it would end? Her visceral fear was gripping at the thought. Would she now join the countless other trans people who had been ruthlessly murdered?

⊰•◦✦◦•⊱

The beeps and whirs of the machine broke through Corrine's unconsciousness. She groaned against the burst of pain that riddled her body in varying degrees of intensity. She felt completely fractured, and her head pounded with enough force to bring on spasms of black dizziness. But even through the depths of all her agony, her attacker was as clear as if he'd been standing right in front of her. Those damn eyes. And the knife.

It hurt to breathe, as if something was sitting on her chest. As much as it ached, she lifted her lids and took in short, shallow breaths that stung her lungs like a pungent vapor.

The hospital room was sterile and reeked of antiseptics. Through her disorientation, Corrine saw she lay under a mint-green blanket, her right arm on top of the sheet in a cast. The curtains had been drawn open to reveal the kiss of dusk against the ombre sky. A vase rested on a nearby table with a bouquet of bright sunflowers, roses, irises, and mini carnations that added a splash of color to the otherwise bland room.

The door clicked open, and Gina walked in, a Styrofoam cup in hand. Her face immediately brightened when she noticed Corrine was awake. "Hey," she greeted, rushing to the side of the bed. "How are you feeling?"

"Like shit," Corrine admitted. Her voice came out hoarse and unfamiliar.

Gina touched her fingers with a sympathetic smile. Her eyes filled with tears. "Well, if it's any consolation, I can't tell," she lied with a chuckle.

It hurt too much to laugh, or smile for that matter, so Corrine did neither. Instead, her gaze swept her sister's visibly exhausted face, streaked with dried tears. After Mom's death, she couldn't even imagine what Gina had been feeling as Corrine lay teetering on the precipice of death.

"Where is Vanessa?"

"She's with a friend of mine. I didn't want her to see you like this."

"Thank you."

Gina paused for a bit. "Why would Pat do this?" she asked the burning question.

Corrine sighed. If only her sister knew the truth. She had become so numb to the physical abuse, the bruises like a second skin, the scars like accessories of tattered ribbons she no longer noticed. But what probably wounded her the most was seeing that look of pity on Gina's face. And for that, she felt the most remorse.

<hr />

Corrine was sick of the hospital, and she couldn't wait to get out of there. It had been two weeks, and she had been tested and operated on out the ass. Plus, the nurses' constant poking and prodding didn't leave her any room for rest. But in the midst of her annoyance, she was extremely appreciative for the medical staff, because she was healing. Physically, at least. She would have to work on mending her emotional and mental damage on her own.

Gina visited nearly every day, and if she wasn't there, Tangie was, bringing with her a constant rotation of flower arrangements or food, which Corrine did appreciate. It certainly helped her recovery process having that support from the two people she loved the most.

On the fourteenth day, Corrine was sitting up in bed watching TV when a knock came at the door. She frowned and stabbed the button to lower the volume on the remote. It was one of those rare occurrences when she was alone. Gina was at home with Vanessa, and Tangie had a photo shoot. Corrine had just returned from a CAT scan and she had been looking forward to relaxing without her usual visitors. So, who then, could this be?

"Come in," she called.

The door eased open with a cautious swing before Bridget appeared in the doorway. They both exchanged uneasy looks, the other hesitant to speak first.

Finally, Bridget cracked the silence. "May I come in?" she asked.

Corrine nodded and watched as she closed the door behind her and crossed to have a seat on the pullout couch near the window.

"I know I probably shouldn't be here," she started, her hands playing with each other in her lap. "But I felt I needed to come."

"How did you know I was here?"

"I called your phone, actually," Bridget confessed, dropping her head. "And Gina told me what Patrick had done."

Corrine sighed, laying her head back to rest on her pillows.

"It took me a minute to come visit, because I wasn't sure what to say," Bridget went on when she didn't speak. "I wanted to apologize."

"For what?"

"I saw the bruises before. And I didn't say anything. I feel like it's partially my fault."

Corrine squeezed her eyes shut and shook her head. "No, it's not your fault."

More silence, the only sound coming from the lowered volume on the TV's program.

"Why were you calling me?" Corrine asked, opening her eyes again to stare at Bridget. "After everything that's happened. After going to the police, why would you call me?"

Bridget's lips thinned into a wire-thin line as if she were hating to share the answer. "I know you and Roman had been seeing each other." Her voice remained dispassionate. "And that you told him I couldn't have kids. We had a huge fight . . ." Bridget shook her head as a shadow fell across her face. "I want to be angry with you, Corrine," she added, her voice strengthening. "God, when Gina told me what had happened to you, my first thought was that you were reaping what you sowed. But your sister told me a little bit more about you, and I can't bring myself to be mad, despite everything you've done."

Everything she had done. What had she done other than want to be loved?

"Did he know you were trans?" Bridget asked. "Is that why this happened?"

Such a loaded question. Corrine didn't think Bridget was ready for the complete truth, so instead she said, "Do you know why we don't like to reveal our gender identity?" She kept talking, not really expecting an answer from her. "Because it's damned if we do, and damned if we don't. I'm a woman and I want people to see me as such. But that point becomes moot if I say I'm trans because now that image is what's in your mind, despite what you see. No matter when I tell you, my life is in jeopardy. So, it's a catch twenty-two."

Bridget looked like she wanted to object, and Corrine already knew she wasn't prepared to understand this conversation. This issue of disclosure was so controversial, because for a cisgender woman like Bridget who never questioned her gender, it seemed nonsensical to conceal the facts about Corrine's past. She just wanted to live her life without the fear; fear of judgment, fear of being hurt or killed. Fear of *living*.

"If we're being honest with each other," Corrine murmured, "I need to apologize, too. For everything."

"I guess my big question is, why, Corrine? Why me?"

Corrine wished she had a better answer. She craved the love and attention that Bridget received, but some part of her figured it would make Patrick jealous, too. Neither had been the case. "I really don't have an answer for that, other than Patrick picked you out in a bar." Corrine lifted her hands and let them fall back on the bed. "With you, I don't know. It was different. You had it all with Roman, his daughter, hell, you even had my husband and didn't realize it. No matter what I did, it was never good enough, and you had the life I thought I wanted and deserved." She paused, watching Bridget's reaction. "I'm sorry, Bridget. I really am."

She nodded, as accepting of the circumstances as she could be. Though Corrine knew Bridget would probably never understand, no matter how much she wanted to. And that was okay. She couldn't be her any more than Bridget could walk a mile in her shoes and know her struggles. There had been times Corrine felt like a stranger in her own body. How could she put that disconnect into words to convey how much she wanted—no, *needed* to feel what Bridget felt? No matter how fictitious? But at least they had begun the journey to bridging the gap. Baby steps.

"So, what's next?"

Good question. Corrine had made so many sacrifices for the past few years she had lost herself. Never again. "Living my best life," she said.

Bridget rose and walked closer to the bed. After only a brief hesitation, she leaned down and hugged Corrine, warm and forgiving. "Good luck with everything," she said against Corrine's shoulder.

"You too."

She watched her walk to the door. Unsure if she would ever see Bridget again, she decided to go ahead and clear the air with one more thing. It was only right she knew.

"Bri?"

Bridget turned with her hand on the door.

Corrine's sigh was heavy, her eyes already brimming with empathetic tears. "It wasn't Patrick that did this to me. It was Roman."

To her surprise, the news didn't seem to surprise Bridget. In fact, her face slackened in despair. Finally, she lifted her chin and kept her gaze level on Corrine's.

"If you don't lock the bastard up," she said, "I will."

———

"You going to be okay?" Tangie asked as she cut off the engine.

Corrine looked through the windshield at her home. The place was the source of her happiness and misery. It had been nearly three weeks since she had come home that day while Patrick was at work to pack some clothes. She had left in an ambulance, fighting for her life.

For the longest, Corrine thought Patrick was her biggest threat. Hell, she had run out of the house ass-naked with only her purse and she had been twirling on the edges of insanity thinking he was going to come after her any minute. But he didn't know she was camping out with Tangie, and when he hadn't bothered calling after the first week, Corrine had let her guard down thinking she was safe. She wished she could go back in time and tell herself how wrong she was.

It had honestly pained her to reveal the truth about Roman, partially because she was still in disbelief herself. And to see Bridget's disheartened face, she knew the news had rocked the woman to her core. But Bridget had believed her, and more importantly, supported her. That had been enough.

Corrine had wanted to blame it on her injuries, so sure Patrick had come home early from work that day and finished what he had set out to do. Or even worse, because her mind had made Roman out to be so special over the past few months, it was her defense mechanism to taint his idyllic image. But no matter how hard she tried to unsee the truth, there was no denying her attacker. And that wonderful man that had her acting so desperate and irrational had shattered like glass as soon as she felt that first blow.

Corrine pressed the door opener and watched the garage slide open, disclosing the empty stall. Patrick wasn't home; they'd driven by his job first just to make sure. And now that she had pressed charges, she slept much better knowing Roman was in a jail cell somewhere. Still, having Tangie with her made her feel safe and gave her the extra boost of confidence she needed.

"Just let me go in and get a few things," Corrine said, reaching for the door.

Tangie's hand on her arm had her stopping to look over to her friend. "You sure you don't need me to go in?"

Corrine nodded. She needed to do this alone. She needed to find her own strength. "Yes, I'm sure. Just stay right here. I won't be long."

It was as if time had stood still for a few weeks. The house was, surprisingly, just like Corrine had left it, and whether Patrick had cleaned or hadn't been home, nothing was out of place.

Corrine journeyed up to the master bedroom. She paused at the door, swamped in the memories. Patrick was in no way close to perfect. In fact, he was a downright asshole, if she could be honest with herself. But he was still the first one that had opened her up to love, no matter how toxic. She had feelings for the man that she hadn't even had for herself. He had been her strength and her weakness. And for that, she would always appreciate her own growth in dealing with a man like him.

She was headed to the mirror when she stopped and took a long look at her reflection. She looked like porcelain. A strange comparison, but it seemed fitting. Her fragility was evident, despite her composure; the swelling was gone, but the marks remained. Corrine lifted a hand to her face, the beautiful mask aged with turmoil. *Baby steps*, she had to remind herself.

Her phone chimed in her purse, and Corrine used her one good arm to dig through her junk for the device. Probably Tangie reconfirming she was okay. Corrine eyed the text message, a relieved smile touching her lips. No, not Tangie, but Bridget. The two words she had sent harboring so much understanding in their simplicity that Corrine felt weak with the renewed liberation. **Thank you.** That was it. But that was all that was needed.

Epilogue

Bridget could remember three instances in particular that had made her especially happy in life, the first being her wedding. Roman was pure perfection in human form, and she was head-over-heels in love. That was the first day of the rest of her life. Which had made the second instance of her elation all the more ironic: when the signed divorce papers had come in the mail a few months ago and her name had legally changed from Pierce back to Hall. The third instance was this very precious moment happening right now.

There were more people than Bridget had expected. And they were all there to celebrate her. The bookstore had set up a booth with her recently published book *Finding Your Inner Badass: A Boss Woman's Guide to Success* stacked on the table in a neat arrangement. An accompanying retractable banner was front and center on display showcasing her book signing event.

Within a month of release, Bridget's book had hit both the *New York Times* bestseller list and *Forbes*'s Best Business Books for Women. And she couldn't have been more proud of her achievement. Plus, all of the positive press had done nothing but catapult Brinique Lux Affair into the most prominent and elite circles, despite Marco's personal feelings about severing ties. They hadn't needed to do damage control after all.

Bridget had dressed formally, as her literary agent had suggested, in a sleek, white ankle-length dress with a knee-high split up the front. Skinny straps journeyed over her shoulders and crisscrossed down to meet her dress at the small of her back. She had pulled her hair back from her face and sent it sprouting down from an elegant ponytail. Now, a few strands had escaped and delicately tickled her cheeks. Bridget wore little makeup, a light shade of lipstick and some eyeliner, with diamonds glittering at her wrist, neck, and ears.

Bridget was honored when Nikki insisted on planning everything for her. Barnes and Noble had closed the entire store for the exclusive affair, and Nikki had brought in Champagne and small appetizers for the guests. Bridget had read a little from the book, answered questions, and had a raffle giveaway for a free consultation from Brinique Lux Affair. Afterward, guests had lined up at her table so she could autograph their books as the professional photographer captured pictures of the momentous occasion. Now, the event was drawing to a close, and she was grabbing a quick bite to eat before her parting speech.

Bridget stood at the small buffet table that was covered by a branded linen cloth and then smothered by platters of finger foods and pastries. She used a toothpick to pluck a piece of chicken from her plate and pop it in her mouth.

"Bridget, there you are."

Bridget put on a smile and turned at the voice, watching her agent maneuver through the crowd toward her. Allison Daniels had been right; the woman was a beast with her clients and Bridget could only attribute the book's phenomenal success to her.

She was dressed professionally in a red silk blouse and black skirt that brushed her knees. Those blue eyes of hers, now twinkling with excitement, stood out plainly against her milk-creamy skin. "Are you ready?" she asked. "It's almost time for your speech."

Bridget had memorized the words she'd scribbled on the index cards the previous night, but now, nerves had her mind drawing a blank.

"Girl, I hope I don't make an ass of myself," she mumbled and had Allison laughing.

"What are you talking about? You've given plenty of speeches. Hell, the book talks about that, too. Just speak from your heart. You got this." She used one of her manicured nails to brush a strand of Bridget's hair out of her face. "Finish mingling and I'll announce you when it's time. Good luck." She patted her arm for comfort and then disappeared back into the crowd.

Bridget nodded and took a breath. *She had this.* Being met with unfamiliar faces, she headed for the bar to grab a drink. Anything to calm the anxiety.

"Excuse me. May I have your autograph?"

Bridget turned to eye the young lady who had a copy of her book in her arms.

"Absolutely."

"Thank you so much!" the reader gushed, passing the book over.

Bridget took an extra second to eye her cover, her name embossed in gold script on the front. This feeling would never get old. She flipped it open to the title page. "Who can I make this out to?" she asked.

"My best friend, Corrine."

Bridget paused with her pen on the page. Her head whipped up, and sure enough, Corrine stood in front next to the lady, a shy smile plastered on her healing face. She was dressed casually in jeans and a silk blouse. Her hair was back to normal as well, and she looked like the woman Bridget had first met in the restroom that day. Only this time, she looked happy and genuinely at peace.

"I hope you don't mind," Corrine spoke up quickly. "I don't want you to think I'm stalking or anything, but I just wanted to support." She gestured to her fingers that gripped a plastic bag overstuffed with hardback books. "If it's any consolation, I did purchase twenty for my support group. So, do you mind signing all of them?"

Bridget nodded with a smile of her own, her heart swelling with pride. Without hesitation, she stepped forward and pulled Corrine in for a hug. It was so good seeing her.

"This is my friend, Tangie," Corrine introduced the woman who had first approached Bridget. "Tangie, this is Bridget, my . . ."

"Other friend," Bridget finished on a chuckle and extended her hand to Tangie's for a shake. She looked back to Corrine. "Hey, I'll be done here in about an hour," she said. "Do you want to go grab something to eat?"

Corrine's smile was cautious. "I would like that. Only if you're sure."

Bridget's breath was one of relief. "Yeah," she agreed earnestly. "I'm sure."

Everyone's chatter began to subside, and all eyes went to the stage area. Bridget watched Allison strut to the podium, cool and confident, and her heart skipped with every step the woman took.

"Good afternoon," Allison began, panning the crowd. "I am Allison Daniels, Bridget Hall's literary agent. I met this amazing woman a year ago on the beach in Cancún. She was writing this book, and the way she was working let me know the type of passionate person she was. And I knew I wanted to be part of what she was doing." Allison then lapsed into the formal introduction about her client's knowledge, expertise, and accolades.

Bridget snuck a look at Corrine and could only smile at how far they had come. Such a beautiful person who had been dealt a shitty hand. But it was inspiring to see her getting her life back on track.

". . . so without further delay, I am extremely honored to present, *New York Times* bestselling author, Bridget Hall."

Thunderous applause erupted, and Bridget worked her way through the cluster of people and up to the podium. "Wow, thank you all for coming to my official book launch," she started, her voice projecting loud and strong from the microphone. "It has certainly been a journey to get to where I am today. A lot of changes took place in my life, and I wasn't even sure I had it in me to continue. For example, as some of you know, I got divorced, because my husband was not who I thought he was. But it was that type of change in my life that pushed me to continue, because I needed to share my gift with the world and not be stifled by what others thought I should be, do, or how I should act."

Bridget paused, letting her words resonate to the spirits who needed her message. She was relieved when she felt some of the tension easing away. She was beginning to feel more comfortable; like she belonged up there and was exactly where she needed to be. "But I have to thank my friends, my family, and all of my support system for keeping me motivated," she continued, eyeing everyone as she started her personal acknowledgments. "To my parents and my siblings, I love you all and thank you so much for your love and guidance. To my best friend and business partner, Nikki . . ." She eyed Nikki, standing off to the side next to Dennis, looking like a goddess with her bulging pregnant belly. "You are my rock. I love you and thank you for your patience and your constant motivation. As you see, I've dedicated this book to you for giving me the idea, and of course my future goddaughter."

Nikki beamed and turned to kiss her fiancé, appreciative of Bridget's words.

"And finally," Bridget turned and looked Corrine in the eye, "a special thank you to Corrine. Your strength is remarkable. To be honest, you are probably one of the strongest women in my life. I know we met under unique circumstances, but you are the type of inspiration I didn't even know I needed. So, thank you and here is to spending life out of the shadows."

COUPLES WANTED

Briana Cole

ABOUT THIS GUIDE

The suggested questions are included to enhance your group's
reading of Briana Cole's *Couples Wanted*!

DISCUSSION QUESTIONS

1. What was your initial reaction to the book? Did it hook you immediately, or take some time to get into?"

2. Corrine grew up in difficult circumstances. What scars does she carry from her dysfunctional childhood? How does her past influence her actions in the present?

3. How did the dual narrator format between Bridget and Corrine affect your reading experience? Do you think it worked well within the novel?

4. What did you like most about the book? What did you like the least?

5. Were there any quotes (or passages) that stood out to you? Why?

6. Bridget and Roman seemed to have an idyllic marriage, however there were some issues between them already bubbling under the surface. Do you think swinging was the catalyst that ruined their relationship or was their marriage not going to last much longer anyway?

7. What were the main themes of the book? How were those themes brought to life?

8. Which character or moment prompted the strongest emotional reaction for you and why?

9. What were the power dynamics between the characters and how did that affect their interactions? How did Corrine and Bridget influence each other?

10. Were there times you disagreed with a character's actions? What would you have done differently?

11. What scene would you point out as the pivotal moment in the narrative? How did it make you feel?

12. Did your opinion of this book change as you read it? How?

13. What "rules" or boundaries do you feel need to be established for a non-monogamous relationship to work?

14. Were you satisfied with the book's ending? Why or why not?

15. What songs does this book make you think of? Create a book group playlist together!

16. If you could talk to the author, what burning question would you want to ask?

Connect with

Visit us online at
KensingtonBooks.com
to read more from your favorite authors, see books
by series, view reading group guides, and more.

for sneak peeks, chances to win books and prize packs,
and to share your thoughts with other readers.

facebook.com/kensingtonpublishing
twitter.com/kensingtonbooks

Tell us what you think!

To share your thoughts, submit a review,
or sign up for our eNewsletters, please visit:
KensingtonBooks.com/TellUs.